Journey Back to You

by Leigh Shalloway

© Copyright 2025 Leigh Shalloway

ISBN 979-8-89747-018-1

All rights reserved. No part of this publication may be reproduced, stored in a retrieval system, or transmitted in any form or by any means—electronic, mechanical, photocopy, recording, or any other—except for brief quotations in printed reviews, without the prior written permission of the author.

This is a work of fiction. All the characters in this book are fictitious, and any resemblance to actual persons, living or dead, is purely coincidental. The names, incidents, dialogue, and opinions expressed are products of the author's imagination and are not to be construed as real.

Cover design by Danielle Koehler

Published by

3705 Shore Drive
Virginia Beach, VA 23455
800-435-4811
www.koehlerbooks.com

JOURNEY
BACK TO YOU

journey back to you

LEIGH SHALLOWAY

VIRGINIA BEACH
CAPE CHARLES

PART 1

Chapter 1

It's less than three months before my emancipation! I'm excited, scared, and everything in between. In August, I'll start my first year of college at Northwestern University in Chicago, a whole eight-hour drive from my current home of Hilltown, Pennsylvania. I chose Northwestern because no one in my high school is going there, and it's three states away from my controlling father. Okay, so it is freedom with conditions; my father will insist I major in business, join the *best* sorority, and graduate Phi Beta Kappa. At least I won't have to endure the weekly school updates he demands now. He likes to continually remind me of the one B I earned at my accelerated private high school, Country Day School, which is in Park City, an upscale community near our house. That B made me the salutatorian, not the valedictorian. For my father, Jonathan Hill, our town's namesake and owner and CEO of The Hilltown Steel Mill, coming in second is never good enough. At the graduation ceremony, he didn't bother to stand up and clap after my address was over. I was so embarrassed. I shouldn't have been. Secretly, I'm hoping to graduate early. The less time under my father's thumb, the better. I just need to last the next four years.

What is so weird is that my father insisted that I hold a huge, elaborate high school graduation party. The party list included all the seniors from my school, even the ones I don't know that well, all teachers and staff, but most importantly, a special seating section for my father's friends and business associates. It's held at the local country club. Who else but my father would turn my graduation into a business event, especially when he didn't seem happy with my high school performance? Appearances are everything for my dad. He's the richest person and the biggest employer in Hilltown and the surrounding area, so I guess the party was something to remind everyone of his elevated status.

The party is being held in the main ballroom of the club. The room is decorated with perfect yellow roses (my favorite), and there is a magnificent dinner buffet, followed by an even more elaborate dessert bar. Dad knows my weakness for sugar, so he made sure there was a ton of sweetness in all forms. Included are chocolate cake and a raspberry filling with "Congratulations Kathleen" decorating the top, crème brûlée, fresh fruit with whipped cream, and my favorite, chocolate mousse. Everyone, especially my friends, thinks it's great, but they don't have to live with the man in charge.

I look for my mom. I find her sitting at the largest table in the business section, quietly sipping her favorite chardonnay. I breathe a sigh of relief. She looks like she did when I was little. She's wearing a classic Prada one-shouldered white silk cocktail dress, her naturally light blond hair in a simple twist, with her makeup perfectly applied in a way that enhances her natural porcelain skin. She is talking to one of Dad's senior managers but looks up at me with a smile. Now I understand why my father married her; she's flawless tonight. It looks like there won't be any "incidents" with hard liquor, where she ends up embarrassing herself and making my father angry.

Near the end of the evening, I notice my principal walking up to the podium in the front of the room. *Oh God no*, I think. This is the last thing I want: a public spectacle at a party I never wanted in the first place.

"I'd like to thank the man who gave us this amazing event to celebrate his beautiful daughter, Kathleen, Mr. Jonathan Hill." The guests applaud politely. "Now let's all give a shout-out to tonight's honorary guest, Miss Kathleen Hill. Come on up, Kathleen!" All my friends start chanting my name as I make my way up to the mic. Balloons and confetti rain down from the ceiling. The vice principal places a silver tiara on my head, reading "The Graduate," and the principal hands me a bouquet of roses and orchids. A matching sash with my name on it is placed over my head.

The sash drapes perfectly on my Stella McCarthy designer frock, and the crown sparkles to great effect. My hair is pulled back, with soft blond waves floating down my back. I'm just glad I took a lot of time putting my look together for the party. I know I'm expected to say something, so I start. "Thank all of you for coming! I've been lucky to have such great friends and a wonderful staff at Country Day. I'd especially like to thank my dad for this great party, and my mom, who helped me get through the last four years. I'll miss everyone, but I'm really excited for the next chapter. Thanks again!" Then there are more merry claps and cheers.

I walk down the podium, where a line of my father's friends are waiting to shake my hand. I can barely hear the acknowledgments because Daniel, an ex, is shouting plans in my ear about the next event of the night. "Kath, meet me at the limo in fifteen. We're heading to Brian's. His parents aren't home, and the liquor cabinet is open for business!" I'm too busy watching the cleanup crew removing the desserts. I didn't get any, so I grab the mousse bowl before it disappears. I stick my fingers into the bowl and scoop up all I can hold. It tastes sooo good. Next, I steal into the first bathroom I see and promptly take off the crown and the sash, dumping them into the trash can. I am so over this fake celebration!

I decided not to go to the next party at Brian's. I'm way too tired to stay up any longer, and I don't drink. My friends tease me for being such a "lightweight," but I remember the night that I got really, really drunk at my friend Julia's slumber party. It ended with my head in the toilet and my favorite sweater ruined. Then there's Mom. She's stuck in a loveless marriage and seems to spend most of her time in an alcohol and pill stupor. It's embarrassing and heartbreaking.

Graduation parties continue all week. It seems as if most of my friends want to extend high school, whereas I feel like it is something to endure so I can get out of Hilltown. But I smile, cheer, and pretend to drink another beer along with them. Then I sneak out when no one is looking. I don't know how I'll stay sane this summer.

The next day, I finish poring over my "Freshman Checklist" from Northwestern. I notice that it's almost four. I jump in my car and head to town to pick up flowers for my mom. I have a standing weekly order of fresh, white roses, her favorite, at the floral section in the town's grocery store. There are not many things that make my mom happy these days, but this is one of them. Carrie, the manager of the department, adds greenery and baby's breath every week and arranges them in a classic white box wrapped with a matching ribbon.

I park my car and walk inside, heading straight to the flower desk. I'm met by someone I don't know. Her name tag reads "Sondra." She turns and smiles at me. "How can I help you?"

"I'm just here to pick up my roses." She looks mystified. "Where is Carrie?" I ask politely.

"I'm sorry, but she had a family emergency, so I'm filling in for her. She'll be back on Monday."

"I have a standing order of white roses that I pick up every Thursday. They're important."

"White roses came in at noon, but I put them where the other roses are. I wondered why they sent only one bunch." I look at the other roses; none are white. They're gone.

I can feel pressure building in my chest. If I'm lucky, they may have them at the florist in Park City. Then I look at my watch, and it's too late. They'll be closed by the time I get there. "Can you please check in the back?" I ask.

"Of course." Sondra walks into the flower storage area, then returns. "There aren't any other white roses. Let me look at her notes." She looks up from her paper with a worried expression. "Are you Miss Kathleen Hill?"

"Yes."

"I'm so sorry, Miss Hill, Carrie did leave instructions for the flowers. There is even the box and ribbon. It's been so busy that I didn't have time to read the notes until now. Can I help you with another bunch? The soft pink are beautiful."

I walk over to the pink roses, pick them up, and show her the bottom of the flowers. "These have already been recut. They are at least a day old. That's why I make a special order, so they will be fresh." I know I sound bitchy, but my mother looks forward to them. It's one of the few things that I can do to make her happy.

I stand there tapping my feet, ready to talk the manager into firing Sondra, but the sane part of me will not do that. I won't be like my father. He would definitely have her fired.

"I couldn't help but overhear. Here are the white roses." Someone hands them to Sondra. "I'm sure my aunt will be just as happy with the pink ones." I look up to thank him. Oh my God, it's Jase Thompson. Everyone knows who Jase Thompson is. Lots of my friends have snuck into the local "townie bar" Joe's, where they don't usually card. He tends bar there for a couple of nights a week. They all swore that they would do "anything" to spend a night with him. Apparently, he wasn't interested. He's Hilltown's best-kept secret. He certainly lives up to his "gorgeous" reputation.

He really is the most beautiful man I have ever seen. He's not the "gym on steroids" look like the guys from my school. His body looks as if it's come from hard work, not barbells. He's long and strong and handsome in a manly way, not in the typical high school preppy boy way that I'm used to. Jase wears his black hair down beyond his shoulders, and he has chiseled cheekbones. His eyes are brown, with lashes so long that I'm jealous. He's wearing jeans and a flannel shirt embossed with "Joe's." I guess he's ready for his next job.

Jase is a manager at the Hilltown Steel Mill. He is kind of a rising star. I've heard the managers praise him and his work when they come to our house to give my father updates. I actually met him at one of the Mill parties my dad dragged my mom and me to. It was the best part of the night, even though it was only for a minute. Whereas the other managers nervously introduced themselves to me, probably scared of offending my father, Jase was polite but indifferent.

My father likes to pretend we're a happy, normal family. He's also always trying to get me interested in the Mill because he thinks my future husband and I will run it one day. What my father doesn't know is that I don't have any intention of returning home after I graduate from college. I still need his money for the next three or four years. After that, goodbye, Hilltown.

I'm sure Jase Thompson heard everything I said to Sondra. I know he thinks that I'm a spoiled and bossy little rich girl. I just acted like one. There is no way I can tell him why I need them so badly, that it's the one thing I know my mother gets happiness from. All I think to say is "Thank you." He glances at me and leaves.

Sondra looks at Jase like he's God. I, on the other hand, look like the devil. "Sondra, can you please get me some baby's breath and some greenery, and I'll arrange them?"

"I'll be glad to do that for you, Miss Hill."

"I'm sorry for being rude earlier."

I see Jase getting in his truck when I leave the store and think about explaining myself. But one look at his serious face, and I decide against it. He's busy, and I acted like a brat. I'll leave it at that.

When I walk into the house, my father is sitting in the den with a scowl on his face. He must be analyzing the latest steel orders. The mill production must be down. My mom is reading the most current copy of *Vanity Fair*. She notices the familiar white box. "Darling, you always remember my favorite roses." She gets up, and I hand her the box. She goes into the living room to get last week's flowers and her "special" vase. Then she goes into the kitchen to arrange the new roses. Her gait is steady, and I breathe a sigh of relief that she hasn't hit the wine and pills too hard yet.

Seeing as everything seems pretty calm here and my mom doesn't need me to save her from my dad's derision, I'm going to head out to the retirement home. My favorite part of high school was my civics class. As a part of the homework, we were given a list of different charities that we were supposed to volunteer at. I chose the Hilltown Retirement Community. Most of the residents worked at the Mill. I only had to volunteer for two weeks; I just kept coming back even though I was done with the class.

From the moment I first walked in, it felt like home. I mean a real home, not like the place I sleep, where I always have to take a minute, before entering, to leave my heart at the door. I was immediately welcomed by the staff and residents. Since starting to volunteer there, I have been the recipient of many hand-knit sweaters, homemade jewelry, pottery, and other homemade gifts. All the graduation prep kept me so busy that I haven't been there for over three weeks. I thought I missed the residents more than they missed me, but when I walk in and hear, "Hey Kathleen," I smile because the feeling is mutual.

It's bingo day and I'm in charge of calling out the numbers. Bingo Queen Mary says, "Oh good, you're here. We're just getting started." I walk to the front of the room, spin the wheel around, and grab the paper with all the letters and numbers on it. I announce B-4.

"I've got it," Ted, one of my favorites, shouts out. "Today is my day."

I really want him to win. He plays bingo every time, and in the four months I've been here, he hasn't ever won the pot of twenty quarters. The quarters themselves aren't important; it's winning that counts. I spin it again. "N-7."

"It's me," calls out June. For some reason, June and Mary always seem to win. Did they somehow "fix" the wheel? Bingo here is like war. The motto is to "do what it takes" to win. Of course, it's random. The more you come, the better the chance to win; it's basic statistics.

In this room, however, a competitive spirit keeps it going. I hear that bridge is the same.

Near the end of the game, in walks Jase Thompson. I'm stunned. By the look on his face, so is he. Once his mouth closes, he turns and heads down one of the corridors. It's obvious that he knows the layout of the building.

I say the last code, and Sally, a very dedicated bingo player, wins for the very first time. She jumps out of her seat and races to the front to hug me and claim her pot of quarters. Everyone claps and cheers. It also helps that Sally is one of the sweetest women in the Home. She was the receptionist at the Mill for over thirty years.

Everybody passes in their score cards, and I note Sally as the winner. I lock everything in a locker marked "Bingo." The whole community is excited for tomorrow's Olympic Bingo Tournament. In this game, only people who have won before are allowed to play. The prize is doubled, and it's first come, first go. I've heard that players form a line outside the door and it's standing room only just to watch the game. I decided that I want to preside. I'll tell Beth, the manager, to pencil me in. I can hardly wait.

Players file out, and I stay to straighten up the room. "So, Miss Hill, are you following me?" I look up and see the gorgeous eyes from the man who shared his roses with me. I blush, thinking he believes me, but his half smile and half smirk let me know he's just teasing.

I have to smile back. "I was going to ask you the same thing. After all, I was here first."

"Technically, I've been here since four, so I think I've been here first."

"I'm talking bingo first," I reply. He laughs. Oh my God. His smile was disarming enough, but the laugh makes my knees buckle. I grab onto the chair in front of me to steady myself and to hopefully conceal the blush that I am sure is covering my face and neck.

"Seriously, what are you doing here? Something your daddy makes you do so he'll look like he cares."

I'm hurt. All the friendly banter meant nothing. He was just looking for an opening to insult me. I turn around to get my purse. I don't want him to see how much that remark stings.

"Hey, Miss Hill, I'm sorry. That was a low blow." I turn around, and he does look sorry.

"Did it ever occur to you that my father doesn't completely control my life? In fact, he doesn't even want me to be here, but I love it here, so I come anyway. And my name is Kathleen. You can lose the 'Miss Hill.' Why are you here?"

"I come to visit the people who have no family, and those whose families have just dumped them here. Mill people look out for each other, or at least we try to."

That could be another dig at my father, but I let it go. The look on his face seems more sad than bitter, so I say, "I know. I don't understand that. I have a kind of adopted grandmother who lives here, Sadie Holmes. Her daughter never comes to see her or even answers her calls. We've grown close since I started volunteering. It's a win-win. I get a grandmother, and she gets a granddaughter. I definitely got the better part of the deal."

Another amazing smile. "I know Sadie. She's great. Very spunky. Did you know she's the first woman to work the front line?"

"I don't know what that means."

He changes the subject. "Do you want some help with tomorrow? I can work my schedule around this wild competition." We both laugh.

"I'd like that." We look at each other, and I feel my heart quicken again. Then logic rears its ugly head. There is no way a man like Jase Thompson could want me. I think I look kind of ordinary with my blond hair, made even blonder with highlights. I have my mother's clear light green eyes, my best feature. I stand five feet five, and I wear a size six, which is considered chubby at my expensive private school. Anything over a size four, and you'll hear those girls vomiting in the bathroom. I do love clothes, and I'm good at putting outfits together, but otherwise I think I just look like any girl my age. My ex-boyfriend Brian always said that I was "hot," but he was just sucking up to me because of my father, and I know he wanted to get in my pants. I don't get sex. The few times I've had it were awkward and over before I knew it. I'm sure it's me. Maybe I'm just not good at it.

I look back at Jase and say, "If you're serious about wanting to help, then get here at eleven-thirty so we can set up the room. We can trade places calling out the numbers."

"See you tomorrow then," he says and walks out of the room.

Chapter 2

After Jase leaves, I head down the hallway to see Sadie. I met Sadie in the lunchroom right after one of my favorite residents died. I'm one of the few volunteers who help out in the hospice wing. It means holding a lot of hands and giving a lot of hugs to the families of the patients. A tall woman with bright blue eyes and a cane walked in that day. She was dressed in purple, with a long silver scarf wrapped around her neck and the biggest purple hoop earrings I've ever seen. She sat right next to me and started the conversation. "You look a bit lonely over here by yourself."

"Um, I'm Kathleen."

She held out her hand and I shook it. "I'm Sadie Holmes." Ten minutes later she had me laughing so hard that I forgot all about my sadness. We've been close ever since.

I walk into Sadie's room. I'm so glad she's there. She goes on all the day trips, plays bridge, and is on the leadership team, so Sadie is rarely in her room. "Kathleen, I'm so happy to see you," she says as she gets up to hug me. She holds me at arm's length and says, "What's going on? You're glowing."

"Well, tomorrow is the Bingo Olympics. Are you coming?"

"You think I was born yesterday? Bingo did not put that rosy tint to your cheeks."

I can't hide anything from Sadie, so I don't even try. "Well, I will have another person helping out, Jase Thompson."

"You mean the gorgeous stud that roams our halls?"

"Well, I wouldn't call him that."

"Then you need to get your eyes examined. If I was forty years younger, I would jump his bones in a New York minute!"

I can't help but laugh. "I won't be doing anything along those lines. He's just helping me out. Anyway, I just wanted to make sure you were coming. I've missed you these past weeks. Sorry, I haven't been here."

"No need to apologize."

We catch up for a while, and I find myself, once again, revealing things to her that I can't share with my mother or friends. About how I'm so ready to start my new life, where maybe I can actually be myself, not the daughter of Jonathan Hill. Sadie knows I really want to study psychology, but I tell my dad that I'll be a business major. I'd rather help people than always be looking to make businesses rich. I don't want to live in my father's shadow anymore. The perks aren't worth it.

"If it's one thing I know for sure, Kathleen, it's that whatever you do, you'll be a huge success."

"Thanks, Sadie," I say as I hug her, not able to hide my tears.

I walk to my car and drive up the winding road to our house. It's only ten minutes away from the center of Hilltown, but it's like another world. Our house is a gigantic *Gone With the Wind*–style mansion. I park in the circular driveway and give myself a moment to regroup, just as I always do before entering our home. The house is brick, with a white wraparound porch, high columns, two porch swings, and giant flowerpots brimming with colorful yellow, purple, and white annuals. I love the swings, using them to escape from the underlying sense of anxiety that's always in our house, especially when my father is home. My mother tries so hard to be noticed. She is always dressing up in her designer wear, sharing anything she hopes will get him to listen. All for nothing.

It's unfair. My mother graduated from the University of Pennsylvania with honors in art history and was managing a successful gallery when she met my father at an art opening that she oversaw. But in the years of my father's impossible demands of perfection, there is no way she can thrive. You can only be insulted and demeaned for so long before you start to believe the insults. "Caroline, I hate what you're wearing." "Caroline, you can't get anything right." "Caroline, you're embarrassing." "Caroline, you're a hopeless drunk and pill popper." "Caroline, it's your fault we can't have more children, especially a son." And "Caroline, I sleep with other women because you don't satisfy me." Okay, I haven't actually heard him say that, but it's implied, and the whole town knows of his philandering.

My biggest concern is what will happen to my mom once I leave.

I open our front door as quietly as I can. I listen and don't hear anything. They're probably eating at the club tonight, which means I have an hour of peace to myself, but I race up to my room just in case they come home early. I know that my mother could have done amazing things designing our house, but Dad never really gave her a chance. Our house became what only he wanted: an homage to the old southern plantation owners before the Civil War. I'm sure he sees his employees as slaves, all working to enrich him.

In terms of the house, Mom was allowed to do whatever she wanted in a few spaces: my room, her bedroom (I never remember my parents sharing the same bed), and the downstairs library. None of them would ever be seen by anyone else, which is why my father let her design them. My room is painted an awful Pepto Bismol pink. Her interior designer, Henri, talked her into the color. "Kathleen, I have been assured that this is all the rage in Philadelphia," Mom told me. One wall, I can understand, but the whole room? Worse, all the accessories in my space, the bedspread, curtains, and even my towels are full of pink Pepto Bismol pansies.

I slip into my pink Jacuzzi tub and think about Jase and his amazing smile. Just as the water is cooling, I hear the downstairs door slam and my father's heavy footfall. I hear my mother crying and apologizing and the freezer opening, followed by ice cubes tinkling in what I am sure is my father's highball glass.

"I didn't tell Penny anything inappropriate. I was just sharing some of the ideas I had for the next art museum fundraiser. I thought we could do a—"

"You sounded like an idiot. No one wants to hear your fantastical ideas. They have it covered. Why can't you just be quiet during these things?"

"She asked my opinion, so I shared—"

"I doubt that. Penny has run the museum board successfully for years. Why would she want your opinion on anything?"

I submerge myself in the bath so I won't have to hear anymore. I know in a few minutes my mom will retreat to her room. I think I'll sit this one out and let her fall into an Ambien–induced slumber.

I wake up early the next day and start to pick out my outfit for bingo. Jase will be there, so I decide to wear something casual, with a hint of sexiness. It includes a lacy "Free People" kind of blouse, the jeans that make my butt look perfect, my Tiffany bracelet, gold hoops, and Tamara Mellon sandals. Once I hear my father leave for the Mill, I head out to the country club. The club has an Olympic–sized saltwater pool. When I was in middle school, I was on the swim team. I spent three hours a day, five days a week, here. I switched to soccer in high school, but I still go to the pool when I need to get my head together. Being in the water is so soothing and solitary. It's like I'm in a completely different world, where only my breathing and the rhythm of my strokes matter, back and forth, back and forth. No fighting parents, no boring school assignments, no outside pressure. I never count my laps, after all; the whole point for me is the freedom of following what my body tells me to do.

I take my time getting ready at the club; they have an amazing marble bathroom. I straight iron my hair and put on wine-colored lipstick. I want to look a little edgy. Then I come back to the present and berate myself: *I'm just stupid, stupid, stupid! He's just a crush, an impossible crush.*

I take myself out for breakfast, a triple-shot latte, and a blueberry scone in the town's only coffee shop, Wake Up. Then it's time to get to the Home to set up for the grand event, Bingo Olympics. I still can't believe I'll be pairing with Jase Thompson to lead the game. *Why am I nervous?* There is very little chance that he is viewing this as anything but helping seniors, but I feel differently. In that one moment yesterday when we talked, I felt a kind of kinship.

I make one more stop at the grocery store to pick up some Godiva chocolates for the winner and colored helium balloons. Just some things to make it more special. When I get to the Home, I notice the line already forming outside the activities room.

It's exactly 11:30 a.m., then 11:40, and still no sign of Jase Thompson. He probably forgot about it. I feel stupid that I took an extra hour getting ready, and he isn't even going to show. I go to the bingo locker and get out the pot of quarters and score cards. I need to hurry because I was waiting for him. The tables are already set up in rows, so I quickly place chairs behind the tables. Beth, the manager, brings in pitchers of iced tea, cups, and potato chips.

Jase arrives at 11:50, looking frazzled. "Sorry I'm late. Something came up at work."

"No problem," I answer nonchalantly. "Can you get the Bingo Olympic banner and put it on the wall, and the bingo wheel with the letters and numbers needs to be by the podium?"

I bring out my pad with the names of the winners in the last two months. I can't give any nonwinners a chair. I look at Jase and ask him, "Can you handle the line? I don't want anyone to jump ahead."

He laughs. "Sure, can't have that happen!" He's obviously amused.

The door opens, and residents begin to file in. I check them off my list, and they pick their places. When all the seats are filled, I announce, "Twenty more people can come watch." I hear the usual grumbles when that number is up, and half the people without seats shuffle out of the room. "Don't worry, you'll have a chance to watch the next one," I say as consolation.

As I stand at the podium and introduce Jase as my cochair, I hear a few catcalls and "Jase, you can look over my shoulder anytime!" and "Jase, call me!" I see he has quite an effect on women of all ages. He ignores the whistles, but I can see a slight flush to his cheeks. Good to know he's not impervious to being worshipped.

I feel nervous instead of the usual excitement. I take a deep breath and start. "N-2." No one answers. Then Jase calls out, "I-6." The game goes on and on. Jase and I change places until, finally, the winner stands up.

Jase yells out, "We have a winner: Mister Lou Neal." Everyone applauds and pats him on the back.

We take a break for refreshments. Sadie comes over to me and whispers, "What do you think of the new guy?"

"Jase is doing a good job, don't you think? And the women obviously love him."

"Not Jase, silly, Lou. He just moved in a couple of weeks ago. He'll get plenty of attention. New guys are always very welcome, and he's cute." Sadie's eyes are even brighter than usual, and do I dare say, it looks as if she took a little extra time with her appearance too. I see a slight pink hue to her cheeks and a silver scarf I haven't seen her wear before.

"Go talk to him," I nudge. "At least one of us has a chance at romance."

She looks straight into my eyes and says, "Kathleen, you're beautiful. Stop giving up before you've even tried." Some more of Sadie's sage advice.

She walks over to talk to Lou, and I start straightening up. Jase joins me in picking up the discarded cards, cups, and plates.

"Thanks so much for helping. It made the whole game easier and more fun," I say. "I can take it from here. You probably need to get back to work."

"Kathleen, I was late. The least I can do is help you clean up."

I'm shocked that he even remembered my name.

I didn't expect that. He's beautiful and thoughtful. I open the bingo locker, and we place everything inside. He doesn't seem to be in any hurry. "You do this every week?"

I would if you come and help me so I can stare at your body, I think, but instead, I answer, "I used to when school was still going on. Now things are a little crazy. If you ever want to help, feel free. It's always Thursday, late morning."

"I'll see. I've taken on training some new people, so I'm pretty booked."

"I understand," I say. I'm disappointed.

"Kathleen, I'm not saying no." He laughs. "I'll come if I can."

"Hmmm." I smile. I stay in the room, pretending to be busy, when all I want is to spend as much time with him as I can.

Chapter 3

Now that school is over, I can't use the excuse that I'm studying at Julia's or Danielle's anymore to stay away from home. I've got to find more alibis; otherwise, I will be under the scrutiny of my father all summer. I remember all the mail in the foyer, including another freshman information packet, and it dawns on me. I could make up fake precollege classes that I will tell my parents I'm attending to help me get ready for college. My mother knows nothing about computers, and my father is only interested in financial news. But I know *everything* about computers. I write a letter to myself saying that the classes are twice a week, on Tuesday and Thursday evenings, in Pittsburgh. I create an ad hoc website and make the syllabus and activities look real and professional. I'll even show my father some of my "homework." I'm hoping this will give me some time to hang out at the Home with Sadie, and maybe I'll even see Jase. Even if that doesn't happen, at least I'll have some alone, unscheduled time. It's something I've never had before.

The next day, while I'm hanging out at the mall with Julia, Danielle, and some of our other friends, Shawna and Susan, I'm hardly paying attention to what they're saying: who is dating who, who got drunk and barfed last night, who's sleeping with each other, and whose parents are out of town so an impromptu party can be scheduled. I'm not listening. If I'm honest, it wasn't ever interesting. I just pretended it was to fit in. But I don't want to do that anymore. In ten weeks I will be out of here, and I will never have to feign interest in someone barfing in a Park City mansion again.

I cut my time with my friends short and head home. I don't see my father's car and breathe a sigh of relief. It's short-lived because my mom calls for me when she hears the door open. I follow the sound of her voice to her room. She's perched up in bed, reading *People*. On her nightstand is a glass of iced tea, not the usual bottle of chardonnay, and by the look of her eyes, she hasn't taken any of her benzos yet. I sit on the bed next to her and fill her with the lie that I was spending time at the mall. I tell her there are some cute sandals at Nordstrom and that we should go there to look at them. "Mom, let's go college school shopping. I have to look good for rush." Joining a sorority is a must. I don't want to pledge, but I've learned to pick my battles.

Her face shifts to sadness, and she says, "I'll miss our shopping trips."

"I know, Mom," I say, holding her hand. My mom and I bond over shopping and traveling. My father usually doesn't join us on our trips, which is fine by both of us. My mom comes alive in Italy, Paris, Greece, anywhere there is art and history and . . . well, anywhere that is away from her husband.

"But I'll be home over the holidays, and you can always come see me as well. Chicago has so many great museums and shops."

She pats my hand but doesn't say anything. I know what she is getting at, and it's not just about missing a shopping buddy. I'm the only one who sees her and talks to her in this house, and I know my presence protects her by offering my dad a distraction. He can always hound me about my grades and take a break from criticizing her.

I want to help my mother feel that she has a purpose. I always reassure her that her love and opinion matter. I know there is a talented and brilliant woman inside, but it's been beaten into submission by years of neglect and emotional abuse. I used to wish she'd divorce my father, but I know that my father would never admit to making any mistakes. It wouldn't look good to the community.

I used to think he was noble for providing well-paying jobs to the town, but what I overhear people saying at the retirement home is that he was incredibly demanding and not always ethical. Jonathan Hill offers almost no healthcare benefits to his workers, who do backbreaking labor. He challenges every worker's compensation case and usually wins.

My mom and I chat some more about our summer plans, and then I excuse myself to go over my precollege work. At least that's what I say. Really, I just look Jase up on social media. I am not surprised to find he has zero presence. I feel foolish doing so, it's a high school thing, but at the same time, I can't say I wasn't hoping for some hot pictures of him without his shirt on.

Instead, what I find is a few articles about how he was promoted, twice, at the Mill. It appears he's made his mark, especially for only being twenty-one, and his department always exceeds its goals. My father would still lose his mind if he knew I was spending time with Jase, but it makes me even more enthralled with him. Smart, talented, devoted to his work, and unbelievably sexy. Who is this guy?

The rest of the week is boring, and I'm counting down the days until I might see Jase again. He hasn't been to the Home since "the Olympics," but a girl can hope.

This time, when I arrive, Jase is already setting up the chairs. Yeah! He looks quite pleased with himself, even more pleased when he sees the surprised look on my face. There's an even longer line forming this week, and I can't help but think it's due to women wanting a chance to ogle Jase. I see Sadie walk in with Lou and give her a surreptitious thumbs-up, and then I walk to the podium to begin the game. Mary wins again.

While cleaning up, Jase asks me about my week and Sadie. I'm not used to this. Guys in my high school tended to be narcissistic and do all the talking. They certainly never ask me about Sadie or care about anything past their own little world. Once the game is done and we're done cleaning, I hang around again. I don't want to leave while Jase is still here. This is a serious crush.

Jase sits on one of the tables and looks straight into my eyes. "Heard you graduated and will be leaving for school soon."

I was shocked. "How did you know?" I can't look away from those dark brown eyes.

"Kat, everything that happens at the Mill is common knowledge. Your father makes sure that everyone knows about things he thinks are important, even if we don't."

I'm so embarrassed. Especially since my father never let me know that my graduation meant anything to him. He did let me pick out a new red Audi to replace my old BMW, not that I even wanted one, but as always, appearances mean everything to him.

"College is my get out of jail free card." I can't believe I just blurted that out. I've always kept my feelings for my father closely guarded. Jase and I continue to stare at each other.

He looks away. "Interesting" was all he said. He gets off the table. Then he looks back at me. "Kat, see you next week."

I'm shocked. I'll see him again! Other than our Bingo Olympics, he never gave me any indication about when he'd be back. I'm in heaven. I especially like that he called me a name that nobody else ever does. Does that mean that he's interested, or am I just an acquaintance? For now, I'll bask in the promise of the next bingo session. It's become my favorite game!

On Thursday morning I pick out my clothes. I've already curled my hair, soft and wavy. I don't want it to look fake; natural is what I'm striving for. I keep my makeup simple: mascara, pink blush, and matching MAC lipstick. I decide on a black pair of Kate Spade jeans. They have little white dots on them, so I go with a classic white buttoned-down shirt, Alexis Bittar funky dangling earrings, and black flats. I finish my look with a white Chanel bag. The thing is, I'm pretty sure Jase couldn't care less what I look like. He's never "looked me over," engaged in flirty conversations, or even mentioned any other activities we could do together except bingo. By the time I've left my house, I've convinced myself that he just cares about the community, and the game is something he can do to let the residents have more fun.

I need to just get over him. That's going to be hard. He's real, doesn't make empty promises, never brags about his success at the Mill, and seems genuinely embarrassed by his looks.

The game is easy. It helps that Jase and I have done it before, so we're a well-oiled machine. Ted finally won, so I am thrilled. Just when I'm done putting stuff away, Jase asks me, "Can I show you something?"

"Sure." I laugh nervously.

He grabs my hand and leads me out to a dark blue Dodge truck. I pause because I assumed he meant something in the Home, not in his car. He senses my trepidation and tilts his head to the side. "You okay?"

"Yeah, I guess," I say. Of course I'm okay. I'm thrilled.

"Don't worry, we'll be back in an hour," he says as he opens the passenger door. I climb in. He goes to the driver's seat, starts the truck, and drives out of the parking lot.

What the hell am I doing? Is he going to kill me? I picture my body left in the woods as he makes a quick left onto a back road away from the town. We continue on the road for several miles, and he takes another left onto an old gravel road, leading us even further away from Hilltown. No one knows where I am, and I'm on a deserted road with a man that I don't know very much. All of the "stranger danger" and "don't ever be alone with a man you don't know" talks I've been given are thrown out the window. I'm an idiot and everyone will know it if I end up on the news later this week.

We continue slowly down the road until we come to the edge of an old bridge. He hasn't said a word, and my mind is spinning, but strangely, I also feel calm. I realize I don't fear him or his intent. I mean, how bad can a guy be who hangs out at a retirement community and buys his aunt roses? Plus, everyone in town seems to adore him. If I'm honest with myself, I have to admit I'm really excited to be alone with him.

He stops the truck and crosses over to my side to help me out. The bridge is old, almost as old as the town. The sun is setting, casting a pink hue to the sky. The air is still. Silhouetted against the sky, the smokestack of the Mill shoots gray clouds of smoke into the air. We stand by the truck for a few moments, taking in the silence. Then he sits on his truck, and I follow his lead.

"Have you ever been here?" he asks.

"No. I always wondered what this road led to, but I never tried to find out."

"I've been coming here for years," he says while rubbing his chin. "It's the only place I can be all alone. I don't have to think about work, my family, or what girl I'm seeing. I only have to think about what I want to do with my own life, my own future."

I'm a little stung by the "what girl I'm seeing" comment, but otherwise I get it. It's like my porch swing; it offers me solitude and the chance to figure out what my future might hold, without other people's expectations.

"So, you bring all the girls here." I try to laugh off my comment, but his face looks as if I slapped him.

"That's not who I am, Kathleen," he says sternly.

"I know. I'm sorry, when I'm nervous, I just blurt things out."

"I get that. And I don't want you to be nervous, so I will answer your very rude question and say no, not all the girls. I just came here with my old girlfriend, Vicky."

"What was she like?" It's none of my business.

He looks at me to see if I really want to hear about her, and when he can tell I meant it, he answers, "Smart, really smart. She was valedictorian and funny as hell. In our sophomore year of high school, she sent me a note in biology saying, 'Do you want to be my boyfriend?' There was only one box to check, yes. Of course, there was no guy in high school who wouldn't check that box. She was a cheerleader but wasn't stuck up like the other ones. She was naturally beautiful, no makeup, long black hair, and a smile that could light up a room."

Wow, no way I can ever compete with that.

He drifts off, and after a moment, I ask, "What happened with you guys?"

"Vicky went to State, and I went to Southwestern. We tried the long-distance thing, but it didn't work out."

I think he is going to change the topic, but he continues and tells me about his "sick" father, which I think means alcoholic, who he had to look after, and his younger brother, Brook, who it sounds like Jase raised with his aunt Anne.

"My father, Sam, lost his job at the Mill because he missed too many days with hangovers. His team members finally got sick of covering for him. He refused treatment again and again, always saying that he could kick it on his own, but—" Jase shakes his head. I search his face for anger or resentment, but instead mainly see indifference. As in, *these were the cards dealt to me; I just coped with it.* I also see some sadness.

I am so impressed that he isn't full of pity or looking for a badge of honor for basically taking care of his family since he was only a teenager. Then he adds, "Since Sam was fired for cause, his pension and union benefits were invalidated." I wince hearing that, knowing that was probably my father's doing. Doesn't Dad know alcoholism should be treated as a medical condition? Of course not. He would see it as weakness, just like he does with Mom.

"When I left to go to Southwestern, I was planning to get my business degree. By the end of my freshman year, Brook was just a sophomore in high school, and my aunt Anne's veterans and social security benefits weren't enough to keep the family afloat, so I dropped out. I needed to sort out my family and the mess that my father caused."

Oh my God, I thought. *He became the official head of his family at the age of nineteen.* He started working at the Mill during the day and taking shifts at Joe's Bar at night.

"Vicky was great through all of this, but I never had time for her." Again, I search his face for anger, but I don't see any. He starts grinning and says, "I don't usually spill my guts to people I hardly know."

"I'm glad you told me," I say and touch his arm. "Why did you bring me here?"

"In a way, we have a lot in common; we're both stuck. I have to do everything for my family, and you do everything you can to escape yours. Different sides of the same coin."

We sit in silence for a few moments, and then my nervousness takes over and I say, "If you could go anywhere, where would it be?"

He looks confused by my random question but quickly answers, "The Great Wall of China."

Everything about this man mesmerizes me. I figured it would be something to do with motorcycles or flying planes, but he didn't hesitate.

"Why the Great Wall?"

"I love history, and from all I've read, there is nothing like it. Imagine a wall spreading miles and miles to protect a country. I have a lot of places I'd like to see, but that's first on my bucket list."

I love history. I'd love to see it, especially with him.

"What about you?"

"The Blue Lagoon in Iceland. I went there once with my mom, and it was magical. The water supposedly has all of these healing elements and makes your skin feel so silky. The scenery is stunning. You can sit and soak right in the middle of a lava field. It's so amazing to think—" I stop mid-sentence, embarrassed by how shallow this sounds compared to the Great Wall.

Then he answers, "Sounds pretty amazing. I'll add it to my list."

It's getting dark, and I can hardly make out his face anymore. We've been here much longer than an hour. I know I need to get back, but I don't want to leave.

"Kat," he starts, "no one can know anything about this. It could hurt my family. If your dad or anyone at the Mill knew I was here with you, it would be really bad for me. It would probably mean the end of my job. I can't afford that."

I want to say he's wrong, but I know he's not. "But . . . but, can we come here again? I won't tell anyone, I promise. I'm really good at keeping secrets. Basically my whole life is a secret."

He hesitates and opens my side truck door. "Do you understand what you're asking for?" He's already taken a huge chance just bringing me to the bridge. "I need to get you back."

He doesn't answer my question. I take it as a no. We drive back to the retirement home in silence, and I figure this will be the last time I'll ever get to be alone with him. When we arrive back at the parking lot, he says, "I have to decide whether seeing you again is worth the risk. But if I do, I could meet you at the bridge next Thursday at seven-thirty. If I'm not there by eight, it means I'm not coming. Oh, and Kathleen, wear something that's easy to take off."

I don't even try to conceal my smile. I spontaneously give him a quick kiss on the cheek. I'm also nervous that someone will see us as I get out of the truck. He waves at me as he drives away, and I think, *I can't wait until Thursday!*

Chapter 4

I spend the better part of the next day on my swing. I google everything I can on the Great Wall, and I'm fascinated to learn it took over 2,000 years to construct. I drift off thinking about Jase and our conversation. He's not like anyone I've ever met, and I really want to know him more. I hope he decides it's worth it. That I'm worth it.

Ironically, I also have some real freshman information forms to fill out for college. Once I'm done, it's still only three. I open the door and yell to Janice, our house manager, "I'm going to run some errands."

I drive to the retirement home, and I'm glad Sadie is free. She's the one friend I know who can keep secrets. We both get some coffee in the cafeteria and take it back to her room.

"Well, give me the news. It looks like you're here for something," she says.

"Now this is super, super secret. Remember when you told me to get to know Jase?"

"How could I? How could any woman forget him?" I smile. "Good for you!" she interrupts. "You're young and beautiful. I dare say, you deserve some fun. You're far too serious." Her twinkling eyes tell me she's teasing me but is also telling me to loosen up. "Well, I have a bit of news too. You remember Lou, the new guy?"

"Who wouldn't?" I answer with a smile.

"Well. We've eaten lunch together the last week or so. He's totally ignoring Betty and Rosie, our home floozies."

"He has good taste."

She fills me in more on Lou and their budding romance, which I have to admit is far surpassing whatever it is I have done with Jase. I get up to go, and she reassures me that my secret is safe with her. I never doubted that for a moment. When I hug Sadie, she looks me in the eye and says, "Don't let your family take your joy."

I'm confused because I never talk to Sadie about my family. But then I remember, Sadie knows everything.

When I get home, I have a meeting with my father about my "classes." He wants to invite everyone in the "study group" to our house. *No way!* That cannot happen. There is no study group.

"Daddy, it's a getting-to-know-you kind of thing. Like me, the students are serious about getting ahead of the game. I'll never be best friends with any of them. They're smart, but if I have to define them, I'd say 'nerds.'" I hate sounding like such a snob, but it works, and he agrees to let the idea go.

I tell my father that the classes are taught by upperclassmen and some TAs. Overall, I'm feeling good about my lie. It's pretty thought-out. "Remember, sometimes I might stay in Pittsburgh overnight."

"All right, Kathleen. I'm expecting you to graduate Phi Beta Kappa, so you may as well start off strong."

"Of course, Dad."

Everybody thinks that I have my life in perfect order. In truth, I'm scared, scared that I'll end up being stuck like my mother. My father is grooming me to be a successful addition to the future management of the Mill, and it won't stop there. He'll want to choose my job, my future husband, where my future kids go to school, everything. But I have my own goals and dreams. I keep telling myself that all I have to do is make it through college, but what if I'm still not free then? Sure, I could live without some of this lavishness, but I've read the studies on how little college graduates make, how they're swimming in debt and then have to move back home or take secondary jobs. What if I have no viable options besides working at the Mill? Then I would be under my dad's thumb forever.

I shake off the gloom and just think about Jase. That is nerve-racking as well. I'm not sure he's even going to meet me. And if he does, that makes me nervous too because my father would deem this slumming and fraternizing with a man beneath me. If he found out, what he would do to me would be a picnic compared to what he'd do to Jase.

On Thursday evening I sit in my car and constantly think of more reasons why I should not go to the bridge. *He probably won't be there. Instead of leaving, I should raid my mom's wine and go to bed. He might not think I'm pretty, especially since his last serious girlfriend was so perfect.* Then I decide, *Don't think, just drive.* I start the ignition. Soon, I'm driving down the small gravel road leading to the bridge. My heart races when I see Jase sitting on a rock close to his truck. He came! A huge smile fills my face, and my palms start to sweat. So much for playing it cool. I stop and get out of my car, not sure what to do or how to greet him. He walks over to me, puts his arms around me, and kisses me like I've never been kissed before. So much better than the "hey" I was going to offer. I lean in, and he kisses me again, slower and sweeter. I don't return the kiss, so he steps back and looks questioningly at me. "Did I misread this situation?"

I awkwardly say, "No, not at all."

I'm not used to such directness. All of the high school guys I've been with usually got drunk and then made clumsy moves on me that I am sure they thought were sexy but were not. Now that we're here, I guess I don't know what I want. "I haven't just casually 'hooked up' before, so I don't know how this works," I admit.

He's quiet. Then he smiles that amazing smile. "Kathleen, I don't have preconceived notions of tonight. I'm not a guy who sleeps with every woman I meet. I don't want just a hookup, but I don't want you to assume this is more than a temporary thing. You're leaving for college in a couple of months, so whatever this relationship is, it won't last longer than that." A few seconds go by as I take that in. "Just so you know, I'm clean, but I brought condoms." *Thoughtful*, I think, *but that makes having sex real.*

"I'm still on birth control 'cause of my last boyfriend," I say, feeling slightly embarrassed.

He smiles and walks over to his truck bed, grabbing a sleeping bag. He spreads it on the flattest part of the clearing and sits on it, patting the spot next to him. I join him, and he touches my face while he softly kisses me on my cheeks and then my lips. It's slow and gentle, not fast and messy like my other boyfriends. He continues the soft kisses, gradually deepening them, until his mouth and tongue are a part of the dance. I lean into him. I want him. I never thought I would ever want anyone like this. He begins to kiss my neck, down to where my shirt ends. Then he moves up my neck and to my lips. His fingers run through my hair. I always thought that was a cliché, but I never had anyone like Jase doing it. Everything is slow, but I'm still having a hard time trying to keep up with all the sensations and feelings, physically and emotionally.

"Mmmm," he groans. He pulls me down onto him to give me another slow, deep kiss, then another and another.

I pull his shirt up so I can feel his skin, and he takes my T-shirt off and unclasps my bra. I pull his shirt off and press against him. He makes short work of both of our jeans. Soon, we're naked. He is still kissing me, but I feel like I will die if he isn't inside me soon. He seems to share my hunger.

"I just want to look at you in the moonlight for a minute. You're gorgeous." Then, he pushes himself into me. *Oh my God. Now I understand what all the fuss is about.* He moves slowly, he isn't in a hurry, but each thrust makes me want more. Soon, he moves faster and faster and deeper and deeper, and I can't hold back. I moan my release. He soon follows me, but he doesn't pull out. He just looks into my eyes . . . those delicious deep brown eyes. I can feel our hearts beating together.

He moves and lies down next to me. We stay like that for a few more minutes, holding hands. I want to stay this way forever, next to him, under him, with him inside me. I can see the strain in his eyes, even though he is smiling. It's strange. For once, I don't want to talk. He is staring at the sky. He has a small grin on his face. "Kat, casual hookups look good on you." We both laugh.

I ask him about work. "Busy as always. Another department was going to close down, so I volunteered to have them report to me. I've done their job before, so it's fine. I'm letting Brook take over at Joe's. I was just doing him a favor since his partner left with no notice."

Even more people? Soon, the whole Mill will be under him. I can only imagine the pressure he feels. Seeing him at the retirement home, I know he really cares about people. This man is probably not getting any sleep. I read online that the day before, he was offered another promotion, his third in two years, which *never, ever* happens at the Mill. He would never admit it, which makes me want him more.

My first high school boyfriend, Nate, whined about having to take AP classes to get into Yale, and he never worked a job or even helped his family around the house as far as I could see. His father went there, so I'm sure being a "legacy" helped. My second one, John, was the same way. Only he was going to Stanford like his father did. Most of the kids at Country Day are the same. I guess I'm not that much better. But being with Jase makes me want to be better.

I remember my friend who went "slumming" shared some tidbits of news to me. "I heard your brother is getting married," I say. "Are the wedding plans in full swing?"

Jase laughs, but I can see his jaw tighten. *Uh-oh, maybe I overstepped.* I don't remember who told me about the engagement, but I have definitely been doing my research on all things Jase.

"I think Lyn, his fiancée, is doing most of the wedding prep, as far as I can tell. Brook just likes a reason to celebrate over and over again. He spends even more time and money at Joe's."

"Does he work with you at the Mill?"

"Yeah." Jase pauses, and I wonder again if I'm overstepping. But he continues, "He just got a promotion, in fact."

"That's great," I say, wondering if Jase was responsible for that promotion.

"It is. He's a good worker. Brook dropped out of high school in his junior year. I tried to change his mind, but he said school wasn't for him. He got his GED and started working at the Mill. I always hoped he'd go back to school, because jobs and promotions will be limited for him if he doesn't, but then our dad died, Lyn got pregnant, along came Brooklyn, my niece, and, well, it never happened. Don't get me wrong. We all adore Brooklyn. She's the best. I just worry about Brook sometimes."

"Of course you do. He's your little brother. Are there any other family members who can help?"

"Right now, we're all living at my aunt Anne's. It's great for Brook and Lyn and Brooklyn. An extra pair of hands amid chaos. We're redoing my father's house next door so they can have somewhere to build their life together, and we can help when needed. Annie, my aunt, is always feeding us." He smiles. "But Lyn's family doesn't live around here, so it's just us. Brook is pretty handy, so he's doing the most work at the house." Of course he defends his brother. He looks embarrassed. "Sorry, I'm going on and on."

"Don't apologize. I like hearing about your life. It's far more interesting than what I'm used to. My friends at school think a long line at Starbucks or an acrylic nail breaking is a tragedy."

I regret saying that as soon as it's out of my mouth. I don't want to talk about the shallow world. He has real problems that matter, and I'm sure I look immature and entitled.

I search his face for judgment but don't see any. "Well, lucky for me, you are not like your friends. In fact, Kat, you're not like most people."

I think that's the nicest thing anyone has said to me, and I feel tears fill my eyes. I lean over and kiss him, and he starts kissing and caressing me as if we have all the time in the world. He's breathing deeply, but he still just lies next to me. I pull him on top of me, and he begins kissing the front of my body. I feel laser-focused on his lips, his skin, and his touch. He kisses each breast, but he's gentle, until he's not. Then, he starts cupping them, sucking them. My core is wet, and I don't know how I can be, in some odd way, both restless and rested. He continues until I feel like I need more. His other hand moves to my center, and I feel a kind of pressure growing deep inside me. I've never felt like this before. I cry out. I can't look at him. I'm embarrassed. I'm sure he can guess how inexperienced I am. He gently lies me down so my head is resting on his chest. "Kat, don't hide from me." I can't hide. Ever since I met him, it's like he's looking into my soul. It's a little bit scary. I've never had someone get so close to me.

Then I point out the obvious. "Um, Jase, you never, I mean we didn't . . ."

He smiles back at me and says, "I love to touch you and taste you, and it seems that you like it too. You don't need to feel embarrassed or like I missed something."

"Do you want to see me again?" I ask. *Say yes!* I hope, but I expect a no.

"The day is up to you; the time is up to me."

"Here, on Sunday?" I ask.

"Here. Sunday, at seven," he answers.

Chapter 5

Spending time with Jase is inspiring me to do more than my fake classes and dodging my parents and friends this summer. I decide that I should learn more about the Mill. Dad has been grooming me to join him there since I was in middle school, so I am sure it will be an easy sell. I want to intern there. The real bonus is that it will allow me more time with Jase.

We've spent two more nights at the bridge. He is so addictive. I wonder if I've always been a closeted sex addict. But I always have to get home before I turn into a pumpkin. All of the lying, though, is becoming exhausting. An internship would mean that I can see him every day without having to fabricate any lies; plus, I'll get to see him in the real world. Not that I mind the world we've created at the bridge; it's better than I ever imagined was possible. But the more he tells me about Brook, his crew at the Mill, Annie, and all the other parts of his life, the more I want to know. When Nate, my last boyfriend, talked, I could barely concentrate on what he was saying; it was so irrelevant. And sex? I'm just glad I got out of the relationship before much happened. The more I see Jase, the more I know him, and the more I like and respect him.

The following night at dinner, I broach the subject. "Daddy, I'd like to spend some time at the Mill observing the process of production. It would help me be a more effective manager once I graduate. I think spending part of the summer interning there would give me a lot of information."

My father answers, "Kathleen, I'm impressed. I'll call Art Kramer and have you placed with our best team leader, Jase Thompson. They do the final part of the process, which brings in the most money. I might even have you look at some underperforming departments so you can let me know which ones I should cut."

I'm shocked my dad would be so cavalier about ruining people's lives. I'm horrified to have that responsibility, or any part of it. No wonder Jase was so concerned about the people he works with. I always know who was fired when I go to get my mother's flowers. The people in town put together gift bags of necessities for each of those families. I knew that they would be losing much more than a job; they were losing a way of life. Maybe I could intervene in some way and actually save jobs.

As I lay on the sleeping bag next to Jase the next evening, my head on his chest and my fingers making slow circles on his stomach, I say, "I want to know your world better."

Jase opens his eyes and looks down at me. "What are you talking about?"

"I want to know more about what you do when we're not together."

His face becomes very serious, and I realize I have gone about this the wrong way. He probably feels invaded and smothered. I'm such an idiot. I should just leave well enough alone. We have our time at the bridge, so why am I ruining it?

"Kathleen, I've always been straight with you. I'm not sure where this is going, if anywhere, and not that it's any of your business, but—"

I burst out laughing. "I'm not asking for a list and timeline of every girl you've dated. I'm just saying I'm thinking about interning at the Mill."

I thought this would make him relax, but if anything, he looks even more concerned. And now that I've unintentionally brought up the "are we seeing other people?" question, I don't feel so great, not great at all.

Jase looks at me. "Okay, Kat, what's going on?"

"You're a part of Hilltown, but I know nothing about it. Who lives here—"

"You mean what the townies do with their lives?" I feel mocked, but he's not wrong.

"I have never called anyone a 'townie.' I just want to know the people and things that are important to you—your crew, your friends, your family, your job."

"And why all the sudden interest? You know that if people knew about us, I'd be screwed. I have a hard enough time putting it together myself."

"They don't have to find out. I'll be really discreet."

"I've already asked my father to set it up. I told him that getting to know the workers at the Mill will help me be better prepared for college and future employment, wherever that may be."

"Our lives and jobs aren't just some project, Kathleen."

"I know that—and that's not why I want to do this." I could not be screwing this up more if I tried. "It's just that you care about your people and your job. I want to see why. And I thought it would be nice to be able to spend more time together."

Jase is quiet. "I can't believe you never asked me before setting this up. My people and my life outside our time together isn't something you can just put in some petri dish. I don't want your project to end up costing someone their job."

"I promise it won't."

"Maybe if you're in an office, not on the floor, we could—" My face betrays me, and he stops mid-sentence. "You didn't?"

"My father says you're the best manager to learn from, so yes, we thought it would be a good idea." He stands up and starts pacing. "Jase, I know you're upset, but let's talk about this."

"Kathleen, it doesn't feel like there is anything to talk about. You have it all figured out. After all, you are your father's daughter." He pulls on his jeans, shirt, and boots and storms over to his truck. I hear the wheels of his truck fade away. Then I burst into tears.

Jase and I don't usually call each other, so I don't know how to apologize for the fight. We text occasionally, under the pseudonyms Tim Wilson and Suzanne Jones so we don't blow our cover. But I can't text him, "Hey. Sorry, I had my dad put me on your team and ruined your life." That would not only blow our anonymity, but it also wasn't something to say over a text.

As a distraction, I spend the next day shopping with my friends. My mother demanded I get more clothes for rush week, so Julia, Danielle, and I head out to Nordstrom in Pittsburgh. They joke about my "secret life" with my supposed Northwestern friends. Julia and Danielle have no real interest in the academic side of college, and their grades were dismal. Neither one has good study habits or my photographic memory. Their parents managed to buy their entrance into state college. They're drawn to the extracurricular activities, mostly having to do with college boys and partying.

I know I won't keep in touch with them once I'm at Northwestern. Our connection is not strong enough to sustain the distance. I already feel it waning, and I haven't even left yet.

Once home, I unpack all the bags, but rather than feeling the usual shopping thrill, I feel ill at ease. I spent a small fortune on clothes, makeup, and shoes that I don't need. I look at my walk-in closet, already bursting with clothes, and wonder how much they cost compared to what an average family makes each month at the Mill. I can't believe that shopping used to be one of my favorite activities.

I throw half of the items back into their bags to return. On my way back to the mall, I make a detour to see Sadie. I need a dose of cheer, and she always lifts my spirits.

As soon as I get there, I sign in and make my way to Sadie's room. I hear laughter and a male voice as I knock on the door. Sadie answers, "Come on in." I open it to find Lou, the man I saw at bingo. Sadie told me they had been eating lunch together. It sure looks like more than a lunch buddy. They're leaning in toward one another, knees touching, with huge grins on their faces.

"Kathleen! I'm so glad you've stopped by! Kathleen, this is Lou."

I feel a little awkward having interrupted their fun. But Lou immediately gets up, shakes my hand, and offers me his chair. "Hello, Kathleen! I've been hoping I'd meet you soon. My Sadie has told me so much about you."

"My Sadie" says a lot. Lou is a tall, handsome version of Willie Nelson. Long hair in a ponytail, well-trimmed white beard, twinkling blue eyes like Sadie, and a ready smile. He is wearing a very lived-in Rolling Stones tee and jeans.

"I'm a Stones girl myself," I say, pointing to the T-shirt.

"Seen them ten times, all in their glory days!"

"You are so lucky!"

We lock our eyes. We've sized each other up and both approve.

"Well, I'll let you have your catch-up time." He leans over and kisses Sadie's cheek. "See ya later, darlin'. Great to meet you, Kathleen!"

As soon as he leaves, I say, "Lunch buddy, huh?"

"Well, let's just say he's more than just a friend now."

"You mean he's your boyfriend? Do tell!"

Sadie is giddy. "Let's just say that lunch became dinner too. Then meals turned into talks and then other things!"

I am astounded. "Other things, huh?"

"Kathleen, I'm old, but I'm not that old! Still going strong in some departments."

I lean over and hug her. "He is so handsome and seems really nice. You deserve each other. I just hope I'm as sexy as you are when I retire!"

"You will be, dear. You have good genes. I've spilled. Now, your turn. What about you and your guy?"

I stop smiling. "Sadie, I think I blew it. I set up an internship for myself at the Mill, thinking—"

The look of horror on her face tells me, once again, what a mistake this was. "Did you at least talk to him about it first?"

"No. I thought it wouldn't be a deal. If anything, shouldn't he be flattered that I want to be around him more? And I'm willing to work for free."

Sadie takes a moment to gather herself for what I know will be a lecture thickly veiled in concern, so I won't feel lectured. And if I can let my stubbornness go for a minute, I may even learn something.

"You've invaded the last bastion for Jase that doesn't include you or his family. He seems to be a great person, and when he's at work, it's kind of a brain break. You just invaded his space, not to mention, you are his boss's daughter, so—"

"How did you know that?" I never volunteered my last name while at the Home, and if asked, I said it was Jones. I didn't want them to act any differently around me if they thought I was a Hill.

"Dearie, everyone knows that and always has. You were never fooling any of us. We may be old, but we're not stupid, and everyone knows the Hill family."

"I'm an idiot," I say as I cover my face with my hands.

"No you're not, and don't ever say that about yourself. We women put ourselves down far too often. You're brilliant and strong. Own that. But you may be a bit naive about life matters and situations."

"Thank you for not saying 'the real world' or something to point out my privilege. I mean, I know I'm privileged. I just wish it wasn't the first, and sometimes only, thing people see about me."

"It's not easy when you literally live in the town named after your family."

We both crack up. "Good point." I laugh. "I guess there's no way for me to hide who I am in this town."

"You can't hide that you're a Hill, but that doesn't mean you can't show everyone, especially that young man you're hot for, who the real Kathleen Hill is."

"What if I don't know who that is? At home I have to pretend so much of the time, it gets confusing."

"Well, let's start with the internship. Why did you set it up?"

"I wanted to learn more about the Mill, how it works, and the people there. My father always speaks of it as an entity, profits and losses, mainly, and never about the people who actually work the lines. But Jase does. And he speaks about them as whole people, with families, and who are good at what they do, even if it goes unnoticed by my father. I guess I wanted to see this world myself."

"Well, that is exactly what you will tell him when you apologize."

"I already did, and he stormed off. He's really mad at me, Sadie. I think I blew it."

"Nonsense. It's not over until it's over. He probably just needed to blow off some steam."

"I don't know what, if anything, I mean to him. I know he cares, and his touch makes me feel so much, but we're just hanging out."

"Is that what you want?"

"I guess, at least for the summer, but it's complicated. I'm leaving in a couple months. I had my fling. I think I should just let him and the internship idea go."

Then she looks knowingly at me. "But you love him."

I look back at her, ready to deny what she said, but then I remember it's Sadie. She knows everything. "But I love him."

And with her wisdom, she answers, "Well, at least that part isn't complicated."

Sadie also knew when to give me space, and this was one of those times. I say goodbye and drive around before heading home. I need time to think. I end up by the bridge, admittedly hoping I'd find Jase there. His truck is nowhere to be seen, so I try calling him. He doesn't pick up. He's probably helping at the bar. I consider going there to see him, but I decide against it. I'm not twenty-one, and he'll be busy; plus, it would blow our cover. But I need him to know I'm sorry. I try his cell again. Finally, he answers this time. "Hey, Kat," he says with a little too much hesitancy in his voice, but I persevere.

"Can we see each other sometime tomorrow? I want to explain myself and apologize."

"I don't think that will work. This is just too much lying for me."

"But I'll only be following you around and helping for about a month. No one will get in trouble because of me."

"I'll see you at the Mill then." He hangs up.

I'm deeply disappointed. Maybe I shouldn't have pushed so hard, but I honestly want to know about the town and the Mill and all the people. I still know almost nothing about it.

Sitting in silence after our brief phone call, I realize how hard it is for Jase to be with me. He's a straight shooter. He's always honest, even if I don't want to hear what he has to say. To be under the radar and deceiving people is hard on me, but I've been doing it forever; he hasn't. Unlike me, Jase isn't a person who lies.

I think about canceling the whole intern thing, but in the end, I don't. I know I am being selfish, like the "princess" I hate to be called. But he's already mad at me; maybe, this way, I'll at least be around him and can possibly get him to forgive me.

Chapter 6

On Monday I drive to Hilltown and it's as if I am seeing the Mill for the first time. The smokestack continuously churns gray clouds out of the enormous chimney. I always thought of it as a blight on the beauty of the town. Now I see it for what it is for the people that work there: the vital source of their livelihood.

I had called Art Kramer, one of my father's top managers, to set the internship up on Friday. He was deferential on the phone, like everyone who worked there has always been.

"Hello, Miss Hill. I'm excited to hear you're coming. Your father wants you to be assigned to Jason Thompson's group. That won't be any problem. He's our top rolling shift manager."

Of course my father had already set it up, and at the time, I was thrilled to be on Jase's team; now I'm not so sure. Mr. Kramer had said the shift starts at 6:30 a.m., and "Knowing Jase, he'll probably come in at five-thirty and end around six in the evening. You can choose whatever times that work for you while he's here."

I was shocked at the length of his day. "Is that the usual amount of time most people work?" I asked.

"No, but Jase puts in a lot of extra time. Your father gets his money's worth with him. He's known to be very loyal to his workers. I don't have to pay attention to what he does. His teams get things done on time and usually under budget. Workers vie to be on his teams, but there is very little turnover. Maybe you can see what it's like to work for him. I may have him train other managers. Last month he took over managing additional people because the other manager wasn't up to the job. Instead of letting the guy and his crew go, he added them to his team. He didn't want them to be laid off."

It's like he's Superman, saving everyone.

I park my car in the lot and head in to meet Mr. Kramer and the HR people. Mr. Kramer shows me around the offices, not the place where I will be working. He mentions with pride that the Mill never closes. "We're lucky to get a steady stream of orders, unlike some of the other mills. Hopefully, that will continue."

"Hopefully? What does that mean?" I ask. "Is the Mill in trouble?"

"Well, manufacturing in general has been hit hard the last couple of years. The Mill has to operate twenty-four seven. If it doesn't, it's too expensive to keep the fires burning. The Mill has its own savings when there's a drop in orders, but there's only so much we can do about that. Even though we're a union mill, if we show cause, we can temporarily lay off employees during slow times, cut hours, or freeze wages. I don't like to have to make cuts, but it's better than shutting down departments. Your father always expects a profit."

I hear some hesitancy in his voice. He clearly cares that the Mill performs well, but I hear concern. I didn't realize how vulnerable mill jobs were. Work hours could always be cut if my father didn't get the money he expected. As the head of all the operations, Art Kramer was responsible for the Mill's financial success. I don't envy him.

I head home to strategize how I can get Jase to forgive me. I promise myself that I won't be a burden to him and his team. I arrive at five o'clock the next morning. I decided to get there before Jase. I want him to know that I'm serious about learning.

The first things I notice when I walk in are the fire, the heat, the noise, and the smell of soot and sweat. It's the end of the night shift, so everything is happening all at once. Mr. Kramer introduces me to Don Lincoln, the nighttime manager. Don is a short, slightly chubby middle-aged man with a bald spot, who has decided the "comb-over" look is still in style. He greets me with a smile and an apology. He can't show me around yet. I assure him that I'd prefer to look by myself. He thanks me and hands me a pair of earplugs. No one notices as I survey the floor.

What both impresses and bothers me is the physical strength required by the employees. The work appears to be difficult and exacting. No wonder Jase is so strong and Sadie has to use a cane to get around.

Everyone is immersed in their jobs. My father's complaints about workers' compensation stand in stark contrast to his people's obvious dedication to their jobs.

Mr. Kramer returns to take me up to the second floor to Jase and his crew. Jase is cool and distant, but polite.

"Jase, this is Miss Millford." I had asked Mr. Kramer to call me my mother's maiden name, but I now realize how ridiculous that is. Everyone in this mill knows who I am, especially Jase.

I interrupt. "You all can call me Kathleen."

"Kathleen will be interning with your group for part of the summer," Kramer explains.

During the first few days, the employees seem wary, and Jase completely ignores me. In some ways, that's a good thing. The people would never believe that there was anything going on between Jase and me. We keep our conversations strictly business. By the end of the first week, Jase and his crews are used to my presence. I even started eating in the company cafeteria, but, of course, no one sits next to me.

I get to observe how Jase works with his teams, and I am immediately impressed by his competent and caring demeanor. Throughout their shift, Jase makes sure his men and women take breaks. Before lunch on Thursday, he calls a short meeting. "Are any of you willing to donate time off or extra work hours to Kevin Kersey? I know that you have been great about your generosity. The baby seems to be thriving, but she remains in the hospital." Everyone raises their hands.

"Great. I'll tell him. It will put his mind at ease."

It seems that Jase wants nothing to do with me *at all*. He ignores me at the Mill and doesn't answer his cell or the texts I'm sending him. We haven't gone to the bridge since the last horrible date. Being close to him day after day just makes me want that passionate connection back. But I have definitely been ghosted.

I have a daily routine. I get to the Mill at 7:30, and I'm usually exhausted by four o'clock. I feel like such a lightweight. I know Jase gets in by 6 a.m. and never leaves before 6 p.m. I see him taking charts and notes home with him, probably schedules and progress reports or plans for the next day. I don't know how he has any time to visit the retirement home or do extra training for new employees. No wonder he usually fell asleep after our lovemaking.

I've been coming to the Mill for a week, and I'm determined not to be ignored any longer. I go to the breakroom and wait. Jase won't be finished for a couple more hours. I periodically peek out to make sure he didn't just leave.

When Jase finally heads to the exit, I run to catch up with him.

"Can I do something for you, Miss Millford?" I ignore his sarcasm.

"Jase, you haven't even texted me, but I've tried to reach you like a million times."

"Kathleen, you get to watch me at work, but you don't get to follow me afterward."

"I promise that I can get obnoxious if you keep punishing me. I have stayed out of everyone's way. I've watched your group and have learned a lot about product rolling from your team, especially Stephanie. I also eat in the lunchroom, and I haven't ever interrupted anyone. My dad wants a 'report,' and I plan on giving everyone an A-plus. What else can I do?"

"You forget, Kat, that I never wanted you here in the first place." Then, he takes a deep breath and stares down at me.

I'm sure he's going to say no and storm off, but he actually pauses. It gives me a moment to look at him, *really* look at him, not the furtive glances I sneak all day at work. I see he's as gorgeous as ever, and my heart quickens, but I also see the strain in his jawline. Even Superman gets tired sometimes. Whether it's the fatigue or my girlish charm, he sighs and says, "Fine, follow my truck."

I nearly jump for joy. He ruins the moment by lecturing me, but I guess I have it coming.

"We're visiting the Kersey's. Remember, this is their home and family, so don't overstep. You need to show some respect. If you act insulting, we're leaving, and I won't let you come again. And in case you didn't know, I do pull rank. Your father wants the Mill to run efficiently, so if I tell Kramer your presence is impacting my crew, you'll be quickly transferred out, and you'll have to take your father's shit. He doesn't personally care about his employees, but he does care about profits."

"Deal," I say, but he's already turned to get in his truck. He knew I'd agree to just about anything he wants. I should be annoyed by his arrogance, but instead it makes me want him even more. As I follow him out of the parking lot, I think about how everybody knows about my father's greed. I never knew my grandparents, and I wonder if this was their dream. Somehow, I don't think so. What would they think of the way my dad had management constantly change people's jobs so they never could become experts and be promoted? His unrealistic projections and almost no interaction between management and staff? Under my father's direction, the Mill feels like it's built on quicksand and could be drowned easily. No wonder Jase is always stressed.

He slows down in front of one of the neat two-story homes in a neighborhood full of houses on gentle hills. All of them have the same design, with large front porches so everyone can easily visit. Some have gardens, some have children's swings and tree houses, some have fenced-in backyards, and some have everything, like this one.

I follow Jase to the front door, and he knocks. A tired-looking, dark-bearded man opens it. In the background, children scream and play, and the smell of chili greets us.

"Jase! Good to see you. Thanks for coming." The men embrace, and then he glances at me and then back to Jase questioningly.

"Hi, I'm Kathleen, and I'm interning at the Mill this month, and Jase, I mean Mr. Thompson, was generous enough to allow me to shadow him today." I stick out my hand to shake the man's, but he just grins at me and then at Jase. "Any friend of Jase's is a friend of ours. Come on in," he says as he sweeps his arms to show us his home. "I'm Kevin." I follow Jase to the living room, which is cozy and cute. A pounding of footsteps cascades down the hall, and then two curly-headed boys run toward Jase and pull him to the ground. "Hi Jase!" beams one.

The other says, "Jase, let's wrestle, and then you can watch us ride our new bikes!"

"Look, boys, you can go play your video games for fifteen more minutes. I need a little more time here with Jase," Kevin says.

Jase looks at the tired man. "Hey, Kev, we got you another week of paid leave. When you come back, let me know what shift you want. I'm sure everyone will be flexible. How's everything going with little Emily?"

"Thanks so much for asking. They think she can come home in a few days. She's put on almost all the weight she needs, and all her tests have come back negative."

Jase looks at me and explains, "Kevin and Josie have a little one, Emily, still in Parkland City Hospital. She came a bit early and needed to gain more weight before coming home."

A young, dark-haired woman walks out of the kitchen. She looks exhausted. Too exhausted to even smile, so she just stares at me. "Hello, Mrs. Kelsey, I'm Kathleen. Thank you for letting me barge into your home. It sounds like it's been a busy time for your family."

I am so relieved when the woman smiles and stops looking at me like I'm a security guard. Josie, as she introduced herself, offers me some iced tea, and I follow her into the kitchen. The boys come with us. Kids always have a sixth sense of when someone could possibly offer them food and ask for a snack. "Please, Mom!" one of the two begs.

"No, we'll have dinner soon, and I don't want you filling up on garbage," Josie replies as she stirs the chili.

The boys, Jaden and Jesse, protest, but without vigor. They tell me they knew they were going to be denied snacks and their ulterior motive was to come check out the girl with Jase. Fortunately, I am fluent in video game speak, so I ask them all about Fortnite and Minecraft.

"Do you like Battle or Save the World better?" I ask the younger one, Jaden.

"Battle!" he says, to no surprise.

The boys start demonstrating the moves from the game and their karate class, so I offer to take them outside. Josie says, "That's not necessary," but I can tell she's just being polite.

"It's no problem," I say. "I'd actually love to get in a few roundabouts before I go home." The kitchen looks over the backyard, so I hope Josie feels comfortable enough letting a stranger hang out with her kids.

Fatigue is in my favor once again, and she says, "That would be lovely. Thank you."

The boys and I demonstrate our moves together until Jase pokes his head out the door. He looks mad at first, but upon seeing my failed block punch, landing me on my butt, he cracks a smile.

"Ready to go, Bruce Lee? I think we need to let this family have their dinner."

I brush myself off and say goodbye to the boys. Kevin and Josie walk us to the door. She looks so frail. I have to do something. "Um, I don't want you to feel uncomfortable, but I'd be glad to come over if you need someone here to watch the boys while you go to visit Emily. I can't imagine it's easy dragging them with you. Or I could just take them to the park or something if you wanted to rest. Maybe that's weird. I'm sorry, you don't even know me—"

Josie looks behind me, where Kevin stands with Jase. My face turns red with the thought that this was exactly what he told me not to do: "Don't overstep." Some slight, almost imperceptible communication occurs between Kevin and Josie, and Josie's face softens. Jase must have noticed it as well because, to my surprise, he chimes in, "I'm sure Kathleen would make a good sitter, and her internship hours are flexible."

"We'd appreciate it. It has been kind of hard. I don't have the energy to run around with them like I used to, so I'm sure they'd appreciate an hour playing soccer at the park. If it's not too much to ask," Josie says.

Hard is an understatement, I think. "I'd love to. I can come anytime tomorrow and Wednesday. I'm happy to stay for a few hours so you can get to the hospital if you want."

Josie finally smiles and softly replies, "Thanks. My sister has tried to help, but she has a full-time job in Park City, and Mom's getting older."

"I can stay for three or four hours. If you need more time, just let me know. Does that work for you both?"

Josie answers, "Thank you so much. The boys take the bus, and it drops them off at three-fifteen."

"Great, I'll come at three, if that's okay, to make them a snack before we head out to the park. And I'll make sure they do their homework. I better make sure it's okay with them." I head upstairs, where I hear children's laughter. I walk into a festive green room with a TV and games, Posters of "The Rock," boy clothes on the floor, and twin beds against the wall.

"Hi guys!"

"Hey," they say. Then Jordan asks, "Are you Jase's girlfriend?"

"No, we just work together." They high-five each other. "Cool."

"Well, I just wanted to know if it would be all right if I come and hang out with you guys for a bit tomorrow. We can go to the park or ride bikes or whatever while your mom and dad go to the hospital. Would that be all right?"

"Will you make us snacks?"

"Of course."

"What about homework?"

"You have to do that as well."

The boys whisper and then say, "Deal! Our babysitters are always family. It will be fun to have such a hot girl watching us!" I laugh. I needed it. Jase ignoring me made me doubt my decision to intern—and myself as a person. The boys feel like fresh air. "Well, see you soon!"

I join the adults downstairs, and we say our goodbyes. Jase doesn't say anything as we walk to our cars, but he looks pleased that I was willing to help. At least he's less frosty with me.

"Well, I'll see you tomorrow," Jase says.

I turn to get in my car but stop. "I don't know when you'll trust that I'm a good person. I'm not doing the internship or helping Josie to impress my dad, or even you, for that matter. I'm just doing it."

"I know, Kat," he says, and that twinkle in his eye returns. Along with that sexy grin— half smirk, half smile. "I think it's great what you just did. See you tomorrow."

The rest of the week continues much the same way. I watch and follow the instructions of the crew whenever I'm at the Mill, but where I really feel useful is at the Kersey's. The boys are great fun, and they are teaching me new video games. The second time I babysat them, Jase and I returned together. Not together as in arm in arm, but at least he wasn't scowling at me, and he even put his hand on my lower back as we walked up the driveway. Jaden and Jesse threw open the door and grabbed my hand, ignoring Jase. "Come on, Kath. Today you might even win!"

Josie looked at Jase. "Sorry they were so rude. They really love Kathleen. I think they might have a little crush on her."

Jase looked shocked but smiled that sexy smile and said, "I'm glad it's working out."

Chapter 7

I miss Sadie so much that even though I am exhausted on Friday, I stop by on my way back from the Mill. The staff is cleaning up from dinner. I say hi and run straight to Sadie's room. She turns around and screams, "Kath, I'm so glad you're here! I've been trying to reach you! Lou and I are going to get married in two weeks. I want you to officiate."

"Wow! What? But you guys just met!"

"When you get to be my age, you have to make things happen for yourself quickly!" She is radiant. "So, will you marry us?"

"I don't have any experience or license to do that."

"Then let's get you official!" Sadie pulls up a website where all I have to do is answer a few questions. "How do you know about this?"

"I've officiated a few ceremonies for friends." Of course she has. Sadie is always full of surprises. She presses "print" and hands me my license.

"It's going to happen in the chapel here. We just want simple, practical vows. I'll get the marriage license. Then we'll have lunch here to make it easy. We already have rings we got on the last field trip. We didn't want to wait. It's not like we have a lot of time!"

"Sadie, I'm going to be your wedding planner. No way 'lunchtime' is going to be your reception! I assume everyone in the community home will be invited, so how many staff and residents are here?"

And my questions continue until I have everything I need. I take one of Sadie's dresses for sizing, insisting she needs a new one for her wedding. By the time I leave, I know her favorite flowers, their favorite foods, favorite colors, and, of course, their favorite cake. I have all the names for the invites so I can work on them over the weekend.

I ask Sadie about her daughter. "I've called and left messages, but she hasn't answered."

I don't want to leave on this sour note, so I say, "Sadie, give me your phone so I can put her number in my contacts. I promise not to be obnoxious, but this ghosting is getting ridiculous. I'll use my phone, and she won't know who I am. She's had plenty of time to 'process' your first marriage. It's time you forgave yourself!"

I dial. "Hello?" Thank God she picks up. "Hi, is this Jenna Holmes?"

The woman answers, "Yes, who is this?"

"I'm Kathleen, from your mother's retirement home."

"Is she all right?" She sounds truly concerned.

"Yes, she's just concerned because she hasn't been able to reach you. It's clear Sadie loves you very much and misses you. I volunteered to try to reach you because we assumed something must be wrong with your phone service."

It was quiet on the other end of the line. I was wary. Would she be angry? Yell at me to mind my own business? Or just hang up?

What I didn't expect was her answer. "I, um, have been thinking of Mom a lot. When you said you were calling from the retirement home, I thought, oh no, I've missed my chance to talk to her, and now it's too late. I couldn't live with that. It's just that I'm so ashamed that I haven't reached out."

"Well, I happen to know she would like nothing more than to talk to you. In fact, here she is." I hand the phone to Sadie, but she stares at me in disbelief, as if it's a bomb about to go off.

"Take it," I whisper to her. "She wants to talk to you!"

"Hello," Sadie says, barely audible.

I busy myself by creating the guest list on Sadie's computer and emailing it to myself. I couldn't leave—she is on my phone—but I'm trying to give her privacy.

"It's all right, honey, I understand. It was a terrible time." I hear over and over again from Sadie. And from the other end, it sounds as if Jenna has been processing her childhood a lot and knows it wasn't Sadie's fault her father was so abusive. I think I even hear her thanking Sadie for protecting her from her dad.

I hear sobs on the line and watch Sadie's tears slide down her cheeks. They need to be alone rather than me pretending I'm not there, so I walk out of the room. I ask to use the phone in the office to continue my wedding organization. The receptionist balks at first, stating, "No one is allowed to use the staff equipment or phones." When I explain what I was doing and for whom, she apologizes profusely.

I call and make reservations for the wedding suite in the Best Western between Hilltown and Park City, for a quick two-night "honeymoon." It's hardly the Ritz, but it's the best the area has to offer.

The desk reception attendant tells me, "Breakfast is free, and there will be a bottle of Champagne and flutes in the room, provided they're twenty-one. "

"Well, they are young at heart, but they live in the Hillside Retirement Home."

"That's great! I love different kinds of love stories!"

"You are so sweet! Thank you!" I give him my credit card information and thank him profusely again.

Lettie, one of the managers of the Home, promises to be the designated driver.

I feel almost as excited as Sadie.

Sadie finds me at the front office and hands me my phone. "Kathleen, you've given me the best gift ever by giving my daughter back. She's going to come to the wedding."

We embrace as she fills me in on their talk and the travel plans of her daughter. She drifts off, looking at my legal pad with my list of duties and checking off items completed.

"This is too much. You don't have to do all of this! We don't need it. Besides, you're too busy to be taking all of this on."

"Sadie, you're my only real 'family,' and I want to do this. I would be pissed if you didn't let me. Not another word. It's taken care of. You and Lou deserve a real wedding."

I spend the entire next day meeting with the vendors I thought that Sadie would like. Sondra replaced Carrie at the florist after Carrie left for maternity leave, and we have become friends after my past poor behavior regarding my mother's roses. Sadie loves calla lilies, so we know how to design a beautiful bouquet and a lily for Sadie's hair.

We decide to put one vase on my podium. Sondra promises to deliver the creations herself on the morning of the big day. Mary and June, the "bingo queens," oversee the chapel decorations that I found at the Hallmark in Park City. Plates, silverware, and glasses are easy. Each table will be covered with soft rose tablecloths, with little rose vases in the middle. Both Sadie and Lou like down-home cooking, so I order a huge spread from a BBQ place I heard a lot of the guys at the Mill raving about. I order Sadie's favorite chocolate cake with white frosting. It will have three tiers, with a bride and groom at the top. The bakery and BBQ place agree to deliver everything.

I also hire six waiters from the local high school to serve and clean up. I ask Lila, our maid's sister, to manage the high schoolers. Then, I hunt down a wedding band who assures me that they are experts in music for people over seventy.

Finally, Sadie's dress. I find a pale-pink dress with ribbons under the breasts and ties in the back. It is tea length and perfect. I buy blue earrings that match and a white gold chain with a beautiful heart charm as my personal gift.

I look over my to-dos and smile with the satisfaction of all my check marks. Of course, it's hard to plan a wedding without thinking about my own someday. Would I want roses and lilies or something more colorful, such as dahlias? A simple dress or a sexy dress or a classic bridal dress? Would my mom want me to alter her dress and wear it? I think it's a Vera Wang silk with an empire waist. It's not my style but is classically beautiful. Most of all, I wonder who will be the man standing next to me at the altar. I wish for the impossible: Jase.

When I get to the Mill, the team is short because someone had to leave suddenly. Having been trained by Jase's right-hand woman, Stephanie, I am finally feeling useful. I can even operate some of the equipment used for rolling the metal into perfect sheets. Each one is the same width and height, ready to deliver to eager customers. I still worry I am more in the way than helpful some days, but Stephanie is always willing to explain things to me.

Jase is pleasant but not warm when he sees me at work. It's been a couple of weeks since we've hung out alone together. I miss him, but I know not to push. Maybe it's for the best. I'll be leaving at the end of summer anyway. I don't really believe it but try to convince myself anyway. Later, while going through my mailbox at work, I see a business envelope.

I open it and almost fall over.

To: Ms. Kathleen Millford

From: Jason Thompson, Idiot

Subject: Forgiveness and Groveling

It has come to my attention that your supervisor has been very foolish in his behavior toward his intern, Ms. Millford. Please check the appropriate box and return the memo to said supervisor.

 —I quit. He is too hard to work with.

 —I'm willing to continue our internship but only professionally.

 —I'm willing to give this another try, but with no more stupid behavior by said supervisor. Said supervisor would also be honored if she would come to his house this Wednesday for a simple dinner.

An actual apology and invitation from Jase Thompson? I never expected it, and I'm thrilled, but I'm not going to let him off the hook too easily. I turn it over and ask for two things: for Jase to be monogamous until I leave for college, and for him to attend Sadie's wedding. I understand that we can't act like a couple—half the people at the wedding will have worked at the Mill—but he can still be there. I also agree to the dinner for Wednesday and put the memo back in Jase's mailbox before heading home.

The next day, Jase enters the staff room as I'm getting a Diet Coke. He leans toward me and whispers, "I got your message, Kat. Next Saturday night after the wedding, tell your parents you won't be home until Sunday. Any problem?"

"No problem," I answer and head to my shift with a huge smile on my face.

The rest of the week moves insufferably slow, and I cannot wait for Saturday. When it finally arrives, I give myself three hours to prepare. I take a long, luxurious shower, taking extra care, shaving and exfoliating. Then, what to wear? I assume we are not going to the bridge, but I can't rule out camping since Jase is more of a pitch-a-tent guy than a fly-you-to-Paris-for-the-night guy. I settle on a lavender flowery summer dress and strappy sandals. I put a pair of jeans and a variety of shirts ranging from sexy to warm and cozy in my backpack. I spend most of my time picking out my lingerie.

Chapter 8

On Wednesday I'm excited but nervous. I'm going to meet Annie, who's like a mother to Jase and Brook. I've heard so much about her. I know I'll love her, but will she like me, or will she only see me as a Hill? I feel kind of honored to have been invited, but then I wonder how many other girls have been invited to dinner. I need to let go of my jealousy.

I race home after my shift to change. I decide to go casual since there would be a toddler around: fitted jeans and a pink shirt. I run down the stairs to find my father insulting my mother.

I peek into the den, where the air is filled with tension. "I'm leaving now. See you later."

"Where are you going, Kathleen?" my mother asks.

"Just to the house of one of Jase Thompson's men."

"Kathleen, remember what I told you about getting too close to the town's families," my father reminds me.

"Get real, Daddy. Checking in on people when they're injured or need help is not a crime. You should try it sometime."

I close the door before he can argue with me. I'm sure that Mom will soon go upstairs and pop a pill, but I can't always be the one to run interference for her.

I park the car and walk toward the front door. I drive the back roads so I have some time to get ready to meet Jase's family. When I arrive, it isn't dark yet, so I'm able to see several beautiful gardens on the small but well-tended lawn. One section is all rose bushes; another is a vegetable garden and a small greenhouse filled with flowering annuals and perennials.

I indulge myself and spend a few minutes admiring the roses. They are so beautiful, and they smell a little like fresh peaches. I walk up the stairs and onto the front porch. I take a moment wondering what it will be like. I'm a little nervous. I ring the doorbell, and a pretty, petite, gray-haired woman answers, her blue eyes sparkling, her arms open. While hugging her, I notice sounds in the back part of the house. A small, blond-haired toddler comes tearing out of the back room, bounding toward me. The little girl seems to realize that she doesn't know who I am. She looks up and laughs, then puts both arms up, signaling she wants to be picked up. I reach down and do just that.

The older woman looks shocked. "You know, Brooklyn never does that with a stranger. You must have a way with children."

"Well, I have been babysitting a lot," I reply.

Jase walks out, followed by a small, mixed-breed little dog and a long-haired white cat.

Annie introduces them to me. "This is Mr. Paws, Lyn's dog. Fortunately, he gets along with my dear old sweetie, Snowflake. Of course, both are having to get used to Brooklyn chasing after them and eating their food."

We all laugh. Brooklyn wiggles when she sees Jase, so I hand the little girl to him.

"Thank you for visiting our crazy home. I apologize in advance. My name's Anne, but my friends like to call me Annie. I'll let you decide which you'd prefer, but calling me Miss Thompson is off limits."

This house isn't crazy; it's a family. My house is the crazy one. No wonder Jase is like he is, really caring for everyone. Jase seems to have mastered the art of communicating so people around him feel special.

"I hope you like family fare. We're having meatloaf, salad, veggies, and mashed potatoes. Chocolate cake for dessert. Would you like a glass of wine?" Annie asks sweetly. It really smells amazing, much better than the calorie-restrictive meals our cook makes at home.

"Yes, that would be great," I reply.

Jase puts Brooklyn down and hands me and Annie glasses of chardonnay. He gets a beer out of the refrigerator for himself. "Well, best to start eating now. You never know when Brooklyn will nod off," Annie suggests.

Watching Jase sit with Brooklyn on his lap makes me suddenly feel melancholy. Someone else will get this—this beautiful man with children of his own.

We chat about work, and Jase tries to act casually, but I can see he's exhausted and worried. Some nights he's at the Mill until after midnight. He still has most weekends free, thank God, but I hear that there have been more layoffs at the Mill. It's making people nervous. I don't want to think about that now. I'm stuffed, but in a good way, and at this moment, I feel content. I feel that a lot when I'm with Jase. I always want him, but just being around him seems to take the edge off my nerves in my own crazy world.

Now I know why. Jase didn't have to pretend he's someone he's not. The way Annie's face lights up whenever she looks at Jase or Brooklyn makes me jealous. Funny, I'm supposed to be the girl who has everything, but my parents have never looked at me that way, like I'm enough, that I'm special. Brooklyn has reached the end of her day. She's rubbing her eyes and doing her best to stay up.

"Excuse me, Kathleen. I need to get her down."

Once Annie goes upstairs, I rise to clear the table. "You don't have to do that," Jase says as he wraps his arms around me.

"I insist, as a good guest should. Plus, Annie cooked all that great food." He starts getting up. "Jase, sit down and relax for once."

I clear and rinse the dishes, but Jase insists on loading them in the dishwasher. Annie arrives as we are finishing up and makes a fuss about how we should not have bothered, but I can tell from the smile on her face that she was pleased we did.

I walk over to hug Annie. "Thank you for a beautiful evening. You have a wonderful home and family."

"You are so welcome, Kathleen. Jase, you must bring Kathleen home again." He smiles but says nothing.

Jase opens the front door and walks me out to my car. Suddenly, I'm overcome with emotion. The feelings came on so fast and are overwhelming. Jase just stops and holds me. He doesn't ask me why I'm crying or care if anyone is watching. "I'm sorry. It's just, your family is so warm and friendly. We're not big on warmth and hugs at my house."

I try to laugh it off, embarrassed to be crying in his driveway, but he looks me in the eye and says, "Kat, you deserve all the warmth in the world. You'll find it if you're willing to wait for someone who cares about the real you." The part left out was "like I do." Still, it was a sweet thing to say.

I kiss him and drive to the bridge. I'm not ready to go home yet. The differences between our families are jarring, and I need time to put my armor back on.

Chapter 9

I've checked and rechecked everything for the wedding. Invites were passed out the week before. The caterer, flower department, and bows for the end of each pew at the chapel are all set, and the small vases with tiny roses and plastic pink tablecloths are already set out. All the servers and cleaners are busy at work. Lou and Sadie have been practicing their vows. I'm so glad they took my suggestion and wrote personal ones.

As I'm looking everything over, the director of the Home pulls me aside. "I just wanted to make sure you know what a difference you have been making here. We have always been appreciative of our volunteers, but everyone here truly loves you. Thank you for today!"

I am glad that I wore waterproof mascara. I already need it.

I walk into Sadie's room and see a small, slightly overweight woman with dark brown hair, wearing a white blouse and a swirling peach skirt. She's helping Sadie into her dress. When she turns around, I see the same bright blue eyes. Sadie grins and tells me what I already know: Her daughter is here. I walk up and give her a huge hug. "It is so great to meet you! I'm Kathleen."

"I'm so glad to be here too. I'm Jenna. Thank you for being such a good friend to my mother and for putting all of this together."

Then I have an epiphany. "Jenna, why don't you escort Sadie

down the aisle? What do you guys think?"

Jenna turns to her mother and says, "Of course, I'd love that!" I can see tears in Sadie's eyes as she hugs her daughter. I'm ecstatic.

"Oh, Sadie, I have something for you!" I'm holding a blue, decorated ribbon that I tie onto Sadie's cane. It cascades down, very Stevie Nicks. "Here's your 'something blue.' You already have your 'something borrowed.'" We're using Tod's computer, which is set to play the "Wedding March." "I also wanted to give you another little something from me." I place the long-chain silver heart necklace I got at the dress shop over her head so it hangs down the front of her soft pink dress.

"Oh, Kathleen, it's just beautiful."

"Well, it's beautiful on you!"

I leave them to go check on the last details. When I look around the lobby, I notice an ice chest overflowing with wine, Champagne, mineral water, sparkling apple juice, sodas, and punch.

"Where did this come from?" I ask the director.

"Jase Thompson. He had some guys bring it over earlier today."

Before I can ask more questions, the first guests start to mill about. Barbara, the recreation director, is giving out the programs as people shuffle toward the chapel. There is a special place for all the wheelchairs. I walk up and stand in front of the packed chapel.

Lou walks in, looking very dapper in a gray pinstriped suit. His family is here.

Tod turns on the music, and the "Wedding March" starts. Everyone who can stand does. Sadie is holding onto her daughter. In one hand is her very festive cane, and her vows are in the other one. Jenna stands next to her mom as her matron of honor. Next to Lou is a tall blond, obviously a close relative. I know his family is here, so I assume it's his son. They have the same blue eyes. Jenna holds the rings. I look around for Jase, but he isn't here. He's not coming. I'm disappointed but can't think about that. Right now belongs to Sadie and Lou.

Once they both make it to the front of the chapel, I address the audience. "Hello, everybody! Please sit. I'm Kathleen, as most of you know. Thank you all for being here for this amazing event, where we are here to witness this very handsome man, Lou Neal, join hands and hearts to the most beautiful woman I know, Ms. Sadie Holmes. They met and fell in love in this wonderful community, and they want to thank everybody here for the support and gratitude. They didn't want to have the traditional service, so they asked me to preside over their ceremony. They've written their own vows, which they will share now. Sadie, please begin."

"When I came here, I thought this would be a good place to be for the rest of my life. People are friendly, the food is really good, and of course, bingo! Instead of coming here to die, I'm living and loving again. Thank you to all of my dear friends, staff, and volunteers, and for my special guest, my daughter Jenna. Kathleen, I can never thank you enough for today. But what I never expected was to meet the most amazing man I know, Mr. Lou Neal." She pauses to squeeze his hands and gaze at him. "Lou, you are the love of my life. You have given me fun and laughter, a friend to share my concerns and dreams with, and also the courage to call me out when needed; many of you are happy about that!" There was a lot of laughter from the guests. "My only regret is that I didn't meet you fifty years ago, but I consider myself the luckiest woman to be able to spend whatever days I do have left with you by my side."

The back door opens, and in walks Jase. He's wearing a black suit, a starched white shirt, black shoes, and no tie, and his hair is ever so slightly damp. I'm so happy and excited. He didn't forget after all. I send a beaming smile his way as my green eyes connect with his brown ones, just like the first time I saw him. This time, he smiles back.

"Um, Lou, it's your turn."

"Sadie, I loved you the moment I saw you. It was in the lunchroom, when I was eating a burger. My eyes were taking in my new home. Then, I saw this tall, stylish, and, dare I say, sexy woman. At that moment my heart stopped, and I just knew that I had to have you as my own. It took me a while to work up the courage to ask you on a date, as we were already friends, but lucky me, you said yes! Sadie, darling, I pledge you love and laughter but also shelter from the storm when things get hard. I love you in this life, and I will still love you when we get to heaven together."

There isn't a dry eye in the room. I wipe my tears off and say, "Let both of you exchange rings knowing the love and promises they hold."

Jenna walks up and hands them each their rings. "Oh my God, Lou. Everyone, look at this ring!" Sadie is holding it up for all to see. It is a beautiful band with three large diamonds. The crowd starts clapping. "This is the most beautiful ring I have ever seen." Tears roll down Sadie's face.

"Lou, Sadie, please repeat after me. 'Bless these rings. They are a token of your love.'" They followed. "As a token of your commitment"—I pause again—"and most of all, for the joy and fun you bring out in each other. Please place these blessed rings on each other's hands." It takes a little longer because of arthritis. "For the power vested in me by the state of Pennsylvania, I now pronounce you husband and wife. Let me be the first to congratulate you, Lou and Sadie Neal." People are clapping and cheering.

Then, my final words: "I would love to send a thanks to everyone who helped with this blessed occasion; you know who you are. Please proceed to the dining room for some delicious food, drink, and dancing."

The celebration is probably the most important event to happen at the Home in years.

Everyone slowly moves to the dining room, each person finding their seat. I'm at the main table with Sadie, Lou, Lou's son Joey, Lou's daughter Maggie, and Lou's granddaughters Britney and Allison, as well as Jenna. My chair is marked with my name, and next to me is an empty chair simply marked, "Friend." I look around for Jase. Luckily, he is really tall, so I spot him and run over to grab his hand, bringing him back to my table. Lou just looks at me and winks. I blow him a kiss.

At first, Jase seems a bit reserved, but that ends quickly. It's as if he knows we're in a safe space. Everybody loves the food; then comes the dancing. I've never had so many partners for so many songs, from classic rock to more formal waltzes.

Jase is a gentleman and asks numerous ladies out to the dance floor. Of course, they are thrilled. Then comes "Unchained Melody," and Jase walks over to me and holds out his hand and I take it. When I am in his arms, time stops. It feels like there is no one else in the room—just this man. I know it's the same for him; I feel it.

He whispers in my ear, "Do you want to get out of here, or do we need to stay longer?"

Let's leave now! I internally beg. *A whole night with Jase.* "I'm ready for that to start as soon as possible, but I need to check if Sadie still needs me."

I walk over to her. Everyone is surrounding her, admiring her ring. "Sadie, I'm so happy for you! I really mean it. Do you need me to stay for anything, anything at all?"

"Are you kidding, sweetheart? Please leave now. I insist! I can never thank you enough, Kathleen, ever. You gave me my Jenna back and joined Lou and I together." We both have tears in our eyes. I quickly hug Jenna and walk over to Jase, who is waiting by the door.

Chapter 10

I'm still tired from the wedding, but the event, especially the dancing, was worth all the hours I spent working on it.

I lock my car, which is staying at the retirement home. Jase pulls next to my car, and I get out to greet him. He picks me up and kisses me in a deep, all-consuming way.

"Hi." He grins.

"Hi," I say back, suddenly feeling very shy around him.

He grabs me and kisses me again, then pulls away. *What have I done wrong?* I wonder.

He looks at me, throws his head back, and laughs. God, how I missed that laugh. "Kat, let's get the next adventure started, but don't expect glamorous."

"I don't care where we go. As long as I'm with you."

While driving to our destination, we chat about work, the huge order we have coming up, the boys, and little Emily, who is home from the hospital. I realize how much I have missed him. Sure, I see him every day at work, but that almost made it worse. To not be able to talk to him, really talk to him, and touch him, has been excruciating.

In about half an hour, we pull up to a nondescript motel just outside of Hilltown. It's nothing fancy. I never noticed it before, but it looks well-maintained. Jase opens the truck door for me and leads me to the room at the end of the row, the one with the most privacy. Jase uses the key card and opens the door to reveal candles and roses everywhere, Champagne on ice, dark chocolates, and a nice comfortable comforter. I see the murky brown one shoved under the bed. He thought of everything. He has so little free time, yet he did all of this for me. He walks over, and we fall onto the bed together. I still remember it like it was yesterday.

He throws off his jacket, unbuttons his shirt, and begins to unzip his jeans. I see boxers, whereas every other time he has gone commando, and I start laughing. "I finally learn whether Jase Thompson wears boxers or briefs!" We both laughed about that.

He unties my dress. "I'm really glad you got a dress that's easy to open." Then, he stopped, in shock. "Jesus, Kat, you're a Victoria's Secret model."

Actually, it's Rihanna's Fenty goodies, but who's going to argue when a man looks at you like he is looking at me. I am glad I followed my intuition and wore a tiny pair of panties, a garter, stockings, and a bra with underwire pushing up my breasts, all in cream and black silk.

He swallows and mumbles, "I'm not sure where to begin."

Then, I whisper, "Just think of me as dessert."

"Dessert, hell," he says. "You're a five-star meal."

"Let me help." I kiss all the way down his chest. He is hard, so I take him in my mouth and suck him. I hear his moans. "God, don't stop." I kiss him gently back up his body and sit on top of him. I move my panties to the side and let him slip inside me. I move slowly at first, then start speeding up. I can tell how turned on he is by how hard he is, the way his hands are holding me near my bent legs, and the way he is moaning. It doesn't last long. With one movement, I feel him filling me and then collapse. He is still breathing deeply as I move off him and lay by his side. After some more kissing and caressing, he gets up, pops the cork, and hands me Champagne. It's perfect. I need to replenish my body.

"Babe, you turn me on so much, I couldn't help myself. I'm sorry.

I promise next time to make sure you come."

"I didn't want to. You did all this, so I wanted to give you a present."

"Best damn present I ever got." He laughs and turns toward me, inserting his fingers in me while massaging my clit. He knows how much I love that. It doesn't take long for me to come.

There are two more amazing lovemaking sessions, one where the Champagne plays a very important part. I'm lying on top of him. The only thing left on my body is the bra. It appears that my lover has a thing for my breasts spilling over the top. He spends plenty of time holding them and sucking on them through the bra, but he doesn't take it off.

"God, I've missed this," he says spontaneously.

I'm glad, but I wish he had said he missed me, not just the pleasure we give each other.

"How about a bath?" he asks.

"Sure." He holds my hand and leads me toward the bathroom. It's full of candles and a bottle of French bath soap. The bathtub, though, looks a bit small, especially for someone as tall as Jase. But hey, I'm up for anything.

He turns on the water and pours in the soap, which immediately starts foaming. Jase periodically checks the water's temperature and turns it off. He finally takes off my bra and kisses my neck. Jase steps into the bath, and I follow him. He shifts so he is sitting up. Our legs intertwine, but as I expected, there isn't enough room for us to do much, especially when we're trying to wash each other. The soap is wonderful, but it makes the tub slippery. Soon, Jase slips down while I'm doing my best to stay in my position, sitting up on the other side. I am so uncomfortable. Next, I'm leaning against all the gadgets, and soon I slide down too.

"I think it's time to get out," Jase suggests.

"I totally agree." There is a major problem, though. We completely filled the small bath, so neither one of us has the room to maneuver into an upward position. We're stuck in the tub. I hear a "shit" from

Jase, but I start laughing and can't seem to stop. Soon, he joins me. It's a ridiculous situation.

Finally, after much twisting and turning, Jase is able to stand up. I'm still laughing as he helps me out. Jase grabs the bath sheet he brought and wraps us both in it. Soon, we've managed to make it to the bed, where we fall onto it, with the bath sheet still surrounding us. Jase apologizes, but I start laughing again. It's one of those laughs that you can't stop; it's way down in my stomach. He seems to enjoy my mirth. The laugh feels so good, a release of the stress I've been holding in for what feels like forever.

I'm tired. I mean, *really* tired. I know Jase must be because he's been working nonstop every day at the Mill while I've been planning the wedding, babysitting, and interning. We fall asleep, wrapped in each other's arms.

I wake up to the feeling of his body holding me. I arch my back and move into him. It is a lazy day of lovemaking, slow and mellow, soft and sweet. When it is over, I turn around and kiss him, deeply. He's hard again, and I'm ready. This time, straight missionary position, but intense. He always fills me with pleasure. I want to spend my life in this bed, with Jase naked and inside me. Impossible.

"Hi." Jase smiles down at me.

"Hi back."

Jase gets up and puts on his boxers. I grab my bag and put on a regular bra and oversized T-shirt with "Hilltown Mill" on the front.

He reaches into the small guest refrigerator and brings out a bowl of perfect strawberries, with yogurt on the side. He also got brie cheese and white cheddar. There are also my favorite chocolate croissants on top of the little refrigerator, complete with paper plates, cups, and plastic silverware. Shockingly, Motel 99 has a Keurig coffee machine. Perfect. Everything about the night has been perfect. I remind myself to hold onto the moment so I won't ever forget it.

Jase is checking his phone. Then, I hear, "Yeah, I'll be there in an hour or so." I'm eating very slowly, as if doing so will make time stand still. He turns to me and says, very seriously, "Time for a quick shower." He pulls my T-shirt off and unhooks my bra. We both attempt to walk in while removing our underwear. In the shower, very little cleaning takes place. As I dry myself, I feel melancholy. It's time to leave our own little world. "Kat, I need to drive you back to your car."

"Okay. I plan to go to the Mill today too."

"You don't have to come in on a weekend. Last I checked, your internship is unpaid."

"No, it's fine. I know we're behind on some orders, and Stephanie showed me what needed to be done for the swing shift."

Jase says, with a smile, "I might have to pull you into a storage closet."

"You have my permission." I hope he will, but I know he won't. His people and his job are more important than my sexual gratification.

"Kat, will your parents ask you about last night?"

"Jase, chill. I told them I was helping with the wedding and I would be staying at one of the guest rooms in the retirement home. It's an easy and sort-of-true alibi."

"Just checking."

"I promise I'll let you know if there is any blowback."

"Okay."

Jase drops me off at the Home. When I get home, Dad is at his desk and Mom is still asleep. *Surprise!*

"Hi, Dad."

"Kathleen." But before he can say anything, I interrupt with my calculated lie.

"Hey. Going in today. I know it's a Sunday, but we've got a big shipment coming up, so I'm just going to change and head in. Oh, and to give credit, Jase Thompson has been working crazy hours. You might let Kramer know to thank him."

"I'll see to it. I'll drop you off, and then one of the managers can bring you home."

It wasn't an invitation, probably just an opportunity for him to lecture or interrogate me.

"Wow, that would be great. Let me throw this stuff in my room." I run upstairs and change into nicer jeans, a new "Hilltown Mills" T-shirt, and a casual pair of gold hoop earrings. I put my hair up in a ponytail. My father always insists that I make a good presentation at the business that bears our name.

I was right. My father spends the drive peppering me with questions about my experience and knowledge of the Mill and steel production. I was prepared for this and surprised it hadn't happened sooner. The only thing that really surprises me is that, for once, I'm not pretending. I actually do know a lot about the Mill and production.

All Monday morning, I do my best to figure out the scale for next month's large workload. I'm hungry, and I didn't have time to wait for our cook to fix lunch. In truth, I like eating in the cafeteria. The food is better and normal (no beef tartar, yuck). Once I pay, I look around and see that Lyn, Brook's fiancé, is sitting alone. We've never talked, but I met her once when Brook and Lyn came back to the house after their "date night." I saw her again when I started my internship. There is nobody at her table, so I walk up to her. "Do you mind if I sit?"

She looks surprised. "Okay, take a load off." She is a very pretty woman, with short brown hair and perfect cheekbones.

We eat silently for a while, but I'm still not always comfortable with silence. "I don't know if you remember, but I met you when you and Brook got home from your date night. I got to meet Annie and your daughter, Brooklyn. I love how her name combines yours and Brook's."

"Thanks. It's different, and sometimes I even get confused." We both laugh.

"Jase told me that you and Brook go on date nights. Did you have fun?"

She hesitates, then answers, "It's great if you like going to a nice restaurant, where your partner embarrasses you by drinking five beers in a row instead of eating, and then having to get our waiter to help him into the car."

I'm silent. What can I say that doesn't make things worse? I try. "It seems like he's still celebrating his raise."

She looks sad. "No, he's drinking away his raise. If it wasn't for Jase, we wouldn't have the money for the materials to renovate his father's place, and without Annie, I don't know what I'd do. I know that Brook loves Brooklyn and me and the *idea* of being a dad, but sometimes he acts like he's still in high school. I'm sorry. I shouldn't be bothering you with this."

"No, please, I understand. My mom has some bad habits too." I look at her, and she looks relieved. We have a sort of kinship: people we love, who only make our lives harder.

"Lyn, let me know if you need any help with Brooklyn. I'd be glad to watch her if something comes up. You can ask Josie and Kevin if you need a reference."

She looks at the wall clock. "Well, back to work. And thanks for the babysitting offer."

"Bye." I like her a lot, but she is so young to have to deal with so much. I'll mention my offer to Jase. He might get a bit peeved because I didn't go through him, but he can't help everyone by himself.

When I get home, both of my parents are at the house when I walk in. My father looks up at me from his chair in the living room. "Kathleen, it's time you started getting ready for school. You've spent enough time at your internship."

I answer, "As I wind things down, I just wanted to see the night shift. I've spent most of my time in the product rolling team and felt it would be good if I looked at other parts of the business."

I thought this would appease him, but he looks exasperated. "Kathleen, don't—"

"I know, I know. Don't fraternize with the 'help.' But I like them, and they work hard. I'm going away soon, so I don't think it's a big deal. I feel kind of honored. They could have been standoffish since

I'm the boss's daughter, but they tried to help me understand what they were doing.

"Well, I'm glad you took the time to see the Mill's operation, especially since you seem to relish being there. There will be a lot more training once you graduate. However, it's time to end your internship and start getting ready for school. I also want your report on the Mill."

"I'll start packing tomorrow. But I warn you, I'll be spending some time with my friends. I haven't seen them much this summer, and I want to celebrate the next step in our lives. I also have to go to the last couple classes before Chicago, and we'll be having a celebration, so I might be in Pittsburgh this weekend. You have to admit, I've accomplished a lot this summer, Dad."

"Hmph" is all he says to that, but that's about as complimentary as he gets.

I race up to my room with a smile on my face. Jase had asked if it was possible for me to get an entire weekend away, and I just set the stage so that can happen.

I can't wait for Friday to come, and when it finally does, Jase and I meet at the bridge for our mystery weekend. He hasn't told me where we're going. He only smirks when I ask and says, "I can guarantee you've never been there." I get out of my car and see Jase has packed a gigantic cooler, blankets, pillows, sleeping bags, fishing rods, and inner tubes. We have fortifications for at least a week. I look at my bag full of clothes. I guess a weekend in New York City is out, not that I really imagined that's where we would be going. I feel guilty that I haven't contributed anything for the weekend, unless lacy lingerie is considered a contribution.

I hop in his trunk and leave mine since no one ever comes to the bridge but us. We laugh and catch up during the hour drive and then pull up to a fence and gate surrounding a wooded area. He scans my face nervously; then I see his shoulders relax.

Jase shares with me, "As a kid, we came here all the time. My aunt knows the director of the church camp, and he said it was vacant this weekend, and we could use it. It's not fancy, but the lake is fun, and it's all ours until Sunday."

He gets out of the car and presses a few numbers into a lock. Nothing happens. He tries again. Nothing. "Shit! They must have changed the code! I'll call my aunt or—"

"Don't be such a wuss." I climb over the fence, jump down, and unlock it from the inside. Jase starts laughing. "Not the best security. But that was impressive."

We follow a concrete path leading to a very sparse habitat with four or so wooden cabins surrounding a small, glimmering lake. There is also a central bathroom and shower, and plenty of grills and charcoal. We walk up to the cabin closest to the lake to drop our stuff off. It's empty, except for two bunk beds with bare, clean mattresses. Compared to the bridge, though, it's like the Ritz.

Jase dumps our stuff on the floor of the cabin. I look at him, and he has a mischievous smile. He throws off his shirt and runs into the water, screaming, "Time for a swim!"

I pull off my sundress and follow him into the lake wearing my underwear.

"I wanted to get you naked as soon as possible." He swims over to me, pulls off my panties, and throws them onto the shore as he kisses me gently. His fingers rub my clitoris. He deepens the kisses and uses his middle finger to move in and out of me, while he continues his intimate massage. I come hard. The water is shallow, so we can stand up. I put my legs around him as he pushes inside me. It's like my first night with him. I'm overcome by my emotions and the incredible sensations he brings out in me. What I feel is way more than a crush or lust. I love him. But he'll never know. If he knew, he would be gone.

The weekend is full of fun, and sex, and more sex. Everything blends together. We swim, we fish and catch nothing, we swing into the water, and we tube around our little lake. It's amazing how leaving the world for a little while brings such contentment. Contentment, always the word I feel about my time with Jase. Of course, the second word would be passion. Contentment and passion? Best combination ever.

Growing up, my family never went camping. My dad considers anything below a five-star hotel camping. I never even thought about it, but now I see how much I missed out as a kid. The only time I've been anywhere like it was with a friend when I was in the first grade. I met her at Bible study before I dropped religion. Her family used to spend a lot of time together, happily, and I always tagged along. I was heartbroken when she moved away. Come to think of it, I think her dad was laid off from the Mill.

After making Jase go on the world's most boring hike around the camp, it's time for a shower. After all, we have real running water. I walk back to our temporary home, get my dependable travel kit, and head to the shower room. I'm surprised to see shampoo, conditioner, and body wash on the wall, like a hotel. I'm busy washing my hair when I hear footsteps. Jase steps into my stall.

"You know, Kat. I couldn't find another shower." I start to turn around, but he says quietly, "Stay where you are." I don't move. He finishes rinsing my hair, massaging my scalp. I'm so relaxed that I could literally lean against Jase and fall asleep. He has other ideas. He reaches for the body gel and begins to anoint my body with the soothing soap, rubbing my breasts, kissing my neck. Then, he moves to my clit. He knows how sensitive I am there. Jase moves me so I'm bent down, my legs slightly apart. Then, I feel his cock pushing into my vagina from the back. I feel so full. I moan, and that makes him push even deeper. Jase puts his arms against the wall, filling me, over and over. I feel an orgasm and scream my release. I stop, but he's still hard and inside me. He moves his arms as his hands hold my breasts, gently squeezing them. He whispers, "I love how you feel when you're coming." He moves faster and deeper. His cock fills me, and I'm soon coming again, Jase following me. We're both out of breath.

This time he leans against me, still inside my body. He slowly moves out and whispers, "I can't get enough of you."

And I answer, "You never have to."

I grab the towel I brought. Jase just looks at me with his signature half smile, half shrug. I giggle. "Okay, I can share."

"Well, I could air dry," he says.

"That would just undo getting clean."

He turns me around so I'm facing him. He picks me up, and I wrap my legs around him as he starts fucking me again. We come together. He slowly pulls out of me. I can barely stand. He starts drying me. His mere touch makes me want him all over again, but I need some rest. He picks me up and carries me to our little cabin, where he's laid out the blankets and sleeping bags and made it homey. Jase gently puts me down and lays next to me, with his arm around me. We both fall asleep. When I wake up, he's staring at me. He rolls toward me and moves into me, but very slowly. Our orgasms come quickly, but neither one of us wants to move.

Jase is the first one to talk. "I think we both need sustenance." He gets up and pulls on a pair of worn jeans. Soon, I throw on another sundress, flip-flops, and panties and go to the barbeque, where Jase is prepping hamburgers.

I smile. "Those look so good."

He quietly says, "Not as good as you look."

My heart is full of him.

Jase cooks. I clean. I never knew burgers cooked over a fire could be so yummy. And of course, s'mores, God's gift to all mortals.

It's Sunday morning, and we're both eating Honey Nut Cheerios in paper cups on the floor of our cabin. Jase is looking very serious.

"Hey, this has been perfect. What's wrong? Is it because we have to go back to the real world?"

"Kat, I can't see you on Tuesday."

"Okay," I answer. It's a night where we usually see each other. Something very serious is responsible for the frown. I hope he isn't seeing someone else. But he's not one to juggle women. He is already overbooked.

"Right before we came here, I was told that my schedule has

been permanently changed. I'll be working overtime on a regular basis. I'm salaried, but when there are large orders, I'm paid more, and we need the money. One of the other team leaders and half of her team have been laid off, permanently. People expect temporary cuts, usually the newest steelworkers. This time, a major department, the tubular department, has just gone away. A lot of the people laid off are senior staff. The union couldn't do anything, nothing, except extend unemployment benefits. It helps with work issues, overtime, and health insurance, but they can't do anything if management can prove that those jobs are no longer needed and if they aren't pulling in enough money. The number of layoffs has never happened since I've been there. Hell, it never happened when my father worked there. People are on edge."

"I don't understand." I really don't. "I know my father is all about making as much money as he can, but I know that layoffs aren't the answer."

"Well, he seems to think it is. It's even worse because so many people are getting laid off at the same time. I'll be charged with hiring and training five more new staff members."

"Why don't they give the people who were laid off those jobs?"

"Management says they aren't qualified for any new positions, but really, it's that they're too expensive. The new hires will work for a third of the cost. At least my original team is protected right now. Product rolling is the biggest money maker. We have plenty of orders because we can finish what other mills start. My staff will like the overtime, but they are used to being able to schedule it themselves, not just being told what and when they have to work. Kat, people are asking me questions that I don't have answers to. I've asked Kramer about it, but I'm not getting any information."

Although I feel terrible, even guilty about the news, I am honored to be let in on it. "Maybe I can talk to my father about what's happening. I'll ask him to tell me about the different departments, which ones are in jeopardy, which ones are solid."

Then, he looks at me and says, "Enough. This isn't how we should be spending our last hours here."

I crawl over to him and sit on his lap. I kiss him, and we tumble down. That is how we spend the rest of our time.

Chapter 11

Driving to the Mill on Monday is bittersweet. I'm worried. Because of the layoffs, I investigated the success of steel manufacturing nationally, and in Pennsylvania specifically. The statistics pointed to a troubling trend of falling profits. The Mill has been in business for over a hundred years. Could it last another hundred? Or maybe just twenty? I still come to the Mill but mostly to get information for my report."

One of the days I'm there, Lyn texts me that Mr. Kramer wants to see me. I knock on the door, and he motions for me to enter. He was on the telephone and hastily puts it down. "Hello, Ms. Hill. Please have a seat. I wanted to check in to see how things are going."

I know this isn't the real reason I was called into his office, so I give him a perfunctory answer. He nods, barely listening, and then says, "There is a minor matter, nothing to worry about."

When I hear those words, there is always something to worry about, I think.

"There has been some discussion of you and Mr. Thompson perhaps getting close. Someone said they saw you outside of work together."

I'm stunned. It's hard to breathe. If I don't handle it just right, Jase and his family might be harmed. We've been so careful, but not careful enough, I guess. Going on the offensive is my best strategy. "I assume you wrote a letter reprimanding the person who spread such malicious gossip—"

"I, uh—"

"You can ask *anyone* that I've interacted with during this internship. Jase Thompson has been nothing but professional toward me. We share one thing in common: our commitment to the Mill."

"Um—"

"Furthermore, I have gotten to know and like many of Mr. Thompson's team members, and they have been immensely helpful, especially Stephanie Morris, who is second in command. She is the person who has trained me the most. Mr. Thompson oversaw everything and excelled at his job. You'll see that in my assessment."

"Of course, Ms. Hill."

"I assume their excellent track record and numbers will not go unnoticed during their review, and more importantly, what do you plan to do with the person or persons who came to you with this innuendo?"

"I'm so sorry to have to bring it up. Would you like me to write a letter of condemnation, or is a verbal warning enough?"

"My main concern is the accusations and how they might affect Mr. Thompson's career. What might be a good compromise is a verbal warning to the gossips and a letter of recommendation for Mr. Thompson and Stephanie Morris. I assume that you want them to continue to be satisfied with their jobs."

"Of course! Jase is our best team leader and is about to get another raise."

"Then make sure both Mr. Thompson and his crew know what an excellent job they're doing. I've had a very interesting and important time here. I can't believe that this came up. I'd hate for it to mar my impression of the Mill or your leadership."

"Yes. I'm so sorry."

I feel bad about the last comment and wish I could take it back.

Maybe I'm more like my father than I imagined. I remind myself that Mr. Kramer will be fine; he's one of my dad's right-hand men, and I can rest assured that Jase and Stephanie will also be taken care of. I only have a couple more weeks before I have to leave for Chicago, and I want to make sure that Jase's whole team will still have their jobs once I'm gone.

I need to start saying my goodbyes, and it hurts. Why did I wait until my last summer to learn about my town and the people in it? Even six months earlier would have made a difference. Then again, maybe I wouldn't have been open to it. I used to be very comfortable spending most of my time with my school friends.

The first goodbyes are to them. I start with my oldest friends, Danielle and Julia. We met in second grade and have been hanging out ever since. I swear we look like clones. We all have long blond hair, fake eyelashes, and designer clothes. The only difference is that they are committed to a size two—and fake blue contact lenses. They don't need them to see; they just want the color. I also invite the rest of my Country Day clique.

We meet for dinner in Pittsburgh on Saturday night. I take everyone to my favorite Italian Bistro, Mazzio's. I always order my favorite, spinach ravioli and a cannoli for dessert. Whenever I eat it, I smile. The first time I had it was right after I saw *The Godfather*, remembering the famous line, "Leave the gun. Take the cannoli." As always, Danielle and Julia give me a hard time about my food choices. "Kathleen, how are you ever going to drop all your extra weight!" I ignore them. They've been bugging me about my size since we were ten years old. I never wanted to be starving all the time like they did. I loved playing soccer, and fainting from hunger is not a great look on the field.

Everyone wants to spend the night in the city, raiding mini bars, but I decline the slumber party. Ironically, Nathaniel, my old boyfriend, and Danielle come as a couple. I wonder if he's still hitting on everyone that he thinks is "sexy." Nate doesn't understand the concept of being faithful. Oh, well. Danielle knows all that. I shared all my frustrations with her when we were dating. It must be Nathaniel's poster-boy-for-Ralph-Lauren looks, his acceptance to Yale, and his daddy's bank account.

I pretend to be fascinated with their future plans; then I chatter about sorority rush. They all want to know my vacation schedule. I tell them I don't know it yet, and then I leave by ten. I really don't want to spend any more of my time off with them.

Monday, I call Josie to see if I could come and say goodbye to her and the boys. She says that Kevin is working a lot of hours, so I can come whenever I want to. I choose three and stop at the grocery to hug Carrie, my "flower girl," and to pick up maple bars for the boys and a lemon tart cake for Josie and Kevin. When I get to their house, the boys open the door and immediately want to go play soccer.

"I can't, boys. I'm just here to say goodbye. I'm leaving for college, but I'll be back at Christmas."

They look crestfallen but brighten when I show them the maple bars. They grab them and run upstairs. Josie and I laugh, and then she makes me a cup of tea and we sit at the kitchen table.

"I'm really going to miss your family, Kevin, the boys, and baby Emily, but mostly you! I know we haven't known each other for long, but I feel like you're the sister I always wanted."

I see tears in her eyes, "I feel the same way. Kathleen, you literally saved my sanity. I don't know what I'll do without you. Sometimes it gets crazy when there are only kids around. I loved having another adult to talk to. A good friend, like you. Especially since Kevin's been working a bunch of overtime. I mean, the extra money is great and needed, but I just miss him."

"Speaking of appreciation." I take an envelope out of my purse and hand it to Josie. In it are five one hundred dollar bills.

"Kathleen, what is this? I can't possibly take this."

"But I insist you take it. I can only imagine how expensive the hospital bills are and . . ." I trail off and think, *I feel bad that my dad is so cheap and only covers part of his employees' medical expenses, not to mention that there might be another round of layoffs.* I don't worry about Kevin. Jase will protect them. I didn't want to worry Josie or remind her of my family connections. We have become too close to jeopardize causing a divide. I knew if I had any chance of getting her to accept my gift, I needed to make sure her pride and dignity were intact. "Plus, I owe you, Josie. I've been interviewing you about having a spouse who works at the Mill for weeks, and that really helped my internship and my future at college."

"I couldn't possibly," Josie says, shoving the envelope back at me.

"Yes, you can. I want you to spend part of it just for you or for a babysitter so you can have some fun!"

I hug her and leave before she can protest further.

My shift on Monday is almost over when Jase walks toward me and says quietly, "I want to bring you to my home again tonight, if that's okay with you." I couldn't believe it, especially because of my emotional breakdown the last time I came over. I could have kissed him then and there, but I kept up my professional demeanor.

We leave together. We had done that a few times while visiting employees, but it feels like we're going home together. Did I just think of his home as "home"? Based on the way Mr. Kramer looks nervous every time he sees me, I don't worry about gossip. Plus, I'm almost out of here. *Jase and his reputation will be safe when I'm gone,* I think with a heavy heart.

We catch up on work, and before I know it, Jase pulls up to Annie's house. I remember the beautiful flower beds leading to the door, and I notice the vegetable garden again.

"My aunt loves her plants, as you can see," Jase says.

"The yard is amazing. What about the greenhouse?"

"I built it for her birthday last June."

"It's perfect," I say, while thinking, *You're perfect.*

Jase looks slightly embarrassed. He has a hard time with acknowledgments and gifts. I'm careful never to overdo it. He did love it when I found one of Lou's Rolling Stones T-shirts in perfect condition off eBay. Later, he showed me his appreciation.

We walk into the house, and Brooklyn greets us with giggles. I spontaneously pick her up and spin her around. We both collapse on the floor laughing. Annie walks into the room and hugs me. The giant mansion I live in always feels empty, even though there are always people there: the cook, the maid, Joanne, the assistant, or my parents. A house should feel like Jase's—filled with love, not people you pay to be there.

I look up and see Jase studying me while stirring something that smells delicious. He seems lost in his thoughts but smiles that beautiful smile at me. After another incredible meal of chicken and dumplings, I start to remove the dishes.

"Kathleen, I can get those. You're the guest, and you both look tired," Annie says. "Jase, why don't you show Kathleen your little apartment?"

Jase and I exchange glances. Annie is beyond sweet, but subtle she is not. I have no doubt that she knows exactly what is going on between me and Jase.

"I'm so glad you came," she says as she clears the table. "Feel free to come by anytime. Jase, you need to bring her to dinner more often." But there wasn't going to be more time.

I try not to let this thought ruin my mood and follow Jase down the hallway after hugging Annie and Brooklyn good night. He leads me down a flight of stairs to a large room with wood-paneled, white-painted walls and a king-sized bed covered with a dark blue comforter. On the shelves are pictures of Jase with his family and dusty trophies from high school football and basketball teams. Funny, I never thought of him as a jock, but with his height and muscular body, it makes sense.

There are also framed Matisse and van Gogh prints. There were two full windows on both sides of the door and small ones near the top of the walls to let the light in. The windows themselves are covered with clean, white shades that match the walls. In the corner is a door opening to a small bathroom with a sink, toilet, and shower. Two bookshelves cover one of the walls. They are filled with books on every subject from David Baldacci thrillers to the history of Western civilization. There is also a small desk with a laptop and printer.

I climb onto the bed and reach for him. When he joins me, we start kissing slowly and deeply. He touches my face, kisses my neck, and moves so I am stretched out on top of him. I wonder if I will ever feel this way with anyone else. I doubt it. For me, our relationship is so much more than great sex. We laugh a lot, and he can converse about almost any subject. He is only twenty-one, but in many ways, he seems so much older. I respect him, his work ethic, his relationships, everything about him. I've been pushing back the thoughts of summer ending. We've never talked about it. I just want to hold onto every moment, but those moments will be ending soon.

To shake off my mood, I joke, "So this is your special place, huh? I bet all the ladies love it."

Jase releases his hold on me and sits up. He looks hurt and kind of pissed.

"Kathleen, I don't bring women into my home. I don't bring women to the bridge, and I haven't been with anyone since I met you. I thought you understood that. I gave you my word."

He gets up and paces. I can't believe what I said. I get nervous and say stupid things. Why can't I just stay quiet?

"Jase, I didn't mean it. Sometimes I get overwhelmed about us. Sometimes I feel scared and say idiotic things. I'm sorry."

"Kathleen, have I ever given you a reason not to trust me since we've been together?"

"No. The exact opposite. It's one of the things I admire most about you. I am really sorry. Please don't hold it against me."

"I won't, but don't make it a habit." He leans over and kisses me, softly and sweetly. Then he says, "I need to get you back to your car, and then I need to run some errands. Can you let me know when you're leaving?"

He still looks irritated and has a right to be. He's done everything he promised and more. I'm stupid, stupid, stupid! We're quiet while we drive back to the parking lot to get my car. Reality is now clouding our future.

I can't sleep that night, so at midnight I decide to make cookies as an apology to Jase and a treat for the team. I guess it's a going-away present since this is my last week at the Mill. I find my favorite chocolate chip cookie recipe from my aunt Katherine. She was like a parent to my mother because their parents died so suddenly in a car accident. Unfortunately, Katherine also died young. If she was still alive, I doubt my mom would be the mess she is now. She probably would have divorced my father, but back to cookies. I know the recipe by heart, but I like looking at my aunt's neatly handwritten index card. It takes me three hours to make four batches. I'm pooped, but the cookies are perfect.

The next morning I set the cookies down in the break room, and I am soon the most popular person on the team. Stephanie tells me they're going to Joe's after work and insists I join them.

"I'd love to go, but I'm kind of embarrassed. I'm not of age. I mean, I have a fake ID but—"

Stephanie starts laughing. "Kathleen, no one will care; besides, you're leaving soon, and you deserve some fun before you go."

I hesitate but realize she's right. "Okay, sounds good." We all leave for the bar early.

Knowing this is probably the first and last time I will go out with Jase's team, I choose my favorite dance tunes and drag everyone out on the dance floor. Jase looks on with amusement. Stephanie comes over to me and says, "Dance with Jase. You know you want to."

"Is it that obvious?" I laugh.

"Please, I see how you stare at him all the time at work. Plus, there isn't a woman in this town that doesn't fantasize about Jase. That includes my mom and my ten-year-old sister." She grabs my hand and walks me over to Jase, "Jase, you should dance with Kathleen. I'll choose the song."

Jase takes me into his arms. I whisper, "She thinks I have a huge crush on you, which I do." It does feel good to be able to hold him close in front of other people, like a real date.

Jase looks down at me and smiles, but I can also feel him, and it's like we're both in the same place, wanting each other.

I whisper to him, "Ask me for a game of pool, which I will win, by the way. Then we'll leave separately. You first, me a bit later. We can meet at the bridge."

All of his team comes over to watch the game. I was right; I did win. Jase looks shocked. He never loses. Then, I laugh and confess, "We have a pool table at the house."

"She got you, Jase." Stephanie laughs.

"Well, guys, time for me to get some sleep. Enjoy yourselves," Jase says as he puts his jacket on and leaves.

I say the same ten minutes later. Just as I walk out, Brook and Lyn are going in. "Hi! Isn't tonight date night?" I say.

"What of it?" Brook answers rudely. I can smell something stronger than beer on his breath.

"Brook, apologize!" Lyn says.

"Sorry," he answers begrudgingly. "It's my time to choose, and what would be more fun than Jack Daniels, dancing, and pool?"

I can see on Lyn's face that this is *not* where she wants to be.

"Well, have a great time." Then, I look at Lyn. "You deserve it." She smiles at me, and we go our separate ways.

I arrive at the bridge, and Jase is already there, sitting on the edge of the ancient structure.

"Hey, just stay there and I'll join you."

"It's not really safe," Jase answers.

"I took a lot of ballet classes, so I'm really coordinated." I reach him quickly and sit down.

The festivity from the bar is lost, and he looks serious. "So, tomorrow is your last day?"

"I could stay until the end of the week, but you don't really need me. All the new people are trained, and I'm sure they'll be better than me."

He nods and we sit in silence for a few moments. Eventually, he turns toward me, and we kiss. This time it isn't slow and tender, but fast and deep. He helps me get off the bridge, picks up the sleeping bag from his truck, and throws it on the ground. We can't get our clothes off fast enough. He moves my legs up on his shoulders and enters me. Something about that position really turns me on. I start to come, and soon he follows me.

"Wow," I say, still panting from the encounter.

"When you told me you did ballet, I needed to test how flexible you were." He smiles.

"How did I do?"

"Very limber." We both laugh, and I curl up on top of him, pulling part of the sleeping bag over us. Within minutes, though, Jase is asleep. There were the familiar shadows under his eyes. I knew he was exhausted but am still a bit stunned that he fell asleep so soon. I don't know if it's just fatigue or the residue left from our night in his room. He gently snores, and it seems to startle him awake.

"What happened?" he asks while rubbing his head.

"You're exhausted, that's what happened."

"Shit, I'm sorry," he says. I tell him it's no big deal, but he looks really serious. "Yes, it is. We don't have that many more nights together this summer, and I shouldn't have blown it."

This is the first time we've acknowledged my leaving. It lands like a thud in my stomach.

I sit there silently. Jase seems to be lost in thought.

"Kathleen, I've been thinking," he says. "You know I don't plan on staying here that much longer. I was wondering. What do you think about me moving to Chicago in a few months? I could get a place near Northwestern while I work to establish residency. Then, I could go to a state school or community college."

I'm stunned. I assumed this was a summer thing for him. I feel embarrassed that I was going to tell him about my breaks and see if he would maybe, possibly, be open to seeing me if he didn't already have another girlfriend. But move to Chicago? I never in a million years imagined that.

"Jase, you don't need to do that. I'll get a copy of my school calendar and highlight my break times. I'll be back in November and—"

"Breaks? So I should just wait until you come back, while we continue to play this game of hide-and-seek with your parents and everyone in town?"

"Uhhh. Well, I thought you didn't want anyone to know."

"If we're in Chicago, it doesn't matter. I thought it would be a way for us to be together without having to lie all the time."

I sit there silently. My brain cannot make sense of everything he's saying. Moving with me. I wasn't prepared for that at all, so I say nothing.

"I get it. You want a new life that obviously doesn't include me. This whole summer has been a lie. I hope it's been amusing."

"That's not true. You mean so much to me. I just never imagined going to college with someone I knew. I chose Northwestern for that exact reason."

"So you want freedom, and that freedom doesn't include me."

"That's not what I'm saying! But I'm rushing a sorority, so I guess I just didn't think about how that would work with—"

"A sorority? Why? Aren't you trying to get away from all of that? You always say you hate your rich, shallow friends. Won't the sorority be full of more of the same things you hate?"

I grapple with the answer. "Some of the sororities actually do public service. And my dad says it is great for networking and—"

"Kathleen, you've always been talking about us spending more time together. Turns out, it's a game for you. A summer fling with a townie."

"What? No! I've felt more myself and happy this summer than I ever have in my life."

"But we don't meet your idea of a serious relationship," he says, getting dressed.

This is not how I thought tonight would go at all, and I can't sort out my thoughts. It seems like everything I say just makes it worse, so I decide to be quiet. But when he starts packing up the car, I can hardly bear it. "Jase, please don't leave. Not like this."

"I guess it was only a matter of time before *this* would end, and that time is now. Good luck, Kathleen. I hope you find what you're looking for," he says as he pulls away in his truck.

"Let's talk about this," I say to the empty space before me.

I toss and turn all night, milling over our conversation. I never imagined he would be willing to move for me. He has his family here, work that he loves, so many people that count on him. I could never take him away from that. And he would hate Chicago. It's big and noisy and . . . but his words—"it's just going to be more of the things you hate"—run through my mind. I hate to admit it, but he's probably right. I am going to be living just like I have been here, and with people he wouldn't like.

I claim I'll get a fresh start in Chicago, but deep down, I know I'm only changing my geography. I've been kidding myself. My father might not be in the same location, but he will still be dictating my every move. He's already started. I'm supposed to join the best sorority and get perfect grades. He even chose my major in business. How is that any different from the last eighteen years?

Sometimes I can be so naive. But Jase's willingness to be flexible and move with me is something we both need to talk about. I would hate for him to move there and then resent me for it. It's a lot to process. I want to do that with him, not on my own, so I text him an apology and ask if we can talk. I don't hear back from him, but it's 2 a.m., so I don't expect to.

After a mostly sleepless night, I call him in the morning. It goes straight to voicemail. I decide not to leave a message, still trying to be careful about our anonymity. I focus on packing and then try him again in the afternoon, this time leaving a message. "Jase, call me, please."

By early evening, I'm getting nervous. I've left him two voicemails and a couple of texts, with no response, not even an acknowledgment. I call Stephanie to see if she knows where he is, and she answers, "Jase always skips town before we start a big project. It's his get-off-the-grid time camping, and there's no service where he goes. That's kind of the point. He likes to decompress from everything for a few days. Were you trying to give it one more shot before you go?" She laughs.

"Um, no, it's nothing like that. I have to turn in this paper about my internship, and I had a question. I'll call Art Kramer for the info."

I can tell she knows about us. Maybe not everything, but something. I start wondering how many "somethings" are out there. Paranoia is not a good look for me; neither is delusion. I decide to drive to Joe's just in case Jase is there. A lot of people saw me dance at the pub after my work at the Mill, so no one seems to care that I'm there.

I don't see Jase, but his brother, Brook, is sitting at the end of the bar. I sit beside him.

"I thought you might come here. Let's go outside," he tells me. We walk quickly to the entrance and stand out of the light. He sees my surprise and continues, "I know all about you and Jase. Don't worry. I don't think anyone suspects anything, but I'm his brother, so I pretty much know what he does. I'll give him a message that you're looking for him, but I won't push it. It would be better if you just went to Chicago and left him alone. Kathleen, you're messing with his head. It will never work with you guys. Make it easier on both of you and let it go. I think he's trying to take a break, and I think you should too."

I'm angry at Brook. *What does he know?* But on my drive home, I realize he may be right. I could never ask Jase to leave his community, and I could never stay here. Better that we both just move on.

PART 2

Chapter 12

"Okay, ladies, it's time to party!" Lindsey, president of Gamma Omega Tau, chants, "Party! Party! Party!" and the rest of the "sisters" and the baby "pledges" join in. Rush has been crazy. I almost quit halfway through, but I knew my father would go apoplectic and flood my phone with messages.

It was a week of polite parties, tea, punch, cucumber sandwiches, and mindless small talk. At the end of the week, we all "rush" to our chosen sorority house. My mom made me a list of "acceptable" sororities. Her first choice was her own, Delta Theta Chi, but they were the *worst*! They were snobby, always advertising how popular they are, with their perfect bodies and perfect clothes, and it looked like everyone came from wealth. I did not want to go back to high school, and Jase's words still haunt me. I would prove him wrong, even if I never see him again.

I've been at Northwestern for two weeks, and I still check my phone constantly, but nothing. Even a "leave me alone" would be better than the radio silence. Jase had to have gotten at least one of my calls or messages. I know that Joe, Annie, and even Brook would have at least told him that I stopped by. Maybe I dodged a bullet. I make one mistake, and I'm out of his life. It's time for me to accept that we're over. I need to focus on my new life, which is in Chicago.

After viewing many of my mom's horrible suggestions, I finally find a normal sorority, Gamma Omega Tau. The members come from different backgrounds, races, and religions, and they have accomplished real achievements, like volunteering to teach in poor countries, being involved in politics, or coaching at the nearest boys and girls clubs. Prom and homecoming queen were not seen as achievements. Plus, the girls are fun. Initiation is a breeze. We just learn the history of the sorority and become part of the pledge class. Once that is done, we have a "secret" meeting where we learn the sorority song, special flower—lavender—and the secret password, used when we need a private meeting with one of the other sisters.

We're popular, but not in the cookie-cutter culture. We have a rom-com and pizza night for pledges scheduled tonight, and I'm wondering if I should skip it. No, I decide, it might be fun. If I start getting weepy, I can always talk to somebody. The good thing about being in my sorority is the instant friends. I'm sure many of them can relate.

I've lucked out with my dorm roommate. Ironically, her name is Suzanne, my made-up name for myself with Jase. She has an asymmetrical haircut, dyed bright pink, and loves classic grunge rock music. Joan Jett is her idol, and I love her too. Nothing like classic eighties rock. Her boyfriend is a tattoo artist in the city, hence her incredible ink masterpieces on her arms and neck. Sometimes I want a break from all that sisterhood and want to just hang here with Suzanne, or by myself, as it seems she spends a lot of time at her boyfriend's apartment.

Northwestern's campus is beautiful in the early fall, with large oaks turning from green to gold to velvet red. I usually do my reading under one of the stunning trees. It's already cool in the evenings, and I love "sweater weather." It reminds me of a time when Jase and I met at the bridge and it suddenly started raining really, really hard. I was getting soaked as Jase raced around the truck, putting on a tarp. He quickly threw the sleeping bag to cover the truck bed, followed by the blanket and a pillow on top of it. He pushed me up and onto our little "tent" and followed me. I was shivering, and he surrounded us with the blanket. The air felt like now: clean, cool, and snuggly. But there isn't any Jase around to warm me. Dammit, I hate when those memories seep through. They make me feel happy and sad at the same time. I'm just hoping that they'll go away eventually.

That Friday we go to a party at Sigma Tau so we can meet and mix. There isn't any real food at these events, just a keg of beer and a punch bowl full of cranberry punch. My big sister, Abby, the upper-class Gamma who helps me navigate all things Greek, has already warned me about these parties and vows to stay by my side for the night.

"This one is open, meaning other frat guys may be there. There are a lot of great guys, but there are also a lot of 'sharks' who go to these things to pick up girls," Abby warns me.

When we get there at eight, the music is blaring, but a tall preppy guy pauses it to announce, "Tonight we have the pleasure of welcoming the new pledges of Gamma Omega Tau!" This is followed by "Gammas! Gammas! Gammas!"

I look around and notice that the guys are kind of interchangeable, just like in my high school. They are all good-looking, wearing expensive short-sleeved shirts, linen shorts, and loafers, probably from Brooks Brothers, and they all seem to want to get me a drink. I must have "freshman" stamped on my forehead. One guy grabs my hand and says, "Hey, pretty girl, where did you come from? Let me get you some punch." Then, he stumbles away, and another one takes his place. "Here's some punch. You look thirsty." He grabs my hand and leads me to a corner of the very full room. I swallow most of the glass; I really am thirsty. A few minutes later he tells me, "Be right back with another one." He returns and hands me another red Solo cup. I start feeling dizzy when he says, "I would love to show you around the house," then something about being a vice president, and Abby walks over, takes my glass, and pours it on the floor, making sure that most of it lands on the vice president guy.

"Get off, shark!"

"Abby, give a guy a break."

To this, Abby responds, "That's what's wrong with you, Robert. Everybody gives you a break!"

He walks away, muttering "bitch" under his breath.

"I'm so sorry, Kathleen. I feel like I've failed you, but it won't happen again! I just wanted to say hi to my guy, the cute one over there playing pool, who is losing badly." He is tall, with short red hair and a ready smile. He looks up and blows a kiss at Abby.

I reassure her, "It's okay. I just feel a little off."

"I'm going to take you back to your dorm, but let me give you some important freshman information: At frat parties, *never* drink the punch! It's always spiked with the strongest alcohol that's legal, Everclear. It has no taste. Then it just hits you. *Bam*! Second, always keep your drink with you. Some guys might want to spike it to make it stronger. There are rumors that some even use the date rape drugs. I've never seen it, but it's possible when things get too wild, too late, and too crowded. And remember that 'players' are sharks. Stay away, unless you're into bad, short, mindless sex. With these guys, make sure they use condoms! Or better yet, two condoms."

"Sounds scary."

"Actually, most are stand-up guys. I'm just letting you know about the very few. Soon, you'll know what to look for yourself."

She helps me back to my room and into my PJs, hands me some Advils, and tucks me in. "I promise to never leave you alone until you learn Frat Parties 101. Tomorrow, more Advil and crackers. Call me if you need anything."

I'm not a huge fan of frat parties. I like it more when all my sorority sisters and their boyfriends pile into cars and drive to Lake Michigan. We build bonfires, often followed by skinny-dipping in the lake, no matter how cold it is.

I go on a lot of dates but never let myself become involved. For some reason, this makes me one of the most sought-out freshman coeds. Even junior and senior guys want to date me, but none of them are Jase. Plus, I want to get into the business program, so focusing on school and my sorority is enough. At least that's what I tell myself. But at night, when I'm all alone, I can still feel Jase surrounding me and holding me close.

For Christmas break, my father keeps saying that he wants me to come home for training. I can't. I just can't. It still feels way too early to possibly run into Jase or one of his friends. I call my mom and ask her if we can go to Canyon Ranch Spa. My mom loves it, and I know if I'm there, she will actually do the yoga and hikes instead of sneaking in liquor and passing out every night. She agrees and I take the short plane ride to Arizona. While we're there, my mom, the real Caroline, emerges. She eats well, takes classes, soaks in herbal pools, rides horses, and actually has fun. My dad briefly joins us for a day and then claims he has work to do and flies home.

Christmas day is quiet and restful. Neither of us give each other packages full of stuff we both already have too much of. We don't call my father to wish him "tidings of comfort and joy." He isn't a sentimental person. When it's time to leave, we both cry. She tells me how wonderful I am. I tell her how wonderful she is, and we can barely let go of each other at the airport.

Spring semester is a blur of classes and more sorority events. I'm planning on double majoring in psychology and business, but I haven't told anyone yet. By anyone, I mainly mean my father. He doesn't respect psychology, because it deals with the messy subject of feelings, and he doesn't have any, as far as I can tell.

Surprisingly, psych is a very competitive major. Lots of students want to get in the program. Psych requires the same GPA as the business school, which is really demanding. Psychology is interesting in a way that business isn't. There are a lot of studies and statistics, but there are also a lot of intangibles, like looking inside myself and having empathy for others. Part of the requirements is to volunteer at a place that helps people, like suicide hotlines, Head Start, or battered women's shelters. I choose to intern at a center for troubled teens, and I'm already learning a ton about addiction, depression, suicide, bullying, and horrible stories of sexual abuse and homelessness. Reality mixed with science.

The business requirements are more straightforward: economics, marketing, formal presentations, mathematics, AI, and high-tech knowledge and experience. I want to stay at Northwestern for the summer. My adviser recommends that I take extra classes and work in "the real world" for both majors. I especially need to focus more on the business requirements, like a possible internship in a medium or large company. He said we might be able to turn it into a job. I'm so into my psych major, and I need to pay more attention to my business knowledge. I know that I must get into the business program. That's what my father is paying for.

He's been talking about how he expects me to shadow him at the Mill during summer break, which sounds awful on so many levels. I don't want to work directly under my father, or worse, see Jase. That night on the phone, I explain to my dad that with the summer classes, I will officially be a sophomore, and I can turn in my application for the business school. I tell him that getting my application in early may help my chances. That's accurate, but I know I'll be accepted with my near perfect GPA and glowing recommendation from the Mill, and hopefully another internship.

My mom and I meet in Europe for two weeks before my summer classes and internship start. My father doesn't even think about joining us, which is fine. My mom is, as always, more relaxed without him around. Her art history degree and knowledge really come alive while we're touring Paris and Italy. I wish she would just leave my father, but all my suggestions are ignored. She definitely has Stockholm syndrome. She is staying with my dad, her jailer, metaphorically.

We just missed Sadie and Lou, who are on a riverboat cruise that started in Paris at the end of May. I live for my biweekly calls with her.

They are having so much fun, and Sadie sounds just as in love as she did when she first met Lou. It makes me see aging in a brand-new, much more positive light.

Chapter 13

A month into my sophomore year, I'm studying my nemesis geology with one of my sorority sisters, Mara, in the student union. I meant to sign up for geography but waited too long to change classes, so I'm stuck. Mara is my roommate. I gave up on the dorm this year since I never really stayed there much of my freshman year, and I lost touch with Suzanne. I think she dropped out and works with her boyfriend now. Mara is equally as hilarious, minus the neon hair, but she is also a rock whiz. I hate the class, and my great memory makes no difference. Mara doesn't understand my half-closed eyes and sighs. She thinks it's all very fascinating.

A handsome guy, with blond hair and blue eyes, so good-looking that I don't have anything to compare him to except maybe a young Paul Newman, approaches us. He sits down and announces, "Hi, you're the famous and elusive Kathleen Hill. I'm Richard Sumners. You guys look like you could use more coffee. Let me get those for you since I'm the one crashing the party. Grande lattes?"

We both nod and murmur, "Thanks."

Mara looks flustered and says, "Kathleen, do you know who that is? That's Richard Sumners. He is top of his class and president of Delta Omega Tau. He's even going to graduate a semester early. Everyone loves him. Plus, Richard's family is super well known in

Chicago. He is on *every* girl's wish list to date, sleep with, or even say hi to. Be nice."

He gets back to our table and puts down the lattes. Mara stands up, gathers her coffee and textbooks, and says goodbye.

"I hear that you're the BMOC," I blurt out. Not very delicate, but at least I'm being sort of nice.

"Yeah, you're pretty famous yourself. You happen to be on the men's bathroom wall as the 'most mysterious sorority girl.'" We both laugh. When he smiles, I see what Mara was talking about. Cute and charming, with just a hint of cockiness. Too bad he reminds me of most high school guys back home.

"Truly, I'm not mysterious. I'm boring."

"I doubt it."

"Well, I need to keep studying these stupid rocks."

"Why don't I help you?" He takes the book from my hands and starts quizzing me on the rocks and their qualities. His swagger diminishes, and he's really helpful. Almost modest.

When we're done, I look over at him and say, "I think I owe you a real drink."

His face breaks open in a grin, and I can see the seven-year-old version of him. We take his Mercedes to the favorite college pub, Charlie's. The food is awful, and the drinks aren't any better, but they never card, hence the popularity. The conversation flows easily. I like that he's so focused on me, but not in a fake "let me get you to bed" sense. We talk about our families, our goals, our favorite stuff, like food, cities, movies, and more. It's the first time that I've had fun with a man since Jase.

I look at my phone. Three hours have passed, and it felt like minutes. "Wow, I need to go. Sorority thing."

"Only if you agree to have dinner with me tomorrow night."

I'm a bit taken aback but answer, "Of course."

"Do you want exquisite or deep-dish Chicago style?"

"The latter, please."

"Great. I have my little brother for a couple of hours in the late afternoon. So why don't I pick you up around eight?"

"Great, I live in—"

"I know. I'll wait outside."

I wonder how he knows where I live, but I guess it's logical to assume I live in the sorority house. Instead, I say, "Is your little brother a freshman?"

"He isn't my real younger brother. That's Christopher. He's eighteen. I'm talking about the big brother program. It's for disadvantaged youth who need someone to have fun with, help with school things, and give them a steady male role model. Mine is Brad and he's ten years old. I try to see him at least once a week."

I'm impressed by his commitment and values. "I know the program. It's wonderful. Brad is lucky to have you." I tell him about my summer internship with the homeless teens, thinking we can swap mentoring stories. He nods a few times. I wonder if he's listening. He takes my hand as we cross the street to his car.

A tall, dark-haired, very thin model-looking woman walks up to us. "Richard, how can you do this to me? Get with another girl before we've even broken up?"

"Carla, as I've told you before, we were never exclusive. I'm starting to feel harassed."

She looks at me. "Good luck. This one will break your heart and make you question your sanity."

I'm taken aback and second-guess my date with him. But I know Mara wouldn't have given the okay if she wasn't sure about him. She looks out for me.

"God, Kathleen, I'm so sorry you had to deal with that. I went out with her a few times. It was very casual. We were never exclusive. This has happened twice now. I hope it's the end of it." We get to his car, and he opens my door. He looks me straight in the eyes. "Kathleen, just so you know, I'm not a player. I'm always straightforward in relationships. I'm really hoping we can get to know each other more and that this incident hasn't marred your perception of me."

"I appreciate your honesty and I'd like to get to know you more too." Still, the interaction with the woman has shaken me up a bit.

For our date, I dress in a simple black shirt (just in case I spill tomato sauce all over it), jeans, and black ankle boots. I add small diamond studs. To top it off, I put on a casual black fedora. I love hats. I'm an old-movie fan, so a hat feels like it completes a look. There aren't many milliners in the States, so I always pick one during my European visits. I curl the ends of my hair because that will look better with the hat, and I complete the look with the first black leather jacket I ever got. My makeup is simple, except for bright red lipstick, kind of Taylor Swiftie.

Richard is right on time. He gets out and opens the door for me. "You look great. So many women dress the same, but you mix it up, and it works, probably because you're so beautiful."

I flush a bit. I like that he notices the details and holds doors for me. He takes charge, but not in an overbearing way. We head downtown to a kind of run-down brick building. There is a long line of people waiting to get in, but Richard holds my hand and walks to the front of the line. An older, short, Joe Pesci look-alike rushes to greet us.

"Richie! So glad to see you. I thought you had disappeared. And who is this beauty on your arm?"

I put out my hand, and he kisses it. "Kathleen Hill."

"I'm honored, Miss Hill. I'm Bernie Desalvador, owner of this humble abode." What a character. "Jenny, put Richie and Miss Hill at the table near the wall, away from the door."

I feel like I'm in a glorious fairy tale. Our relationship evolves quickly. Every time Richard takes me out, people know him, and we get the best tables in the most exclusive restaurants. But not in a sycophant way like people were with my father. With Richard, it's all handshakes, back slaps, "How's school?" and "Who is this lovely lady?" questions.

He knows everyone by name too. When we're seated and served off the menu, it feels like we're family, not the king lording over someone.

We go to the symphony, museums, opening nights at the theater, exclusive parties full of very wealthy people. I've always been too busy with school to even consider a boyfriend. Richard is different. It's like he's royalty. I can't believe he wants to date me. He is on a much grander scale than my experience as the "princess" of Hilltown.

Richard is planning to graduate a semester early, from the business school, and is already working on his MBA application. He told me that he plans to go to law school once he's done with his business degree and is already studying for his LSATs. He says he wants to be a lawyer and "fight for the underdog." I admire him for that. I know that his father has a large accounting firm that he could easily go to work for. I'm impressed that he wants to strike out on his own. More we have in common.

After a month or so of dating, we were just finishing a delicious meal at his perfect condo with a lake view. Richard looks at me. "I think it's time we had sex." I nearly choke on my food.

I look at him across the table. Something feels off. I should be really excited; after all, he is gorgeous, intelligent, caring, and ambitious. Richard continues to talk. "Kathleen, I know you are naive in sex, having only two boyfriends in high school and none in college. I'm clean. I get checked regularly, but we'll use condoms until you can get on regular birth control. I'm glad you aren't some slut, sleeping around with a bunch of guys."

My thoughts go wild. *What? Oh my God. How does he know about my high school boyfriends, sexual history, and birth control?* At least he doesn't know about Jase. But really . . . his thinking is archaic. Why does my sexual history even matter?

He stands up and puts our dishes in the sink. Then he takes my hand and leads me into his very large, mauve, monotone bedroom. Everything is huge. A dark king-sized bed, a modern montage of art, and a gigantic flat-screen TV. I've never spent the night before, and nothing much has happened between us except lots of passionate kissing. He puts his hands on each side of my face and proceeds to kiss me, gently at first, then very deeply and with lots of tongue. He reaches for the bottom of my dress and pulls it over my head. I'm glad I wore a pretty bra and panties. He announces that I'm so sexy. It's starting to feel kind of like high school.

Finally, he sheds my underwear, puts on a condom from his bedside table, and pulls me onto the bed. He starts kissing me a lot, murmuring how beautiful I am. He sucks on my breasts through my bra. Then he enters me. He doesn't look at me; his eyes are closed. He moves faster and faster until he comes. Then, he abruptly gets up and goes into the shower.

Wow! That was different. I feel like I'm being treated like a proverbial bird in a cage.

When he returns from his shower, he lies on his back and falls asleep. No good-night kiss, no holding me; he doesn't even bother to say good night. In the middle of the night, he wakes up and starts kissing me again. We're still in the missionary position, but Richard keeps his eyes open, so I feel a little more connected. I don't come and wonder if I should fake an orgasm, but it's over so quickly, so it's too late for that. Then he kisses my forehead, turns over, and starts snoring. *I'm sure it will get better.*

I feel alone, not connected. With Jase, I always knew I was special by the way he touched me, looked at me, and made me laugh.

The next morning, I wake up to fresh coffee and croissants. Then, he tells me, "I couldn't just let my lady love be hungry."

He may not have rocked my world yet, but he can be endlessly charming, charismatic, and funny, effortlessly drawing people into his orbit. He holds impromptu gatherings at his condo, or sometimes we head to Lake Michigan for our usual bonfire fun. He loves parties and chides me if I have to study. "Kathleen, I'll help you afterward." Which I know will never happen. But then he looks at me with his blue eyes, and I give into his endless celebrations.

Everyone sees Richard and me as the perfect match: intelligent, beautiful, and from "old money." I don't really see us like that. Richard is far more down-to-earth than people give him credit for. And as for me, Hilltown may be a big deal in Western Pennsylvania, but in Chicago, the Hills hardly matter at all.

In terms of our intimacy, it's getting better. I just figure that Jase was more experienced and we had an undeniable passion. Richard is probably the norm. I get the birth control shot that lasts for six months, which is way better than condoms. *But why do I feel like something is missing?*

Chapter 14

Near the end of my sophomore year, my father calls. "Kathleen, it's time for you to start your training as future CEO of the Mill this summer."

"Daddy, I'm planning to stay in Chicago for the summer. I'm getting great training at school. There are a lot of classes I want to take that are only available during the summer quarter. Richard's going to be here for most of the summer too, and I want to spend more time with him."

The real reason I want to stay for the summer is to take as many psychology classes as I can. I earned credit for my internship with the teens last summer by writing some case studies, and I'd like to do the same this summer. I couldn't swing working at the Mill and double majoring. My supervisor from last summer already said that he wanted me back during my second year. I accepted. My adviser thinks it's another great opportunity. I hold my breath, hoping my father will agree to it.

"Sounds like a good idea. Richard's family is very well connected. Next summer I may want you to come home for a couple of weeks. After all, you need to see the changes we've made. The Mill has been streamlined and reorganized. Who else but me can train you? And what would they teach you that I couldn't?"

How to be kind and caring toward my fellow human beings, especially those who are struggling, I think. But I say, "I'll learn about the financial aspects of different businesses. They said I could dive into project management, performance reviews, inventory, and production orders, for businesses different from the Mill. It's the perfect thing to give me well-rounded experience and knowledge." I will be doing none of this at the teen center, but he'll never know. He hasn't been as bossy about my college classes as I thought he would be. He seems distracted most times we talk, which is nothing new, but it seems even more so than when I lived at home.

"That's good thinking. I always knew you had a head for business. But try to come home for a week. Your mother misses you." And he hangs up.

Phew. I dodged another summer at home. I've been back a couple of times to see my mom and Sadie, but I always avoid Joe's, the Mill, or anything near the Mill. I no longer check my phone daily to see if Jase has texted, but I can't say I'm completely over him. Will I ever be?

Every time Richard takes me out or we attend an event, dozens of women stare. It's unnerving. I can't tell if they're glaring at me because they are jealous or they're glaring at him for some reason I don't know about. Sure, Richard is a natural flirt who has, according to rumors, broken more than a few hearts. I tell myself I'm being crazy and that even if he broke some of those women's hearts, it doesn't mean he'll do the same to me. He seems really devoted and respectful, almost too much. Richard's asked me to have dinner with his parents. It's clear that this is a big deal.

He knows everything about me and my life, even things I'm pretty sure I never told him. My life seems like a fast-moving train, going in one direction, heading toward Richard Sumners.

Richard insists on picking out my clothes for the evening with his parents. I'm in a form-fitting simple black Dolce and Gabbana dress and matching wrap, Gucci flats, a Chanel clutch, and a pearl necklace and matching earrings. Richard gave the pearls to me as a surprise before we left. I thanked him profusely, but they made me uneasy about what expectations his parents might have. Also, no bare legs, panty hose a must.

He talks about his parents all the time, so I guess I shouldn't be surprised to find myself in his car driving to a swanky part of Lake Forest Park. Or as far as I can tell, an even more exclusive part of what appears to be one of the best neighborhoods in Chicago. We barely talk on the drive. I can tell he's nervous, which is making me even more nervous. His car hugs the road and makes me slightly nauseated when he takes the curves.

Richard is always pressuring me to buy a "real" luxury car like his new BMW sports coup. But I'm keeping my five-year-old Audi. It's the one thing my parents let me pick out without their interference. It's a source of personal pride and rebellion. Every time Richard bugs me about it, I immediately shut down the conversation. My parents do the same thing. They want me to have a Range Rover or some huge gas-guzzling car so I can be "safe," but I always say that my car is perfectly safe and change the subject.

Richard pulls into a long driveway, and we approach what looks like an estate. It makes our home in Hilltown look tiny. The house resembles Hampton Hill, where Henry the Eighth held court. It has a beautiful fountain next to the driveway. The lawn is immaculate. Hedges have been trimmed to perfection. I want to touch them. Even in winter, there are pots with some type of flowers that can stand the cold. The colors are brilliant, yellow, purple, light pink.

Two men walk up to us and open the doors of the car. We get out. Richard takes my arm and leads me up the steps. The servant scurries to the door ahead of us so he can let us in. A large chandelier, I think it may be a Chihuly, hangs in the foyer, and a gorgeous marble staircase spirals up to meet an open second-floor hallway. The wood parquet floor is buffed to a sheen worthy of a museum, as are the vases and impressionist paintings in the foyer. I think I spot a real Monet. Everything sparkles without a fingerprint or speck of dirt to be seen. The foyer leads us to the living room. Everything is formal, loads of antiques. I'm afraid to touch anything.

Another servant takes my cashmere wrap. Holding my hand, Richard leads us into the living room, where his parents are waiting. His mother, the slender and lovely Valerie, approaches wearing a simple yet perfect dark blue Chanel dress with matching heels. I see where Richard gets his clear blue eyes. She smiles at me, but not a real smile; it's practiced, and she shakes my hand. But her real smile emerges as she embraces Richard. He must be her pride and joy. I now understand why Richard is so into perfection and has scrutinized my outfits so closely lately. He used to compliment my boho chic style; now it's pretty clear he wants me to be a replica of his mother. She may look perfect, but it feels like she's a mannequin in a Sack's Fifth Avenue window: untouchable.

His father, Stephen, is dressed "down" in a Ralph Lauren cashmere sport coat and pants, a Brooks Brothers shirt and tie, finished with leather Gucci slip-ons. His eyes are dark, even when he smiles. His face looks like my father. I wonder if that hard look is just normal on every CEO's face. Stephen holds my hands for a minute too long, then turns to his son and shakes his hand like a business associate. Interesting, one cold and distant father and a loving mother. It could be my house, except my mother is almost always in some state of inebriation, and my father would never hold anyone's hands.

Richard has two siblings, both in college, but it is clear that Richard is the heir apparent. The cocktail hour is easy. I talk to his mother, who is full of questions. Of course, she would want to know about any girl her son brings home. We discuss my academic aspirations and my sorority. Like Mom, Valerie was a Theta Pi. I tell her that I chose to be a Gamma because they have the highest GPAs of all the sororities. I can see his father is listening. I want to make sure I make a good impression. Obviously, his family is very, very important to Richard.

I drink chardonnay and Richard drinks bourbon. A maid walks around offering fresh bread, goat cheese, and caviar. I'm not really a fan of anything except the bread, but I take the appetizer anyway, following Richard's lead. Soon, we're whisked into the dining room, where a huge table is beautifully set. I'm between Richard and his mother.

His father seems pleasant but indifferent. His mother wants to know how we met. Richard answers, "Kathleen was the student every guy wanted to date, but she wasn't interested in having a boyfriend. She wanted to give all her time to academics and her sorority, but I changed that."

I chime in, "Yes, lucky for me I'm still able to keep up my GPA."

Richard frowns at my attempt at lightheartedness, but then he smiles and says, "Nothing but the best for Kathleen."

During the main course of filet mignon with béarnaise sauce, roasted potatoes, and asparagus with a sprinkling of olive oil, Stephen speaks to me directly for the first time. "Well, Miss Hill, I hear you have a town named after you."

I smile and lock eyes with Stephen Sumner. I know that look. My father has it all the time when he's about to make budget cuts or lay people off.

"Well, technically, it's named after my great-great-grandfather because he started the steel mill there, which is still the largest employer in the area."

No doubt he already knows about my background. If he's anything like his son, he's done his research. "Yes, your father has a good reputation as an astute and successful businessman." He smiles with a predatory look. This time I feel uncomfortable. I feel like he's looking me over. I glance at his mother; she has the same look my mother gets when my father is interested in another woman: sad, lonely, and still. *God, what am I doing here?* Then I shake myself. *Of course I'm just making all this up. His dad just wants to make sure I'll fit well in his son's life.*

Chocolate lava cake and after-dinner drinks finish the meal. When it's time to leave, I get a hug from his father that lasts longer than necessary. Then I think, *There you go again, Kathleen, making stuff up when there is nothing going on.* After he lets me go, he comments, "I'm sure this is the first of many social events to come."

I turn to Richard's mother. "Thank you for a wonderful evening."

She says it was a pleasure, and we head to Richard's car, which has been brought around and warmed up for us. Richard is giddy on the drive home. "You passed! You're the only one who ever has. All the other women shrank when faced with my father. Kathleen, you were perfect."

"Thanks, I guess. I didn't know it was a test." But of course I did. It would be the same meeting my father. Suddenly, I feel really weird about the dinner.

"Kath, stay over so we can really celebrate!" Richard says. His eyes look dark, even a little scary. It's the same look as his father had, like he wants to devour me. But I don't want to be with him right now. Too many "Dad" resemblances.

I'm not sure why I feel this way. It wasn't an awful dinner. Richard's parents were polite and interested in me. Then, I remember a dinner where the only thing I needed to do was show up and be me. I was accepted as soon as I walked through the door. No pretenses, no interview-type questions, no butlers or filet mignon. Just a warm aunt, darling toddler, and unbelievably caring, real man. That was a family and home; this was a competition. Now I'm not even sure I want to pass.

I tell Richard that I need to study more, big test the next day, which is clearly not what he wants to hear. He protests and tries to convince me otherwise, but I nearly jump out of his car when we arrive back at campus. I head immediately to the shower at my sorority house. Something about the evening is making me feel dirty, as if I need to purify myself. The water keeps flowing down my body, and all I can think about is Jase, both of us jammed into a small bathtub in the inexpensive Hotel 99, laughing hysterically. And more of the same at the church camp, both in the lake and in the shower. Our nights were always filled with laughter, talking, snuggling, mind-blowing sex, and then more of the same over and over again. I felt nourished and fulfilled afterward, not drained and frail like I do now.

I tell myself it's just because I have such a heavy course load this semester. I'm starting to wonder if a double major and trying to graduate in three years is such a good idea. Granted, my AP classes allowed me to start college with a lot of class credit already, but it didn't take care of any required classes. I also have masses of homework and presentations. It's never-ending. I wake up at 5 a.m. and go to bed at 1 a.m. I could slow down, but then I wouldn't be able to graduate early. I'm on track to finish my business degree and my psychology degree by the end of the year. No one, not even Richard, knows that, except my adviser. I'm not sure why I'm keeping it a secret. I don't want anyone to have input or sway over what I do when I graduate. If my father knew I could graduate early, with honors, he would push me hard toward coming home to work or earning an MBA degree. Richard would want me to have a normal schedule so I could be with him all the time.

Right before spring quarter, Richard was unhappy that I wanted to live at the sorority house instead of moving in with him. My God, I'm only twenty. I don't need to find any role models for early marriage; I just have to look at my mother and Richard's mother. If I give in to all of Richard's petulant complaining, I'll turn into our mothers. I'll be able to throw great parties and smile on command, but I'll have no power or respect from anyone, including myself. Richard and I rarely have sex, and now I'm not even sure I want to. But I tell myself, *Kathleen, shut up. Of course I want Richard. I'm just tired. Maybe I need to slow down.*

I reach for the phone like I always do when I'm feeling confused. "Sadie, it's me!"

"Hello, my beautiful Kathleen."

"Hi. I just needed to talk to a normal person."

"Kathleen, 'normal' is nothing I've ever been called." We both laugh. "So, my dear, what's going on?"

"I'm so tired, and I miss you."

"Dear, your break is only a few weeks away. You'll be here soon enough."

"You're right. I just miss you. What have you guys been up to?"

"Since you called a few days ago?" She laughs. "You obviously think we lead a far more exciting life than we do. But there is talk about moving the retirement home."

"What? Why?"

"Hilltown is changing."

"Changing good or changing bad?" I don't know anything. I've barely been home since I went to school, and I never, ever set foot in the town. I went to Park City if I needed anything.

"I'd say bad. There have been a lot of layoffs at the Mill, and people are moving away from the town."

"More than normal? Is everyone all right?"

She knows what I mean by "everyone." She reassures me, Jase and his family are fine.

"They wouldn't close the Home, would they?"

"There is some talk about moving the community to Park City, but no, I don't think they'd shut it down."

"But that's away from people's families, and it's more expensive."

"I know. It won't impact us, thanks be to God for Lou's money wisdom and his sweet little condo. We'll probably move into that soon, just to be safe. How's Richard?"

"Oh, you know, busy with studying for the LSATs and all his family events."

"Busy with any other things?"

I know exactly what she's asking. I've dodged the question before and give a noncommittal, "Yes, he's busy too."

"If that's all you have to say, sounds like it's missing something."

"Well . . . his predecessor is tough to match."

"Yes, I know, dear. I have no doubt Jason was amazing in bed. One look at him tells you that. But he also respected you; you had fun with him; he was responsible to his family, the Mill, and the town. I'd say it was more than just 'busy' time."

"This isn't helping. I feel more confused now. Distract me and tell me about your latest trip. I can't study while I'm sad, and I have a few more hours of cramming to do."

She concedes, and I hang up feeling better. But when I finally go to bed, all my doubts and confusion returns, keeping me up half the night. I sneak down to the kitchen and steal Mara's Ben and Jerry's Rocky Road. The first mouthful is sweet, chewy, and creamy, with lots of chocolate. It's the perfect medication for the moment. I continue to enjoy my treat. Mara and I have an agreement now that we're roommates: We can eat whatever we want from each other, but we have to replace it. I make a mental note to get to the grocery store the next day because this ice cream is not going to last the night.

Chapter 15

It's the winter of my junior year, and I'm studying for my advanced statistics course at the sorority. Everyone is whispering and pointing. *Oh no*, I think as I begin to realize what might be happening. I'm right. Fifteen minutes later, Richard opens the door with a bouquet of yellow roses. He holds me by the hand and stares deeply into my eyes. "Kathleen, my beautiful girlfriend, I'd like for you to wear my fraternity pin. Although I've graduated, I am and will always be a Sigma Ti Kappa." I hesitate. I don't want to humiliate Richard. My sisters start cheering, whispering, and clapping. I feel like there is only one answer, and that's yes, but is that what I want? I don't say anything, but I smile and hug him. Richard pins the small broach on my shirt and reaches into a large cooler to get out a bottle of Crystal and two flutes. He opens it and pours the perfect bubbling elixir into each of our glasses. There are lots of bottles of Moet and more flutes for each sister in the cooler.

After more toasts, lots of "congratulations," "you're so lucky" tears, and hugs, Richard announces, "Now it's time to whisk my Kathleen away. Party on, ladies!" More clapping. Richard certainly knows how to put on a show. My real problem is how to avoid having sex with him. He's been bugging me to stay overnight with him ever since we went to his parents'. Why am I so reluctant? There was the hug with his father, the depressed, too thin mom deferring to her son and husband, and the weird looks between Richard and his dad. Tonight, though, I relent and stay at his apartment.

The next day, like always, I feel empty, not loved.

I call my parents the next morning. My mother is excited and eager to finally meet the man that her daughter is pinned to. My father congratulates me for making such a "good choice." He is even more impressed when he surveys Richard's family's net worth.

The following day Richard and I go out to brunch to celebrate. When I order the eggs benedict, he says, "No, she'll have the fresh fruit with nonfat yogurt. I got you a dress to wear to the gallery opening tonight. I just want to make sure it fits."

"What do you mean by that?" I ask. "Did you ever think I'd want to be part of the conversation around getting pinned? Or if I have time to go to another gallery opening with you tonight? Or if I even want a new dress?"

He looks pissed, and I wonder if I've gone too far. He's always so cool and collected, even detached in some ways, but the veins in his neck are bulging, and his face is grimaced.

"Of course, that's it." He laughs. "You're just exhausted from all the studying you're doing. After brunch, take a nap and you'll be good as new for tonight. I'll pick you up at seven."

He starts chatting about the artist featured tonight and a host of other things that I don't pay attention to. The waitress arrives and looks sheepishly at me as she places the fruit and yogurt on the table.

After my tiny brunch, I stop by the student union and fill myself up with pancakes and a double latte with whole milk, just to spite Richard. I cram in a few more hours of studying and then get ready for the gallery opening. The outfit he bought was delivered, and I hate to admit it, but it is a beautiful Vivian Westwood turquoise silk cocktail dress. I begrudgingly put it on. It fits perfectly, even with my second brunch, so I feel a little bit better about that.

We're going to Barnard's, one of the most famous art galleries in the city. We get there early to help his mom. Richard parks in "The President" spot and shrugs when I say that it's presumptuous. When we get into the gallery, I can't believe my eyes. The featured artist for the night is Samuel la Fete, an up-and-coming French master craftsman. His favorite medium is oil paint, but he also does original sculptures in white marble. My mom and I saw one of his shows the summer before on one of our European trips.

Each piece has been lit so that the brushstrokes can be noticed. It's a bit like the impressionists: bright colors like van Gogh combined with the elegance of Renoir. Apparently, half of the pieces have already been sold. That's unheard of with a new experimental artist. Proceeds will go to the American Cancer Society.

Valerie does a quick walk-through. Her women's group, Women of Art, has staged the gallery. She is the president.

"You've made the space perfect, Valerie," I tell her.

"Thank you, dear. I wanted you to know all eyes will be on you tonight. Richard has never brought a date to any of our functions. I just wanted to warn you in case you notice whispers. They all wish it were their daughters in your place."

"They all want to be lawyers' wives?" I ask, trying for levity.

"Lawyer? Whatever do you mean, dear? Richard is going to work for his father after he finishes the thesis for his MBA."

"Oh, I thought—" Fortunately, someone interrupts, asking Valerie a question, and I'm spared having to explain myself. Maybe Richard is waiting to get his LSAT scores back before he tells his parents about law school. He might not want them to know so he doesn't get their hopes up. I already know that he wants to do a lot of pro bono cases. He can be prideful that way, always aiming to be the best.

But I'm starting to wonder if I really know him. Come to think of it, I haven't seen him crack a law book in weeks. Maybe months? And what about the LSATs? Is he still taking that? He lied about being done with his MBA. This isn't adding up.

I feel two hands near my neck, ever so subtly massaging me. I turn around and I'm shocked; it's Stephen.

"You're all knots. There are lots of ways to release yourself that I'd be happy to show you," he says, giving me a knowing look.

"Yes, I do, and I have a great massage therapist and your son to take care of me when I'm stressed. Excuse me, I need to go to the bathroom." I practically run away before he can follow me.

I take the first open stall. I need to collect myself. I've been deluding myself that Stephen was just being friendly and his long embraces and leering looks were all in my head. But now I know I was wrong. What's even worse is that Richard and his dad have been sharing weird looks ever since I met Stephen. Do they share women? Gross! But what can I do about it?

I take a deep breath, wash my hands, and open the door, ready to face whatever the rest of the night will bring. Valerie Sumner is a master entertainer. The show is almost sold out. All the guests want one of the artist's pieces. I'm not surprised. They can match any decor, modern or traditional. Some guests have flown in from all over the United States. "The beautiful people," as F. Scott Fitzgerald would say.

I look around trying to find my semifiancé. He is talking to a tall, slender, dark-haired model. She looks a lot like the woman who interrupted our conversation on our first date. I walk up to them and extend my hand to the woman, introducing myself. Richard looks as if he has been caught, and the woman looks amused. She introduces herself as Anna, a "friend of Richard's," and quickly walks away. I think I hear a chuckle from "Anna."

"That was awkward," I say.

Richard looks chagrined. "I'm so sorry about her. We dated for a little while, and she wanted to talk about our relationship, so I shut her down. And I think seeing you just made her upset."

"Richard, I'm not going to throw a fit. I'm just beginning to see things more clearly."

Then I head to the bar. I think I need something stronger than Champagne. Just as I order a gin and tonic, Stephen Sumner sidles up next to me.

"So, my beautiful Kathleen, which one of these pieces do you like best? I want to make sure you get something tonight. It will be from Valerie and I."

I see Valerie looking at us and I recognize the look of sadness and defeat. Just like my mother. I turn around and pick the first object I see, just to get this over with. It's a small but elegant painting of a wineglass on a golden table. "That one."

"Come now, you need something bigger and better."

"Just because it's bigger and more expensive doesn't make it better." I walk away.

I thank Valerie once again and congratulate her and then tell Richard that I'm taking an Uber home. I turn as he's protesting and practically sprint to the door.

I ignore Richard, and the rest of his family, for that matter, for the rest of the week while I prep for the end of the semester. On Saturday, Richard and I are at my favorite casual restaurant. I've been up for twenty-four hours cramming for finals and I'm starving. Richard is barely listening to me talk about my economics final, so I change the subject to his favorite topic: himself.

"Did you get your LSAT scores back?" Enough of his claims that he is going to take the LSATs and apply to law school. I want to see if there is any merit to what his mother said.

One minute into his already-very-tired excuse tells me what I need to know. He's not going to law school. I wonder what else isn't true about Richard. I always knew he put on a great show; I just didn't know that he was the actor. The waiter brings more bread, and I dive in. I love the bread, freshly made sourdough. Better than in San Francisco.

"Slow down there, tiger. You're eating like you haven't eaten in months."

"It feels like it," I say. "I told you I've been cramming all week." This isn't the first time Richard has commented on my eating habits, and I'm getting tired of it.

"When we start living together, you may need to rethink your wardrobe."

"Why? I have plenty of clothes, and I'm sure when I land a job, I'll buy some more."

"Why don't you let my mother take you shopping? I think you would look better in some more elegant and classic styles: Chanel, Caroline Herrera, and for casual parties, Brandan Maxwell. I know you like fun clothes like Johnny Was or environmentally conscious Stella McCarthy, but we'll be meeting and spending time with very, very important people who are also very rich and conservative. Also, I haven't wanted to mention that you've put on a few pounds since we started dating. The new clothes will show the extra weight, so I signed you up with my trainer." When my mouth drops, he mistakes it as being concerned about the cost. "Don't worry. All bills will be paid by my family. I'll have my mother's secretary handle everything."

Richard takes out a list, and I see personal trainer, Pilates instructor, hair stylist, hair colorist, and my own professional dresser.

Again, he misreads my face as acquiescing and says, "As I said before, my mother's social secretary will handle everything."

All I want to say is "check please," but I am still starving, so I finish the rest of the meal in silence. He doesn't even notice. Richard started out so promising. What happened? What happened to working pro bono for NGOs and nonprofits? What happened to helping the underdog? What happened to the guy who volunteered with a little brother? Was that even real? I never met the supposed brother, and after our first date, he never mentioned him again. When I asked how he was, he said, "Brad who?" Maybe Brad was just like the LSATs, a lie. Instead, he spends all his time hobnobbing with his parents and their "associates."

With all the studying and sorority responsibilities, I missed that

Richard is just like Nathaniel, another old boyfriend. Even worse, I've worked so hard to liberate myself from my own father and his judgment, only to have it replaced by Richard, who is ruled by his father. It's clear that if I stay with Richard, Stephen will be included in the bargain.

I need some space. I need to go home for a while and see Sadie. Right now, I'd kill for my pink room with the cheesy Jacuzzi tub next door. Classes end in a week, so I'll book a flight for the following Saturday and leave my car at the sorority house. I'll surprise Mom and Dad. Strangely, they haven't been bugging me about coming home, and Dad hasn't mentioned working at the Mill in a long time. Thank God, because that is not what I want for my future. I may not know what I want, but I am getting a lot clearer on what I don't.

Chapter 16

My plane lands at nine o'clock in Pittsburgh. I get a rental and drive home in the dark, barely able to keep my eyes open. I can't wait to dive into bed and sleep for days. When I finally pull into the circular driveway, the darkness is stark. All the lights are off. That is very different. Someone has always been at the house. We have a gardener, a cook, a maid, and Joanne, who takes care of everything else.

I enter the house, flip on the lights, and see most of the furniture covered with sheets and boxes littered all around the living room. I'm too exhausted to get into it tonight, so I head up the winding staircase to my bedroom. As I lie down, I notice a slight musky scent. The room has obviously not been used since I left. When I open my eyes again, it is after 10 a.m. I follow the scent of coffee downstairs and find my mother sitting at the kitchen table.

"Kathleen, what a surprise! I didn't know you were coming home." She jumps up to hug me, and I see tears in her eyes.

"So good to see you, Mom. I've missed you." I'm surprised when I realize those words are true. "What's going on with the house? Are you redecorating again?"

She looks very uncomfortable and tries to tell me to wait until my father gets out of a business meeting to discuss it.

"No, Mom, tell me. What's going on?"

"We're moving."

"What? Why?"

"Your father sold the Mill. We don't have a reason to stay here anymore, so we're moving to Philadelphia."

My mind is racing with a million questions. "Sold the Mill? But it's his identity. What is he going to do now? And leave Hilltown? But it's your town too. You've been here forever, and it's where our family fortune was made."

"I know, dear, but it's time for a change. We'll discuss it more with your father."

"Okay, Mom," I say, but I'm reeling in shock. When were they going to tell me? When the house sold and all my belongings were given away to Goodwill? Or after they already moved? And what happened to Stephanie, Jase, and everyone else at the Mill? Do they have jobs? Is this what Sadie was trying to tell me, or not tell me, during our phone calls? I need to go see what's happening. But my father makes his entrance and beckons us to the family room. Mom immediately stands up; she's always catering to my father

"Dad, tell me what's going on. Mom said you sold the Mill and you're moving to Philadelphia."

"True, but it shouldn't make a difference in your life. I've met your boyfriend's father, Stephen, at several events. It seems like you and his son, Richard, are forces to be reckoned with and are going to set up a life in Chicago. Besides, I didn't feel the need to tell you everything about the Mill. It was a business transaction."

"Business transaction? What are you saying? Hilltown is our home; it's been here over a hundred years. The town bears our last names and the Mill in the town."

"Kathleen, you need to look at the bigger picture. Having a steel mill is not a lucrative venture these days. The Mill has been bleeding cash for the last four years. I did my best with it, but it's time to move on to somewhere with more possibilities."

"Why didn't you at least tell me? This was supposed to be where I might work."

"Kathleen, we had an excellent offer from a meat processing plant, and I took it. We were lucky to get the contract. Most of the mill towns and cities in Western Pennsylvania haven't been so lucky."

"Lucky? I hardly think selling our legacy to a meat processing plant is lucky. When did you know about this offer?" There is no answer. "When?' I ask again.

"Not that I need to tell you, but we were initially approached when you left for college."

"Three years ago?"

"Actually, a bit before that. But I didn't see the possibilities until later."

"What possibilities? For who?"

"For us?"

"You mean for you."

"I mean for the future of our family. Kathleen, I'm done with this line of questioning."

"What about the town and employees?" I ask politely, but inside I am livid and will not be silenced.

"We've been shedding employees for several years, department by department, keeping the most lucrative departments working until about two years ago. By then, it was over. The product rolling department was still making money, but when Jase Thompson left for school in Camdan we closed everything down completely."

Jase? Camdan? I knew enough about him to know he would have stayed if it meant his people had work.

"What about jobs for the other Mill employees?"

"They either moved or got jobs at the new business. It isn't like I left them high and dry."

Everything in me wanted to scream, but I wouldn't know anything if I did that.

"What about pensions? Health care? Promotions? The Mill itself has supported families for generations."

"We had the best lawyers handling the acquisition. We made sure that everything was above board." Except everything was shrouded in secrecy. How could that be "above board"?

"Kathleen, this move will make you a very wealthy woman when I die."

"We're rich enough."

Then he used the mother factor. He knew that she was my weak spot. "Besides, your mother will have a new suite to decorate and many upscale stores to spend money in."

The clothes she would never wear. The suite she'll sleep in alone.

"Is that what you want, Mom?"

"Of course." Anything to placate my father. She knew all of this was wrong. She couldn't even look at me. I knew she was just going from one prison to a larger, more opulent one.

"So, this is all about money and prestige."

"Kathleen, that is not fair. Our family is making a calculated move to become richer and more respected."

But "the family" had nothing to do with it. It's my father's dream to always make as much money as possible, to be an influential businessman.

"So nothing else matters."

"What else is there?"

"People, Dad, people."

"That isn't my responsibility."

"Actually, it is."

He waves his hand dismissively, letting me know the conversation is over. I feel so stupid. There had been signs that something was off; I just chose to ignore them. I remember things my father said. Most of all, the things Jase said about departments losing employees. I never really listened, never really wanted to think about it. Yes, my father never told me about this change, but then again, I should have asked more questions. I was relieved to stay away.

"What about the house?" I ask.

"The house has been sold to the owners of the new plant and will close by the end of this month. Although we didn't expect you, it is probably good that you flew home. That way you can look through your room and such for things you may want to keep. Your mother and I are leaving tomorrow morning on an early flight, and the movers will come at the end of the month to put any furniture we want to keep into a storage facility. You have until mid-June to decide what clothes and things you want to keep. We'll be getting new furniture. The people buying the house want most of this furniture to stay with the house. Your mother and I have plans this evening. Last night at the country club, but I'll wake you when we leave tomorrow. Once we're settled in Philadelphia with a new house, you can pick out new furniture. We're looking at Lake Forest, the best suburb in Chicago. There are quite a few houses we're looking at . . ."

I tune out the rest and head to my room. One week to go through a lifetime of belongings? I really want to go to town and see if everyone is all right. But I can't do that until tomorrow, not under the watchful eye of my father.

The rest of the day is spent going through my stuff. So far, the only things in the "keep" pile are pictures of my aunt Katherine with my mom when I was little, a shimmering dress I wore when my mother and I went to Vegas, and my favorite jewelry. I come upon a pink envelope hidden in the top drawer of my dresser. On the front is a heart, and the envelope is held together by Scotch tape. I open it, and rose petals fall out. They are from the night Jase and I spent at Hotel 99. I remember spraying them with rose water the day after that magical night and putting them in my desk. Do I keep them or throw them out? It's a reminder of my heartache. I place it in a small box containing mother-daughter pictures and my grade-school diaries. I'm not ready to let them go. Most of my clothes, old trophies, books, and magazines go in the "trash" or "giveaway" piles.

By seven o'clock, I can't look at one more thing. It's exhausting trying to erase most of your life. Or have it erased for you. I wasn't sure which one was happening. Maybe both. I have one more thing to do. I need to call Richard to break up.

It doesn't go well. When I say I'm not coming back, he says, "Of course you are. We have tickets to the ballet next week." I say we are done and his pin is in my sorority room. I say he is free to go there anytime and retrieve his things, and I can pick up mine when I drive back to Chicago. He says, "I'll have the movers come in a couple of weeks to bring your stuff here. I cleared space for your desk and laptop and—"

"Richard!" I interrupt. "We're over. I'm not moving in with you."

He pauses for a moment, and I hope it's finally sinking in. Maybe it is, because he calls me a bitch and says, "Who do you think you are?" and then hangs up. After that, I don't have energy for anything but a bath. I appreciate my pink Jacuzzi tub for once and almost tear up when I realize this may be my last pink bath. I crawl into bed and fall asleep immediately. But it is a restless, dreamless night.

I'm woken up by my mother. She is thinner than I remembered and looks even sadder, if that's possible. "Mom, are you okay?"

"Of course, darling. Just busy. Still feels like we have a lot to do." Why even ask? That was going to be her answer. She's always bowing to my father's wishes. I hug her as close as I can, but she pulls away when my father beckons for us. I get dressed and follow her downstairs.

My father dictates, "When you get done, call Joanne. She'll handle the rest. Remember, I demand that you stay out of Hilltown. There is no reason to go to a place you spent very little time in when you lived here. There are some seedy parts of Hilltown now, and Park City has everything you need."

"Good morning to you too, Dad," I say, but he doesn't smile. And I don't agree to any of his terms. I am no longer a child under his roof; he can't tell me what to do. I have the credits I need to graduate if I want to, and I decide I want to. I've loved Northwestern, but I always stayed in my safe, narrow box: sorority, classes and Richard. I never even studied abroad because I didn't have time with my two majors.

"You guys better go. The driver is waiting." Dad looks at me skeptically, but my mom hugs me again, obstructing my view of his grimace. As soon as they leave, I run upstairs to grab my small suitcase. I jump in my car and head to town.

The first thing I notice is the lack of smoke emanating from the giant chimney of the Mill. It had been the most prominent feature of the town. I hated it while growing up, but then I learned how vital that smokestack was. It paid for the houses, groceries, everything needed for the people who worked there.

I turn onto Main Street and gasp. The streets are dark. Most of the stores are boarded up. Only one small grocery remains. The dress shop, the miniature golf adventure, the large grocery store where I got my mother's favorite flowers—all gone. They've been replaced with a fast-food restaurant, a Dollar Store, and a gas station.

I feel dizzy, like I might throw up. Now I understand Sadie's "change for the bad" comment. I pull to the side of the road and try my best to pull myself together. But in every direction I look, Hilltown resembles a war zone, not the thriving town it had been. I'm not sure how safe I am. Some people walking down the street look like ghosts. They are thin and gaunt, watching my car like they have never seen one before. I begin to drive again, much more slowly this time, through what had once been vibrant neighborhoods. Many houses are boarded up and tagged with graffiti. There are also large signs in the front yards indicating the property management company. They are all from the same group and have the same contact information. I type the number into the "notes" in my phone and decide to look into it later.

Some houses look the same, like someone lives there. But these homes all have fences and various signs, warning against trespassing, Beware of Dog, or names of security companies protecting their properties. Clearly, the people who live in Hilltown feel like they need to protect themselves. The porches where people used to visit each other are not needed anymore.

I get out of my car in front of one of the nicer houses. When I look down, there are needles discarded on the sparse grass in front of the sidewalk. There are also pipes. And spoons. Spoons? Then I remember the summer class I took about drug addiction. The spoons are used to "cook" the drugs, by melting the dry substance with a match and a spoon.

As I carefully navigate the sidewalk, I notice that the house at the end of the block has a lot of people moving in and out of it. Some of the people coming out walk behind the house and into an alley. There are also nice-looking cars. They drive in, stop in front of the house, and pick something up without going in. I get back to the rental and quickly drive away. I intuitively know that it's a place I should not venture. Now I know why Dad said to stay away.

I get back into my car and head the other direction. I think about Annie, Brook, Lyn, the Kerseys, and the other families I had gotten close to. And, of course, Jase. I head to Annie's house. When I get there, I'm relieved to see that it is still in the town, but a large *No Trespassing* sign is where the dahlias used to bloom. Most of the other gardens are full of weeds. I walk toward the house and open the gate. It looks like it has a lock on it, but it isn't latched. I knock on the front door, and a man opens it with a growl and a gun. "Get out of my yard, or I'll shoot you." Once he sees that I am obviously not a threat to his safety, his posture relaxes. "What do you want?" he asks gruffly.

"Hi, um, I'm a friend of Annie Thompson and her family. I haven't been here in a while. Did they move?"

Crouched behind the man is, I assume, his wife. "Don't worry, Arlene. She says she's a friend of Annie's."

"Do you have any information about where they moved? Are they still in town?" I ask.

The man answers, "Annie sold us this house for a song. She was very fair to us and honest. She warned us that the town was changing; we just didn't know by how much. Annie and her family moved to

Camdan a couple of years ago. That's all we know." He looks to his wife, who nods.

"Do you think anyone else might know more about their whereabouts?"

"I would ask Joe at the bar. If anyone knows about that family, he's the one. I know that one of Annie's nephews used to work there. Be careful. You have a nice car, but it won't stay that way for long if you keep it parked in this town. It'll get sold for parts. After that bastard sold the Mill for a pretty profit, everything went to hell. They claimed the new owner would hire a lot of us back, but that didn't happen. Meat-packing and steel are hardly the same thing. We've been doing all we can to stay afloat."

I thank them and hurry back to my car, filled with shame. I dread going to the bar. It is obvious that my father is seen as the man that killed Hilltown, and he is. But I'm sure my choice to never come back contributed to the horror of the present situation. Not to mention that being a "Hill" is not going to put me in good standing with anyone. But I'm here, and there's no way I can leave before trying to find Annie and Jase. That is, if they'll even agree to see me.

I slowly drive to Joe's Bar. I notice the flashing sign in the window and feel thankful that it's still in business. There are only a few cars in the parking lot. A few years ago, it would have been packed.

I get out of my car hesitantly and walk toward the entrance. It's déjà vu. Three years ago, I was scared to enter this place, but I'm even more nervous now. I push open the door. There are only a few customers, mostly middle-aged men. Some look like they are barely holding onto their barstools. One of the men approaches me. "Hey, beautiful, can I get you a drink?"

"No thanks," I reply.

I look around for Joe, the owner, and see him serving a customer at the far end of the bar. When I approach him, he says, "What in the hell are you doing here?"

I flinch but say, "Look, I know you don't like me—"

"Hate is more like it," he responds.

I take a deep breath and continue, "I really understand how you must feel."

"No, you really don't," he spits back.

"I'm just trying to find Annie to make sure she's okay. We were friends. I know they're in Camdan, I just don't know where."

"You're not much of a friend." He is right. "Look, I know you really came back just to mess with Jase, but he's not interested. I'm sure of that. He gets plenty of pussy and doesn't need you in his life."

I guess Jase and I weren't that good at staying undercover. "Like I said, I'm not trying to bother him. I just want to make sure everyone is okay."

"Does it look okay to you?"

"No, it doesn't, and I'm so sorry about that. I've been away for three years and didn't know. That's no excuse. I should have known, and I'm sorry."

He softens a bit at this and slows his almost manic wiping down of the counter. "I don't owe you anything, and neither does Jase, but if it makes you leave and never come back, I'll tell you where he works. Do we have a deal?"

I nod.

"Jase works at a place called The Bar. Annie lives there too in a small house with Brooklyn. Now get outta here!"

"Thank you. I mean that. I really appreciate it."

He turns away from me, and I hurry to my car. The logical thing to do would be to go home, pick up my belongings, and head back to Chicago to figure out what's next for me. At least I know Jase and his family are probably fine. He's working and in school. What else do I need to know? I briefly wonder what happened to Brook and Lyn. How about the Kerseys? What about Stephanie and all of Jase's crew?

Rather than turning left to go back to Chicago, I stop by the house to pick up my suitcase and the few things I want to keep and turn right toward Camdan. I hope I can get some answers to all my questions.

Chapter 17

Camdan is a typical kind of funky, fun college town. Southwestern, the state university, has a reputation as a good school, especially in the fields of engineering, small business management, and its graduate program in social work. It's a beautiful school. Much smaller than Northwestern, but the campus has some lovely antique buildings, and the grounds are full of large, old trees to study under before the snow comes. There are lots of cute boutiques and cafés in the city. In high school, I used to shop here for fun vintage clothes. It's close to Park City Hospital, the nearest and most vital healthcare facility in this part of Western Pennsylvania.

I google "The Bar." It's on the city's main drag. It's been voted the best bar in Camdan for three years. I wonder if Jase has something to do with that. I'm lucky to get a parking place only a block away from the establishment. I get out and walk toward the bar.

I find myself at the entrance. Patrons are going in and out. I think about my visits to Joe's during my last summer in Hilltown. After that, I ran away to Chicago as fast as I could. I never looked back.

But I'm here now, hoping to get some forgiveness from the man I left three years ago. I've never been able to really let him go. My heart is pounding way too fast. I can barely breathe. Does he hate me? Of course he does. I'm a Hill. I keep telling myself, *Turn around.*

He won't want to see you anyway, but that's a lame excuse. I'm afraid, so much more afraid than I was before the first time I met him. I should have snuck a Valium from my mom's stash before she left. It's too late now. If I turn back, I know I won't return. He'll live like a ghost, buried inside my mind and my heart. The worst thing that he can do is throw me out. I won't get forgiveness, but at least I'll get closure, and I need that.

It's raining. My hair is soaked. I'm a wreck, but I utter, "Time to suck it up, Kathleen" and push the door open. It's packed on a Thursday afternoon. It's full of college seniors who have just completed their finals and are ready to launch into the real world. I belong in this group, but my launch isn't full of excitement. I have so many loose ends to clean up, and the biggest one is here. I look around, searching for Jase. The Bar is a lot like Joe's, just a bigger and better version. There's a pool table, a karaoke stage, pinball machines, clusters of small tables overflowing with people, and a dark mahogany bar, too crowded for stools.

I'm pushed to the back of the line by customers eager for drinks and refills. Many of them are young women sporting short cutoffs and tight T-shirts. It's obvious they want to be noticed, and when I follow their gazes, I know why. There he is, Jase Thompson. *Shit*. He looks even better than he did three years ago. Same long black hair, lean, muscular body, and dark brown eyes framed with lashes every woman would die for. There is a difference, though; he looks relaxed. He's laughing. He was always so serious while we were together. But he has the same intensity and focus, filling orders efficiently. I move to the front of the line.

A small dark-haired woman, holding a tray of beverages, walks behind the bar. "Hey, Jase, don't be such a slacker. I need three apple martinis, six Buds, and two shots of tequila. Oh, and three autographs for your most ardent groupies."

"Very funny, Cin."

"No, I'm serious. Can you take one of them home, please? Or better yet, all three? They're in here all the time, and they're lousy tippers."

He smiles and looks up. I know he sees me by the look in his eyes and his startled expression. "Can you take over?" he says to Cin, more as a statement than a request. He immediately walks from behind the bar directly to me and grabs my hand, moving us both to the only small space left in the room.

I'm not shocked by his attitude. We did not part under the best of circumstances. What I don't expect is the visceral reaction I still have to his touch.

"*What* are *you* doing *here*?" He's angry, and he has every right to be. I've crashed into his world, where I don't belong, again.

"I, um, I just want to talk to you."

"We have *nothing* to talk about."

"Jase, please?"

"Then talk away."

"Can we go somewhere quieter?" I am sure he will say no, but I'm willing to beg.

He hesitates, looks at my pathetic expression, and grants my wish. He yells to the waitress behind the bar, "I'll be back in fifteen."

He walks onto the sidewalk, turns right, and keeps walking. I'm behind him, but it's hard to keep up with his quick stride. Thank God it's not raining anymore. He stops at a small brick building. We're right in front of a bakery. *Oh God*, I think. *I do not want to have this conversation in front of a very busy bakery. I want some privacy.* Then, I notice a door right next to the business.

Jase opens it and walks up a flight of stairs, leading to a landing. I'm behind him, but it's hard to walk quickly in wet high heel sandals. He pulls out a key and opens the door. I'm still standing at the bottom of the stairs. He looks down at me and, with great irritation, asks, "What are you waiting for?"

I hurry up and walk into the apartment. It looks a lot like his old bedroom. It's clean but simple. There's a blue couch in front of a flat-screen TV. Blinds, not curtains. At the far end of the room is a small kitchenette. Behind me is a door to the bathroom and a closed door, the bedroom, I assume. I put my purse on the couch and turn around. There he is, the man I can't forget, his touch burned into my memory. We stare at each other for what seems like an eternity. He takes a step toward me.

"Shit," I hear him say.

Then I'm in his arms, his lips on mine. The kiss feels like a waterfall, washing over me, leaving everything but him.

I kiss him back, again and again, but I need more. I reach for his shirt and pull it over his head. He pulls down my leggings and my panties and kicks them and my sandals out of the way. I undo his belt, unzip his jeans. He picks me up. I wrap my legs around his body, and then he pushes into me. He pauses just long enough for me to get used to him. But I'm already so wet, so ready for him.

He continues his assault on my senses, pounding into me again and again. "Oh my God," I moan. I'm so close, so close to my release.

"Jesus, wait for me, baby," I hear him say, but I'm already too far gone. My pussy clenches and pulses around him. He soon follows me. I gasp for air. And then it's over.

I slide down his body slowly, separating us. I reach down and awkwardly pull on my clothes. I'm in shock. I look at Jase, and he looks as surprised as I do. I'm not one for hooking up. I'm not a girl who has casual sex. But this is Jase. This is different.

Then I hear, "Kathleen, you screwed my town, my family, and even me. I hope you got what you came here for."

"What?" His words are so angry.

"You heard me," he answers.

So, this isn't a reconnection; it's revenge. I look at him. "You were many things when we were together, Jason Thompson, but cruel was never one of them." I pick up my purse and run out the door. I need to get away from him as fast as I can.

I almost trip on my way down the steps, but I push against the door at the bottom of the stairs. It opens. The cut in my heart is so deep, I know deep breathing is not going to work this time. I race to my car and open my purse. I drop it so most of my belongings land on the sidewalk, including my car key. I reach down, but that makes it worse. The rest of the stuff in my purse falls out. I can't keep from crying.

I've lost all my dignity, leaning against my car, tears streaming down my face; my clothes are a mess, my makeup is ruined, and I don't care. I knew it would be hard seeing Jase, but I never knew he would use sex to wound me. He never did that before; he was always so gentle. Then, I feel arms on each side of me. I turn around, and there he is, Jase. He touches my arm and says gently, "Kat, come back in."

"No, you're right. My family ruined Hilltown. I'm sorry." I wipe the tears away, ashamed of everything, but even more ashamed of what my father has done to Jase's beloved town.

"No, I'm sorry. That was uncalled for. Please come back in." He picks up my remaining stuff off the sidewalk. Then, he looks up at me and says, "Please?" I'm still so confused. "Kat, I figured I'd never see you again. It's not an excuse for what happened. I wasn't thinking."

I follow him back to his apartment. He raced out so fast that he isn't wearing a shirt, so he looks around for it and pulls it on. He turns to me and says, "So, here we are."

"So here we are."

"I know why I'm here, but why are you?"

"I don't really know," I say. "I haven't been to downtown Hilltown since school, and I had no idea how much it changed." I look at his face for a reaction, but it's neutral. I breathe a sigh of relief. "I graduated early, and I guess I wanted to come home. And I wanted to see you."

"Well, you accomplished that," he says, and it stings. He turns serious. "I didn't use a condom. I'm fine, but I don't—"

"I got the birth control shot. It works for six months. I still think about you. I never really got over you."

He laughs and says, "So you never dated anyone else? I find that hard to believe."

"There was only one. He was a rich frat guy. He wanted to marry me, but I broke it off. He wasn't you; he was a carbon copy of my high school boyfriends. Jase, I'm sorry for how I left, and I'm sorry about what my father has done to Hilltown. But I'd like to—"

"That's just the thing, Kathleen. It's always about what you want. What about what I want? I wanted to join you in Chicago, but you wanted to be free. Now, three years later, you want to just waltz back into my life? You have no idea what I've been through, what the town has been through. You've found me, but now it's time for you to leave, again."

"Jase, I'm sorry about how I behaved that summer, but you can't say there's nothing between us."

"Kat, it was just sex."

"Do you honestly believe that? Because I don't."

"Why is it that women always believe that sex equals—"

"Don't belittle me. You can lie to yourself, but don't put that on me. What we had meant something. If you want to tell yourself otherwise, fine. But I know it was more than sex, and I think you do too."

Jase is silent for a long, long time. I calmly wait. I may just be a bad memory to him. To me, our last night in Hilltown was heartbreaking and confusing. It was like we were in a maze, trying desperately to find each other but never meeting. But to him, it could have felt much worse. Rejection.

Finally, he says, "Kathleen, I don't want to live in the past."

I breathe a huge sigh of relief. It's an opening. Better than that, I want nothing to do with the past either. "I came home because you were right. I started creating something too similar to what I was running away from in Chicago. But I left that. I have changed, Jase. *You* changed me for the better. I hope you'll give me a chance to show you that. And I care about Hilltown. Maybe that's why I came home, to do something helpful. I don't know. All I know is that my childhood home is being sold, and all I want from it is the rose petals from a night with you and some pictures of my aunt. I know I've sprung a lot on you tonight, so I'm going to go. I'm checking into the Courtyard Marriott for a while if you want to see me again. I won't force myself into your life if you don't want me."

"Look, Kathleen, I don't have a lot of free time. Between work, school, Annie, and Brooklyn, I'm pretty filled up."

"Jase, you've always been filled up. I'll make time to be with you, even if it means seeing you really early or late, when you're done with work. And I'd love to see Annie and Brooklyn too, if that's all right."

He hesitates, but only for a moment. "I'll pick you up tomorrow night at six in the foyer. I usually eat at Annie's a couple of nights a week. I'll ask her to put out another plate." He looks at his watch. "My break is way over. I gotta get back. I'll see you tomorrow night."

I wanted to jump up and down. This is way better than I could have imagined. I smile at him and say, "Jase, I really appreciate the invite." Then I walk up to him and give him a long, slow kiss. I head toward the door. Before I leave, I turn around, and he's still staring at me.

Chapter 18

I leave his apartment feeling happier than I have since the summer before I left for college. I also feel a bit frightened at the intense feelings I still have for Jase. My life at school was so predictable, so easy. I've lied to myself for the last three years. Endless classes, sorority events, a double major, my internships, and my time with Richard kept me busy, but I was never satisfied.

I pull off the interstate to check into the Courtyard Marriott. When the receptionist asks how long I will be staying, I answer, "Can we leave that open for now?" I have another twenty-four hours before I'll see Jase again. I hope I can pull myself together by that time. I need some kind of direction about what I'm doing with my life now and in the future. There's no certainty that Jase even wants me back in his life.

Things are different now. My family no longer has all the power over me. All those years of feeling the pressure to run the Mill are over. And I'm relieved, but that also leaves a wide-open chasm. When I left Chicago, I was running away from Richard and a life I didn't want, but what *do* I want? What am I running toward? Jase, obviously, but what else? I can't figure out my entire future in one evening. But seeing Annie, Brooklyn, and Jase should help. I'm certain I want them in my world.

I turn on a mindless reality show and drift off to sleep. Early the next morning I hurriedly drive back to Hilltown again to try and understand all that has changed since I left. What I find is more of the same boarded-up buildings, closed retail shops, and homes that look vacant or neglected. I start to feel depressed but am buoyed by the idea of dinner with the Thompsons. When I get back to the motel, I buy a bottle of wine in the downstairs mini mart and run into Jase. I can't help but gasp at the sight of his tall, amazing body and hair that every woman would kill for. Richard was handsome, but nothing like Jase. For Jase, it's effortless; Richard, you could tell it was part of his act and took a lot of work.

"Ready?" he asks. I nod and follow him to his car, a silver-gray Mazda. I wonder what happened to his truck, but I don't ask. I fear it's somehow related to the Mill closing.

We don't talk much as he navigates the small city's streets. I'm relieved when we pull up to a neat ranch-style house, with flowers leading up to the front door and a greenhouse on the side yard. I smell roses, just like the ones I remember so long ago. We park in the driveway. Before we even get out of the car, the front door opens, and a little girl races out.

"Uncle Jase! Aunt Annie promised you were coming!" She races to his side of the car and falls into his arms. She then looks at me and says, "I am Brooklyn Anne Thompson. Who are you?"

"My name is Kathleen Millford Hill, and I've actually met you before. But that was a long time ago, so you probably don't remember."

"Kathy is my favorite name. Can I call you that?" she asks.

"Of course."

"Kathy, you're really pretty, but I don't remember meeting you. Uncle Jase never brings girls here. Are you Uncle Jase's girlfriend?"

I didn't know how to answer. Luckily, she became interested in something else. "You knew me when I was little?"

"We ate dinner together two times."

"Did you meet Snowflake?"

"Yes, I did. She even sat on my lap."

That seems to pass some sort of test for her. She grabs my hand and pulls me toward the open screen door and into the house. I notice the delicious smell coming from the kitchen. The walls are filled with pictures of sunflowers, Annie's favorite flower, and the furniture is the same. For a moment, I feel like I have traveled back to Hilltown, the way it used to be.

"Coming, coming!" yells a friendly voice from the back of the house. Annie, looking just as I remember her, enters the living room and says, "Kathleen, it's so wonderful to see you again!" She grabs me in a huge embrace. "I was thrilled to hear Jase was bringing you with him. How are you? I'm so glad you're back."

Her hair is a little grayer, her gait a little slower, and her body a little thinner, but her eyes and her smile are just the same. I am so happy and relieved that she is all right and even more that she has welcomed me so warmly.

"I'm so glad to see you too," I answer.

Jase interjects, "Annie, Kathleen is only here for a visit. She's not back."

There's a bite to his words that I'm pretty sure Annie feels as well, based on her look. I was hoping that we could at least explore our relationship, but his dismissive remark makes it clear that Jase has already made up his mind. At least he isn't going to string me along. He is just going to break my heart again.

Annie clears the awkwardness by saying, "Well then, I'm especially glad you were able to make time to come tonight." She announces dinner is ready and tells Brooklyn to wash her hands. "Jase, can you help her?"

Before Jase can answer, I volunteer, "Brooklyn, I have to wash my hands too! Let's do it together."

"Come on, Kathy, I'll show you where to go." Brooklyn grabs my hand and leads me to a pretty yellow powder room. Brooklyn climbs up onto a small bench in front of the sink and reaches to turn on the water. "Auntie says we need to sing 'Happy Birthday' when we wash our hands, to make sure they're clean. So let's sing together."

The conversation is stilted at times, but thanks to Annie's warmth, Brooklyn's cheer, and the delicious roast, it is a mostly enjoyable evening. After clearing the dishes, I'm ushered out of the kitchen. While Jase washes them and Annie supervises, I join Brooklyn for a session of engineer Barbie and matchbox cars.

"Time for your bath, sweetie," Annie calls. "Kathleen, I hope you can stay awhile. I'd love to catch up after I get Brooklyn to bed."

Jase says, "Annie, Kathleen has a busy day tomorrow, and I've got early classes, so we need to be going."

"Jase, bring Kathleen by again before she leaves."

"I don't know—" Jase starts, but I immediately interject, "Of course I'll stop by before I leave." I declare it forcefully.

I hug Annie and Brooklyn and walk toward the car without even glancing at Jase. *Fine*, I think. If he wants me gone that much, screw him. No more thinking about Jase. I'll graduate and maybe travel, go to grad school, or get a job. I'll meet someone who respects me, and we'll do important work together. No more guys trying to control me with their money or guys with grudges they can't let go of.

I open the car door and sit in the passenger seat. I'm fuming. Neither of us say a word on the drive back to the motel. He pulls into the entrance and parks near the lobby. He gets out and walks over to get the door for me, but I'm already walking toward the entrance. I am miserable and hate that the evening is ending on such a sour note, but I'm done apologizing.

I hear him behind me. "Kat, wait."

I turn around. "Why did you even invite me tonight if you were going to be such a dick?"

"I'm sorry," he says. "I thought I could handle it, but then driving with you, seeing you with Brooklyn, how Annie's face lit up when I said you were coming, it was too much. I can't get involved and have you go away again. I've moved on with my life, and it seems you have too. We should leave well enough alone."

I decide to take a chance. If he was still mad and didn't have feelings for me, he would have stayed in the car. "Why don't you come up for a bit? If this is it, that's fine, but we can at least say a proper goodbye this time. We never got that, and I don't want the ghost of Jason Thompson haunting me my whole life." This gets a smile from him, and we walk into the hotel together.

In the elevator, our hands brush against one another, and we smile shyly. I fumble for my keycard when we reach the door. My hand is shaking, and I can't believe how nervous I am. It finally opens, and he follows me in. Just as I am about to offer him something from the mini bar, his mouth is on mine. He pauses to look at me and ask, "Is this okay?"

"God, yes," I reply, and he kisses me again, tasting my lips, moving his mouth lower, kissing my neck. We stumble to the bed and continue our explorations of each other's bodies. Wow, have I missed this body. When he reaches down to pull my dress over my head, I stop him. He looks lost. "Kat, what is it?"

"Before we go there, you need to know that for me, this isn't casual sex. And I hope it's not goodbye sex. I don't know what we're doing, but tonight can't be our only night. If that's all you want, leave now. I barely recovered when you left."

When I look into his eyes, I know that there is no way he is going anywhere. Nothing about our relationship has ever been casual, even though we tried to pretend differently. "Okay, Kathleen. But let's not talk about it now. I have other things I want to do."

I laugh and pull the dress over my head, and he unhooks my bra. My nipples feel engorged. I pull his head down so he can kiss them, suck them, knead them. Jase pulls his shirt over his head, and I help him unbuckle his belt and unzip his jeans. He kicks them out of the way and makes fast work of my panties. Just like the first time we made love, Jase begins by kissing my forehead, moving down to my nose, then gently kissing my mouth. He kept kissing me even more slowly and deeply. He moves down my body, kissing and tasting my breasts, down to my abdomen, and continuing down to my core.

Just when I think I am going to explode with want, he finally enters me. He's buried deep inside me and could stay there forever, as far as I'm concerned. We peak together, and then he collapses onto me. We don't talk or move; we just curl into one another and fall asleep.

Hours later, still drowsy, I sit up and look at Jase. I love watching him sleep. I lean down and kiss him. His eyes open at my smile. He glances at the time on his phone and says, "I love you on my skin and under my skin, but I've got to be going. I've got a nine-thirty, and I need to get Brooklyn to her camp and stop by my place to clean up."

"You're not the only one who needs to take a shower. Why not kill two birds with one stone? There's plenty of soap."

He hesitates, but only for a second. Once he's gone and I'm getting dressed, I hum to myself. This is the happiest I've felt in a very long time. I don't know where we are headed, but I know I will see him again. And for now, that's enough. A small victory, but I'll take it!

Now I need to figure out what to do while I'm here. I have to help, but how? I think of Annie and Brooklyn and decide to start there.

"Hello, Annie. It's Kathleen. I just wanted to call to run some ideas by you."

"I'm all ears," Annie answers.

"Um, I was just wondering if you all might need some help with Brooklyn? I have some free time, and I would be very willing to babysit or run errands or whatever. If that's all right with you and Jase, and Lyn and Brook, of course. It seems like they're still busy working."

I'm met with silence. "Of course, if you all don't need any help—"

Annie interrupts, "That would be wonderful, dear. You see, Lyn and Brook aren't together anymore. Brook is trying to figure some things out, so Jase and I are doing our best to take care of Brooklyn. I would welcome the help for as long as you're here, and I'm sure Jase will appreciate it."

I am surprised and saddened to hear about Lyn and Brook's relationship, but it inspires me even more to volunteer as a babysitter.

Annie continues, "Could you meet me at the preschool so I can set it up for you to pick up or drop off Brooklyn?"

"Why don't I pick you up? We can go together."

"That would be wonderful, and it's very sweet of you. She gets out at noon today. Is that a problem?"

"No, just give me your address, and I'll be there at quarter to twelve."

Later that day, all the needed paperwork is finished, and I am now authorized to pick up and drop off Brooklyn. The little girl is so excited. "Does that mean we can play together lots and lots? What about tonight? Auntie Anne, can Kathy spend the night tonight? We're not finished with our game."

This time I decline. I don't want to spring too much on Jase. That backfired last time.

I'm heading back to the hotel for a nap when my phone rings. "Hey, babe," Jase says when I answer. "Annie told me about you helping out. I'm thanking you in advance."

I'm so relieved that he's not mad. "It's my pleasure. You know I adore your family." *And you*, I think. "How's your day going? Did you get to class on time?"

"I'm pretty beat. Some beautiful woman kept me in the shower, so I was late, but I think I know how she can make it up to me."

"Oh, really? I have some ideas myself."

"I like where you're going with that, but I was thinking more along the lines of helping me at The Bar tonight. Mike says we're already slammed. It's all the college kids. I guess now that they're not in school, they want to party."

"I'd be more than happy to pitch in. I'll just change into some jeans and meet you at the bar at six-thirty. I can't have you too tired to mix drinks," I tease.

"Really, babe, you don't need to do much. I was just thinking I might get to see you this way."

"No, I really want to help out. I did a bunch of waitressing when we had sorority parties and altruistic projects. See you soon!"

I take a second shower. The first one didn't count. A few hours later I park my car in the lot at the back of Jase's apartment.

Everyone who lives in the building uses it. I'm glad it's here. I couldn't find any street parking. Then, I walk down the block to the bar. I stand in front of the entrance, feeling a little nervous. I start laughing. What is it with me, Jase, and bars? The laughter and noise emanating from inside ease some of my nervousness, and I open the door. Jase wasn't kidding. The place is packed, standing room only. There are lines at all the pinball machines, and girls are lined up at the bar. It is obvious they are trying to get closer to Jase and his friend, Mike, the other lead bartender and hopeful co-owner of The Bar. He and Jase are putting in a bunch of sweat equity to buy it from its previous owner, who is looking to retire. Mike is fair-skinned, with blue eyes and shaggy dark blond hair, making him the perfect complement to Jase. Now I understand why the bar is packed, predominantly with girls.

"Kat, come on back." Jase walks over to me and gives me one of his toe-curling kisses. When he's done, I notice a lot of shocked and annoyed looks from the women in the bar. I am flying high with the way Jase welcomed me. It feels so good not to have to hide like before.

"Babe, you just sit here, and I'll keep the rum and Cokes coming."

"Jase, no! Put me to work. I can wash bar glasses, handle beer orders, and do my best at waitressing. Just tell me where to go, and I'll start."

He hesitates. "Okay then, beer orders it is."

Jase introduces me to Mike and the waitresses, Cindy, Michelle, and Sara. He shows me how to pull the amber liquor so it's not all foam and where the beer bottles and pitchers are found. Once that is done, I get to work. It takes me a while to get in the swing of things, but after an hour, I feel like a pro. I have pint glasses filled before Jase or Mike even need to relay the order to me. It's crowded behind the bar, but I hardly mind all the brushing up against Jase. At one point, while I'm filling a pitcher, Jase moves behind me and whispers,

"You're really helping, and I appreciate it. Mostly, though, I just like the way you move." I feel myself flushing.

The time flies by, and soon it's last call. Jase and Mike start filling the last orders and directing people out the door. When I look at the clock, I'm shocked that it is after 2 a.m.

The waitresses pull the tips out of their pockets and begin to tally their earnings. Once they are done counting, they hand me a pile of bills. "What's this?" I ask.

"Your share of tonight's tips," Cindy answers.

"Really, you don't need to give me anything. I was glad to pitch in."

"Are you kidding?" Michelle, one of the other waitresses, answered. "By filing the beer orders, Kathleen, you freed up a lot of time for us to get other orders out. Even giving you your fair share, we've made a lot more money than usual, so please take it. Jase, be sure and bring Kathleen every weekend. She doesn't slow us down at all!"

"Kathleen, take it. You've earned it," Mike says with a wink. He's a little like Brook, just more handsome and self-assured. "Hey, Jase, mind closing up tonight? I have something I've gotta get to." Mike motions toward the door, where a very voluptuous brunette is waiting.

Jase looks at Mike and the girl by the door and smirks. "Okay, but you owe me, buddy. Tomorrow is your turn. I've got something to do too," he says, all the time looking at me.

"It's a deal. Nice to meet you, Kathleen. Be sure and give my buddy hell."

"Jase, just let me know what to do," I volunteer.

"You've already done a lot. It won't take long to finish. Just sit, and I'll get this done."

Cindy brings me a chicken sandwich with a heap of fries and tells me to dig in. "I'm always starving after a shift." We chat and laugh about some of the antics of the evening, and before I know it, Jase is done closing up. He asks me if I want to come over. "Are you sure you're not too tired?" I ask. He smiles and says, "Never."

When we get to the apartment, I follow him into a lavender room with unicorns on the walls. I'm wondering whose bedroom it is. I recognize the bed and some of the artwork. Jase clears some stuff off the bed for me to have space and pulls back the comforter. "What is this?" I ask. Jase laughs. "This is Brooklyn's playroom and bedroom when she stays here. I sleep on the pullout sofa in the living room on those nights. Usually, she's with Annie, but my aunt needs her rest sometimes, so I try to pick up the slack."

I excuse myself to go to the bathroom and rid myself of chicken sandwich breath, but by the time I return, he's asleep. Poor guy. He's trying to buy a bar, in school full-time, and taking care of his family. I crawl into bed as gently as possible, and I'm asleep in minutes.

Chapter 19

The next two weeks fall into a pattern of me watching Brooklyn Mondays, Wednesdays, and Thursdays; then I have dinner with Annie and Brooklyn. The best nights are when Jase joins us.

I regularly help out at The Bar on Fridays and Saturdays. I stay over at Jase's after the shifts.

I never guessed that returning home would mean being with Jase. I came to Camdan to say goodbye, but when I saw him, three years just melted away. Now I want to stay here forever. Jase would have to pick me up physically and move me out of town or leave me in a ditch to get rid of me. Being with Jase again, getting to know Annie, and spending time with Brooklyn feels the same as our past summer so long ago. This time, though, I don't have to worry about getting "caught." My father can't hurt Jase. I've talked to Northwestern, and now I'm officially a graduate. I have them send my diploma to Annie's house. I don't have to hide my relationship with Jase from anyone, but I still need to tell my parents about finishing college. They knew that I took extra courses; they just didn't know how many. I'm not ready for what will probably be a very serious conversation. Dad will try to convince me to begin law school and stay with Richard. Mom will undoubtedly cry and plead with me to live in Philadelphia.

Then there's Hilltown. I don't know what I can do to help it. I lived there practically all my life, and now it's a disaster area because of my father's greed. But it's also my fault. I stayed away from the town except for short visits with Sadie. Sadie and Lou moved into a lovely little home in a gated community. It's for the over-sixty-five crowd. They love it. Some of the other mill worker retirees moved there too. The others stay in a new community home just south of Park City. The old retirement home lies empty.

I drive to Hilltown again to get a more detailed look at the town. It takes almost two hours to get there. The town looks even worse in the light of day. It's impossible to hide from the run-down neighborhoods, boarded-up houses, and abandoned graffiti-painted businesses. I drive to the town's elementary school and park where I once practiced my soccer skills and hung out with my friends. It's been taken over by homeless people. How did everything change in just three years? From pretty little houses and lovely families to a place of disrepair, desperation, and poverty. I only have to look down to see more used syringes and drug paraphernalia on the ground. Public trash cans are overflowing with rubbish. No children are playing on the jungle gym or swings. They've started to rust. I look up and see the giant smokestack, but there is no smoke. The Mill's employees are long gone.

I see a group of people coming from what used to be the Mill. It must be a shift change. These people look tired and expressionless. No one yells out to meet at Joe's. I can see that there isn't any community pride.

It isn't completely ugly. In the sun, I can better see well-kept houses and a few small businesses that aren't spray-painted with gang affiliations. But this isn't a place where people can thrive and create friendships and have dreams.

Meat-packing is hard labor, and you don't have to have much skill for the jobs. The owners don't have to pay people a living wage. It seems like a high number of immigrants work there. They can't organize for better pay or health insurance because they don't want anyone to know that they live in the United States. The new owners must be making a ton of money. I thought my father was a bad leader, but at least he had the union to rein him in.

I make a mental note. Most of the run-down properties are owned by the same company, Miller's Inc. The meat-packing plant is part of their portfolio.

The name is familiar. I remembered that I thought of interning with them. I look them up on my cell. They are a large group, an extremely diversified accounting firm. Real estate is just one of their divisions. Then I remember why I decided to turn down any involvement with the firm. They became rich by buying up swatches of foreclosed homes and buildings and selling them for a profit. If they don't sell, they just let the properties go into ruin, then write them off for tax purposes. Their business model has been successful, but I didn't like the idea of taking a job with a company that takes advantage of the "little guy." Their ethics are questionable.

I drive back to the motel and look up Miller's Inc. just in case I'm wrong. What I see are numerous lawsuits bought by the IRS, several cases of sexual harassment, and an ongoing investigation by the DEA, accusing Miller's Inc. of operating as a money-laundering scheme. A RICO case is now pending in the Massachusetts Federal Court, naming them as defendants. So far, they've been able to skirt the law. Maybe I can change that.

I want to dig deeper into what must be the town's greatest malady: drugs. Based on the needles and spoons I've seen littered everywhere, I guess heroin. But my research leads me to the newest and most dangerous opioid, fentanyl. It's very scary because it's at least fifty times more powerful than heroin. Since it came on the scene a couple of years before, overdoses have skyrocketed. Apparently, the high is so great, but users are willing to risk dying for it.

The site I'm on says there aren't a lot of old users. Most end up dead. The only silver lining is that some street dealers are beginning to cut the strength of the fentanyl because their customers keep dying. A lot of addicts, though, just buy more so they can feel good and stave off withdrawal. Addicts now crave the more potent fentanyl; heroin is not enough. They need the stronger stuff.

The pipes might be used for crack cocaine, crystal meth, or PCP. These drugs have the opposite effect as opioids. The users stay up for days on end. People using these drugs can become aggressive. Meth is probably the worst because the drug damages regular brain function, so there is usually some permanent damage even when someone gets clean.

There are a bunch of small and empty plastic bags stamped with pictures or words on the ground. I remember reading that this identifies the seller or the drug itself. The bags I brought with me look like they are from the same supplier. They are all stamped with a blue star.

The other thing bothering me is that Jase and I haven't ever really talked about what went wrong between us three years ago. I haven't wanted to bring it up, because things are going so well, but we need to address it at some point.

Jase never talks about Brook, who I have yet to see since I've been in Camdan. Whenever I try to bring him up, Jase always changes the subject. All he says is "He's doing his thing to get his life together." Subject closed. Lyn's absence is another "subject closed." I want to know more about what is going on.

That day, when I pick Brooklyn up at school, she asks if we can swing by Jase's apartment to get Little Brooklyn, her favorite doll, before heading to the park.

"Of course," I say. "But we have to remember that your uncle worked hard last night and had classes all day, so he may be napping. We have to be really quiet when we get to his home."

"I'll just wake him up! He lets me wake him up all the time."

"No honey, not today. Let him sleep. He has some exams coming up, and he'll need to study for them."

I have to park on the street because the parking lot is full. A car that I don't recognize is in the driveway. I assume it's a friend of someone who lives there. Brooklyn and I quietly walk up the stairs. When we get to the top, I notice that Jase's door is ajar.

"What the hell are you doing here?" I hear Jase say.

Then I hear a female answering, "Nothing yet, but I'm ready, and it feels like you are too."

I tell Brooklyn to wait in the hall as I head toward Jase's room. I peer in the room, and sitting astride Jase is a naked woman with giant breasts and long red hair. I can't help but notice her perfect body.

He pushes the woman's hand away. "Leave."

"The door was open, so I figured—"

"You figured wrong! Get out of my bed!"

The woman quickly scurries off the bed, looking around for her clothes. She grabs them and races out the door. Then he sees me. He looks frantic. "Kat, this isn't what it looks like!"

In the background, I hear Brooklyn. "Uncle Jase, why is that woman naked?"

Panic takes over my body. I hear Brooklyn whining in the hall but can't get to her. I'm frozen in place. Jase gets out of the bed and puts on his sweats. "Don't go anywhere."

"I need to pee," the little girl tells Jase.

I interrupt, "I can take her. Okay, sweetie, let's go to the bathroom."

"Who was that lady?" she asks.

"No one," he replies.

I want to scream, but Brooklyn is already frightened. I can't fight the tears running down my face.

"Kat," he says as he enters the living room.

"You don't get to call me that."

"Let me explain."

"Look, Jase, we never made any promises. You don't owe me an explanation."

He looks like I slapped him. I'm so confused and hurt. Part of me thinks, *Of course this happened. We weren't exclusive. You weren't anyone special. You really think a guy like Jase doesn't have other women?* But another part of me is crushed. I thought we were recreating something special.

Brooklyn sidles up next to me, takes my hand, and says, "Can we go to the park now?"

"Of course, honey. We're done here." As I walk out the door, I hear Jase plead, "Kat, we need to talk about this."

I ignore his calls. Brooklyn can see through my fake cheer, but I try to hold it together for the rest of my time with her. I drop Brooklyn off at Annie's; she asks me to dinner. "Can I have a rain check? I have a date with Sadie."

I call Sadie as soon as I leave Annie's and nearly weep hearing her voice. I try to act as if I am all right and ask her about herself, but she immediately says, "Get your butt over here. I know something's wrong. I hear it in your voice."

I look at my directions. When I get there, I punch in the code that she gave me. Sadie's move is one of the good things about the Mill closing. I take the first right. Wow, Lou does well. The houses in the neighborhood are very nice. Some are one floor, but some are even two stories high. Annie's house is the first. Her cane makes climbing upstairs dangerous, but she's still nimble.

When I walk in, I am practically tackled by Sadie, who can still hug with surprising strength. Sadie looks even younger than on her wedding day. True love does that for you, I suppose. But loving Jase is hard. Jase promised to be "someone" I can see more than once. He never promised fidelity. I have no grounds to be angry, but I am. I don't think I can do it. Having an "open relationship" would be too much for me. I promised myself that I would never have another one-sided love affair.

I love the new house. Sadie has painted most of it a light green. The motif continues throughout the three-bedroom, two-bath abode. There are a lot of interesting paintings and artifacts throughout the house. "Lou was quite the traveler before we met, so that's what's on the walls. But we've done quite a bit of traveling since we got married."

We're going to Vegas next week. Nothing but over-the-top fun." I look around, and my eyes stare at the unusual but beautiful painting in front of me. It's obviously by the same artist I got from Stephen and Valori. When I get settled, I'll still hang onto that piece. It's not personal to me, but it's probably worth a fortune. I'm sure I can sell it if I find myself low on funds. Right now, I'm financially safe. Dad has been putting money into my account for school, the sorority, and miscellaneous needs. I've saved quite a bit of it because it may take me a while to find my dream job. Hell, with Jase juggling women, I can go wherever I want, whenever I want. It's too raw to think about that yet.

"You look exhausted," Sadie tells me. "You have dark circles under your eyes. Sorry, sweetie, but you're a mess. You're staying for dinner, no arguments! So what's happening that's making you this way? Your man?"

"No, I broke up with him in Chicago."

"Wise," Sadie answers. "So it's the other guy, your real love."

"It's not always about a guy, Sadie!"

"I know that, dear, but your 'I'm worried about school' and 'I'm worried about my mom' looks are far different from your 'I'm all twisted up about Jason Thompson' look, and you're screaming that one right now."

"I thought there was a chance we could reconcile, things seemed to be going so well, but we're over."

"And why is that?"

"I caught him with another woman."

"Did you talk to him about it? Maybe you misread the situation."

"That's what he said! I mean, how stupid does he think I am? A naked woman on top of him is not hard to misunderstand!"

"Kathleen, the one thing you always said about him was that he never lied. Why do you think he's lying now? Was *he* naked? Were they in the act?"

"Well, before I walked in and saw him, he did sound like he was trying to kick her out of his apartment. He was in bed naked.

I'm pretty sure he was just getting up. No wonder he wanted me to babysit, more time with his groupies."

"You sure spend a lot of time trying to ruin something good between the two of you."

I was quiet. "So this is my fault? I didn't have a naked man in my bed."

"No, you didn't, but there may be a reason for that, and maybe it's *not* what you think."

"I don't know what to believe. I mean, we never talked about being with other people. I don't want to become a disgruntled, demanding girlfriend. If he starts another relationship while I'm here, it will make me crazy."

"Well, honey, that's on you, not him."

"But before I went to Chicago, remember, he just disappeared."

"And why was that? I seem to remember that you told Jason you wanted to keep him on the side for your vacations, like a fancy dessert. I didn't tell you this before, because your mind was already made up."

"I did *not* say that!"

"Kathleen, we never lie to each other."

"But, Sadie, you know I changed my mind the next day and went everywhere in Hilltown to find him. I called. I texted. I even tracked down his brother, Brook. All throughout my first quarter, I kept looking at my phone, foolishly, hoping I'd hear from him, but I didn't. That was the end of it."

"Since you saw him in Camdan, have you called him to talk about it?" Sadie asked.

"No."

"Kathleen, you are holding him to impossible standards. You don't believe him. You don't listen to what might be very logical reasons for everything. He took a chance with you before, and it sounds like he's trying to again. Did you ever think that he may be waiting for you to show him your commitment? I think that you might be the one afraid to get more serious. Maybe it's because of your mom and dad. Let's face it, sweetheart, except for Jason, you haven't been the best judge of men." She's the only person who uses his real first name.

What can I say? Sadie is usually right. I never went to church much growing up, only Christmas and Easter, but I'm pretty sure that God gave me Sadie.

I stay for dinner. I have some time to ponder if I was wrong about Jase. Compared to three summers ago, Jase is making an effort this time. He's been calling my phone all day. I listen. He left a reminder text that he has an unusual early shift at The Bar and then a marketing class, so when can we talk? It would have to wait until tomorrow. Damn, I hate to wait. Once dinner and catching up is over, I hug Sadie and Lou goodbye, promising to be back in a week. It's so good to be able to see her whenever I want to now, not just through the phone. I can't believe how much I've missed her. "Hey, Kathleen!" I turn back, and Sadie is smiling at me. "Next time, bring Jason!"

I laugh back. "I promise." It's time to pick up Brooklyn. She stayed at her camp longer for a special pizza and movie. She's spending the night. I get to Jase's apartment and notice that his cell phone is on the counter. It rings, and I just let it go to voicemail. I don't want him to think I'm being presumptuous with his privacy. I also don't want to know if it's another woman. But then it rings again, and again. I check the incoming calls, and it says Park City Police Department, so I answer nervously, going through all of the reasons they could be calling. Maybe something has happened to Annie, Mike, or a coworker at The Bar.

"Hello?"

"Is this Jase Thompson's number?" a gruff voice asks.

"Yes, he left his phone here, and I saw it was the police, so I answered. I'm babysitting his niece."

"Do you know where I can reach him?"

"I think I can find him. He's in class. Can I tell him what's going on?"

The voice on the phone hesitates. "This is Detective Steve Sanders of the Park City Police Department. It's about his brother, Brook. Just tell him it's an emergency and to come to the Park City ER. Tell him Brook is alive, but Jase needs to get to the Hospital ASAP."

I call Annie immediately. "Hello?"

"Annie, it's Kathleen. Can I bring Brooklyn over? I'm sorry. It's about Brook." There is silence on the other end. "Annie?"

"Is he dead?" she asks.

I'm taken aback. *Dead? Why would she say that?* "No, but he's in the ER in Park City. I need to go find Jase and head over there now."

"Of course, Brooklyn can stay here as long as you need. Unless you think I should go—"

"I don't think Brooklyn should know anything yet. She should be with you."

"If you think so," answers Annie.

I pack a small suitcase for Brooklyn, remembering some of her favorite toys. I pick her up and run down the stairs to my car. I don't want to scare her, so I just say, "Jase left his phone at home, and it's really important that he has it." I tell her she needs to stay with Annie.

She's disappointed we aren't going to bake cookies as planned, but I tell her she can do it with Annie. She frowns. "But they aren't as good."

"I'm sorry, sweetheart," I say, my heart breaking. Not over the cookies, but over a fatherless future I fear for this little girl I love. I know what it's like to have a father, but not a real father.

Annie is at the door when we arrive. "Will you—" she says as she reaches for Brooklyn.

"I'll call as soon as I know anything. I'm sure everything will be okay." We both know that's a lie.

Annie says, "You know he'll blame himself."

"I know. I'll go with him and call you as soon as I know anything."

"I hoped he would have talked to you about this. He'll need someone to be there for him, but he won't tell you—"

"I know. I won't leave him alone. I promise."

We both stare at each other, silently acknowledging our unique bond. We both love Jase.

I run to my rental and speed toward campus. *Shit, shit, shit. Which class is tonight? Tuesday. Tuesday. Tuesday.* I berate myself for forgetting the schedule Jase left for me. Then I remember. Marketing—Roberts Hall, a building at the edge of the campus.

I luck out and find a place to park in front of the building. I frantically run up the stairs and into the door. I grab the first person I see in the hallway. "Do you know which room the marketing class is in?"

"Upstairs, room two-zero-three," the startled professor answers.

"Thanks." I find the first staircase and climb the stairs two at a time. I search the room numbers. I finally find it and swing the door open, scanning the room for Jase. He sees me and walks to the front of the classroom and out into the hall. "Is it Brook?"

What does everyone in the Thompson family know that I don't? "Yes. The police called. He's in the ER. They said to come immediately."

Jase looks frantic.

"He's alive. We need to get to the hospital now. Brooklyn's at Annie's."

Jase retrieves his books and backpack, and we run down the stairs and through the front door.

"My car's right here. I'm driving," I say. He doesn't fight me and slides into the passenger seat. I turn the car onto the ramp of Highway 22 and drive as fast as I can.

"Go faster!" Jase says tensely.

We don't talk on the drive, but I keep stealing glances at him. His face is blank, I can't read him, but his jaw and his eyes are tight. *Just keep your eyes on the highway. Don't think too hard. We will get to the hospital safely.* It becomes my mantra. I wipe out any other thoughts.

Finally, I see signs directing us to the Park City Regional Hospital. "When we get there, I'll drop you off at the emergency room and then park the car," I say. He sort of nods, which I take as agreement. I stop the car, and Jase jumps out, sprinting through the hospital's doors. After parking and taking a minute to gather myself, I open the hospital door and approach the registration desk. "I'm here for Brook Thompson."

"Are you family?" the receptionist asks.

"Yes. I'm here with his brother, Jason." I hear shouting in the distance and exchange glances with the receptionist. We both know who that is. She sighs and says, "All right. Go through the doors on the right, and it's room twelve at the end of the hall. Please close the door after you go in. The noise is making the other patients uncomfortable."

"Thank you." I follow the sounds. *Let me get the fuck out of here!* I hesitate briefly in front of room twelve, then open it.

"What in the hell is she doing here?" Brook screams. The police officer—I assume it's Detective Sanders in plain clothes—and Jase are standing next to Brook, who is handcuffed to the bed. The walls of the room are painted a dirty white, and the floors are grainy old tiles. Not welcoming, more like a jail. My presence seems to be the least of Brook's worries. I don't say anything. I'll leave if Jase wants me to.

"She's with me and stays, little brother," Jase answers.

As I look at Brook more closely, I say a silent prayer of thanks that Annie doesn't have to witness such a scene. I barely recognize the easy-going guy from three years ago. This man's pupils are dilated, his arms are covered with needle track marks, and he has a large, open, infected sore on his left wrist. The track marks are everywhere: on his feet, on his neck, between his fingers, on his legs. He is so, so thin. His blond hair has turned a muted brown color, and he smells like vomit.

"Hey, brother," Brook pleads. "I don't belong here. I promise, if you let me go, just for a little while, I'll come back and show you I'm well. I only need a little while, just to take care of some things. Just for a little while—"

Jase just stands there. Detective Sanders interjects, "Jase, can we talk outside?" Jase pulls my hand to follow them.

Once we're out of Brook's earshot, Jase says to the detective, "She can stay."

The detective nods and explains, "Jase, it's really bad this time. We tested him, and he OD'd on a mixture of fentanyl and trank.

Trank is the newest drug to hit the streets. It's actually a large animal tranquilizer, and judging from the wound on his arm, it looks like he's been using it. Trank's being mixed with a lot of drugs, including fentanyl. Dealers are always looking for new ways to addict people. Fentanyl is still popular, but it is getting a lot of attention by law enforcement these days, and none of the drug cartels want to be in the spotlight. Drugs are not going away, though. Dealers just change what they're giving addicts. A stronger form of meth and cocaine seem to be coming back." None of this is good news.

I peer at Brook's arm from the hallway. I feel like throwing up. There's a gaping wound that is pus-filled and infected and eating away at Brook's arm.

The detective continues, "If people use trank often, they can lose their arms or their legs, or even die from untreated infections. I've seen it myself. Narcon, the drug we use for opioid ODs, doesn't work on trank, coke, or meth. and neither do other drugs like methadone or Suboxone that stop cravings. Scariest shit I've ever seen. Right now, the only option is to get the wounds cleaned and cared for while simultaneously treating his addiction to fentanyl. It's harder because we now have two drugs in his body to contend with. If he doesn't get help, serious help, he'll be dead in a few months or sooner. We were lucky. My partner, Andy, found Brook. Andy used to work in the small force that patrolled Hilltown when the Mill was still operational. He knew Brook and called me as soon as he was revived. It took a shitload of Narcan to resuscitate him, and he was caught carrying meth. There was no trace of meth in his system, according to his blood panel. It looks like he's most likely a low-level drug mule. Because he has a car, he's probably moving products to nearby locations and dealers. That might help his case because it would mean he hasn't hurt anyone directly and isn't carrying fentanyl. Fentanyl is now a class-one narcotic, so there wouldn't be room to negotiate around Brook's sentencing or treatment if he was caught with it. But he had enough meth on him for us to charge him with possession and intent to sell. Fortunately, he's never been caught carrying heroin or fentanyl before. I read his file. You should know, though, that he's been using it for a long time. He knows all the dealers, so they probably also use Brook to test drugs."

"What does that mean?" Jase asks.

"Dealers dose him with any new shipment and see what happens. Being a drug tester is a dream job for users. Drugs are free. But it's also a dangerous job. You have no idea what drug you've been given and you don't know the potency. The user is a guinea pig." The detective gets more serious. "Jase, Brook will have to go through withdrawal in jail. It's not a pretty sight, but at least you'll know that he won't be out on the streets. There are healthcare professionals in the drug units to make sure that Brooks makes it through the worst part. They'll clean and bandage the wound. Like I said, the prognosis isn't good if he doesn't get and stay clean. He's using the worst possible combination. Fentanyl poisons his nervous system from within, and the trank destroys his tissue from the outside."

Jase says, "I appreciate everything you've done for us, Steve. You know he's been in jail before, so it won't be his first detox. He flunked drug court and wasted my money when I sent him to rehab. But he's my brother, man. He's still my brother. And he's Brooklyn's dad."

From Brook's room, we hear, "Fuck you guys. You're supposed to help me. I'm dope sick!"

Tears form in Jase's eyes as he says, "Book him. I don't know what else to do."

The detective promises, "I'll try to get him on the docket ASAP. He can't use any outpatient options. His file is pretty damning: public consumption and intoxication, plenty of petty theft arrests, once for resisting arrest, and multiple DWIs. There is also his rehab history. He's gone through withdrawal multiple times in the beds set up at the fire station, only to start using as soon as he got clean. He went to a state rehabilitation facility but left halfway through it. The last one was the private center, where part of his treatment was federally funded, and you paid the difference."

Jase is quiet. I know he's suffering. Then he answers, "He finished that program and learned welding. He was clean and went to meetings for four months. Then Brook lied to himself that alcohol didn't count, but it did. Then the streets called to him. He's been homeless since then."

"Jase, because I know you're a stand-up guy, I'll try and get a good public defender and a judge who is sympathetic to addicts. No promises, though."

"Thanks, Steve." I have never seen Jase look so hopeless or defeated.

Detective Sanders pats Jase on the shoulder and says, "I'm really sorry."

We follow him back into Brook's room, where the detective begins reciting Brook his rights. "You have the right to remain silent. Anything you say can and will be used against you. You have the right to an attorney—"

"Goddammit, cut out all this police crap. What the fuck am I doing here?"

Detective Rogers continues reading his rights. "If you cannot afford one . . ."

My head is spinning with all of this. Sure, I knew Brook drank too much, but fentanyl? And the new stuff, trank? Whoa! I walk over to Jase and take his hand in mine. He's still fighting back the tears and trying to look stoic, but I know he needs me.

Once the detective is done with his rights, he turns to Jase. "They'll send a patrol car with guys who deal with addicts. He'll be in jail with a lot of other men detoxing. It's a dorm setting, and like I told you, Jase will be monitored. You won't be able to visit him for the first week. What happens after that will be up to the judge. You might want to look for a lawyer and outline an action plan. You have to show why your plan will work better than jail."

Brook keeps screaming obscenities, begging for his freedom. But what does freedom mean to him? Being locked up in jail or returning to the streets where he'll keep using and die?

Jase has tears running down his face. I don't know what to do, but I have an epiphany. Because of my monthly allowance and my internships, I have enough money to pay for Brook to go to a great rehab center. I know that a thirty-day program isn't enough for someone as addicted as Brook. He needs to get out of Pennsylvania and cut ties to any of his dealers or junkie friends. They aren't real friends; all they have in common are drugs.

A nurse walks in and straps Brook's right arm to the hospital bed. She attaches a saline drip. She tells Jase, "I've put a mild sedative in the line. It should help him calm down." And eventually, he looks like he's fallen asleep.

"Jase, let's go somewhere we can talk," I gently tell him. The nurse points to an extra ER space. I lead him out of Brook's room and into a cubicle. I close the drapes for privacy.

I know it's important to keep my head clear. I love Jase, and Brooklyn deserves a loving father. I never had that, and neither did Jase.

"Jase, if Brook is given a chance, I want to pay for his rehab."

"No way!" he interjects. "I can pay for my brother."

I don't give up. "Look at it this way. My family is partially responsible for this. It's the least I can do, or I should say, my father can do. I've been racking my brain on how I can help Hilltown and pay reparations in some way, and this can be that. Please, it would be doing me a favor. I feel guilty and horrible about the whole situation."

Jase doesn't agree, but he doesn't protest, so I continue. I have his exhaustion in my favor. He is a proud man who never takes handouts, so I have to be delicate with my pitch. "Jase, I've been doing some research on addiction after seeing so many needles on the streets of Hilltown. Anyway, research shows that short-term, meaning thirty-day, rehab is not nearly as effective as long-term rehabilitation, which has great support and a multifaceted approach, AA, NA, nutrition, classes, and doctors that specialize in addiction. From what I've read, the recidivism rate is high for fentanyl, but Brook has a lot to live for, especially Brooklyn. Let's do our best to give her something we both never had: a loving father."

Jase's shoulders slump. I've overwhelmed him, so I say, "For now, let's just call off the dogs. Soon, the police officers will pick up Brook and he'll go to County, in the detox area. There is nothing more you can do for him now."

"You don't have to do anything. It's not your problem," he says.

"But I want to help. Go on in and say goodbye to your brother. You don't want to watch him go to jail. That will be hard on both of you. Let your brother have some dignity."

Twenty minutes later I'm looking at a man talking to Jase. He looks like he's in his sixties, wearing a lab coat and stethoscope, so I assume he's a doctor. He turns to me. He has a long white beard and hazel eyes. I bet those eyes have seen a lot. He puts his hand out, and I shake it. We walk out of the room again.

"So you're the person who's going to fund Brook's stint in rehab."

Chapter 20

The doctor warns me, "Rehab hasn't proven to be too effective, I'm afraid, so you may lose your money. There are no guarantees. I'd want to vet the program you choose. One good thing is that Brook was at least able to stay clean after one of his programs."

"Of course," I say. Inside, I'm screaming, *Why did I volunteer to give away my savings on a long shot?* Then I look at Jase. He looks helpless. He's very good at taking care of everyone else. It takes a lot to love someone so addicted. I understand a little. My mom is on prescriptions and wine. I've done all I can to help her, but I think she will have to leave my father. I don't know if that will ever happen. It will be up to her. I'm tired of trying to convince her.

Brook wakes up and starts tugging on the handcuffs. When he sees the doctor, he settles down and looks embarrassed. "Brook," Dr. Howard says calmly, "we're going to prescribe some antibiotics, and a nurse will come to clean and dress your wound."

"Hey, Doc, can you tell all the cops to let me out? I'll be fine. You know I don't need to be here. I wasn't going to sell anything."

"I hate that it's come to this, but you have a chance to get sober. You have a daughter. I hope you get to watch her grow up."

Dr. Howard steps out of the room, and we follow him. "You already know that Brook is addicted to opioids. He's in an acute stage. After detox, he'll join the regular population in a minimum-security facility. They will probably give him Suboxone or start him on methadone for cravings. But it's a long, hard journey. You know that, Jase?"

Jase nods and thanks the doctor. The doctor leaves and two nurses enter Brook's room. We remain in the hallway to give them privacy. I ask Jase if he needs anything, coffee or water. He says no. We sit in silence as I measure how and what to ask. I have so many questions, but I don't want to overwhelm him. I start with "Do you know when he started using?"

Jase takes a deep breath. "I don't know exactly. I wasn't living in Hilltown when he started. Brook already had an alcohol problem, like our father, and then he got hurt at work and was given Percocet for the pain. Lyn left him shortly after that, so I know Brock was overwhelmed trying to take care of Brooklyn. Then Annie broke her hip. I went to part-time at The Bar and took time off from school to help with her. Every Tuesday, I'd drive back to Camdan for a couple of nights. One time, Annie called me because she couldn't find her pain pills. We got another script. Then it happened again; her meds were gone. I noticed a big change in Brook. He seemed dazed. Not just tired but out of it. Brook started nodding out, like he was sleeping but standing. I ignored the signs. I kept thinking he was just overwhelmed because the Mill was closing and he lost his job. Then Lyn moved to Texas. She said she would come back and get Brooklyn, but it never happened. I hear Lyn's already gotten married and has a baby. I don't get a mom leaving her daughter, especially with Brook being unstable. Maybe she didn't think that she could be a single mother. That's when Annie and I stepped in."

I encouraged him to continue. "Then Brook did something he had never done—he left Brooklyn home alone. Annie heard Brooklyn screaming. Thank God our houses were next to each other, so Annie went next door and got Brooklyn. She was napping and woke up all alone. She was terrified. Annie called me, and when Brook got back, I laid into him. He promised that he was gone for just a minute. Said he needed to go to the store. It seemed believable, but looking back, he didn't have any groceries with him when he returned. He just had the familiar glazed look. I didn't see it. Or maybe I didn't want to. I was so busy and—"

"Jase, don't blame yourself; this is bigger than one person can handle. You've done so much for your family and the people at the Mill. You can't take care of everyone." I put my hand on his arm to reassure him, but he's staring at the ground. "When did the crimes start?" I ask.

"Like I said, a year ago, he stole Annie's meds. About nine months ago, he was picked up for petty theft. And I finally realized he was on some serious shit. I should have put him in rehab then and there, but he kept saying he was fine, that everything was under control. I stupidly believed him. I wanted to. Now Brook's turned into our father, only worse."

"Does he still have custody of Brooklyn?"

"No. Child Services stepped in, so Annie and I got custody. Lyn didn't fight it. I'll be Brooklyn's dad if anything happens . . ."

One of the nurses comes out to the hallway and tells us that they sedated Brook again. Then she looks at Jase. Twice. He has that effect on women. "If it were me, I'd go home and get some rest. There's nothing you can do for him here, and it's been a long night already," the nurse tells us.

Jase says he's starving and that the cafeteria options look gross. I smile at his attempt to lighten the mood.

"I know just where to go." We go to the front desk first so he can sign the necessary forms. He lists me as a family member so I can visit Brook. Then I lead Jase to my car.

Over burgers and fries at a little-known diner Sadie and Lou introduced me to, we talk about Brooklyn and Annie, anything but Brook. After a long pause, Jase says, "Kat, I don't know what to say."

"You don't need to say or decide anything. Brook is somewhere he can't leave. He may be going through hell, but he's safe for now. All you need to do is sleep. You look like shit, no offense."

"None taken, but I should—"

"For God's sake, take one day off. This whole thing is going to be a long journey, so you'd better rest up. We can look up good facilities tomorrow when you aren't so tired."

There was nothing that he could say. I am a much stronger woman than the one he'd known three years ago. He nods and continues eating. When we get in my car, I start driving to Hilltown rather than back to campus. When he protests, I say, "I'll take you back in the morning. You don't need your car now, and I'm sure the detective will tear up a parking ticket."

"Is this just your way to spend the night together?" he teases.

"Maybe." I smile.

We stagger into my old bedroom. I'm also exhausted by the day and all that we'll have to face tomorrow. But Jase looks at me. "Kat, I wanted to explain about that woman who was with me. I swear, I never invited her over. She's a—"

"Shhh," I say. "It's fine. A very wise woman may have suggested to me that I overreacted. We don't need to discuss this tonight."

He falls asleep immediately, but I can't seem to turn my mind off. I'm afraid my sighing and tossing and turning will disturb him, so I get my computer and start researching fentanyl addiction. We are lucky Brook isn't dead already. People continuously OD'd on fentanyl because batches aren't consistent.

Right now he is going through withdrawal, called "dope sick," and it sounds horrible. Nausea, muscle cramping, migraine headaches, and anxiety, and the user keeps needing more and more for the same high. They want to avoid detoxing, which is a horrible, sickening situation. What I learn matches everything the detective explained to us.

After an hour of this, I turn my computer off and climb into bed with Jase. He stirs and looks at me. I pull the comforter around us and say, "So tired, going to sleep. Night. Love you." And I'm out.

When I wake up a few hours later, sunshine is pouring through the window and Jase's body is wrapped around me. No wonder I slept so well. Then I realize what I've done. I said the forbidden "L" word. We've never said that to each other, and now I say it on the day his brother is in the ER and on his way to jail? I beat myself up for a while, then return to sanity. *There is no way he will remember.* That calms me down, and I shut my eyes for a little more rest.

I wake up, and Jase is smiling down on me.

"You still snore." He used to tease me about it, which I steadfastly denied.

"I do not snore!" I laugh. "I refuse to believe it."

"Kat, could we talk about something?"

"Sure," I say, thinking it's about Brook and rehab and what to do next.

"Do you remember anything while you were falling asleep?"

"Did I talk in my sleep about fentanyl? Sorry, I was doing some late-night research."

"You said, 'Love you.'"

I look up at him to see his expression. I fear he's freaked out, but he's smiling. "Uh, I did?"

"Yep, you did. That was before you started snoring."

I think about denying it or saying I was crazed with lack of sleep, but then I remember what Sadie said: *"You seem to find a lot of ways to ruin this."* "I meant it," I say and scan his face for a reaction.

He smiles. "Is that so? This feeling stuff, you know that I'm not that great at it. I'm afraid of fucking up. Afraid you'll kick me out of your life again."

"Jase, I never kicked you out of my life. You just left."

"What are you saying?"

"The next day, I knew I'd made a mistake. I tried to find you so we could figure things out, but you were gone. I went to your house and talked to Annie, I went to the Mill, I went to Joe's, and I talked to your brother. Brook promised me he would let you know that I needed to talk to you. I tried to reach you every day for a week, but nobody knew where you were. Your voicemail was full. Your email sent an auto-response that you were out of town and not available. I waited and waited, hoping you'd come back before I had to leave for school."

"You seemed pretty clear that you didn't want to be with me, so I was nursing my bruised ego," Jase admits. "Brook never told me about your conversation."

"I get that, but even while I was in Chicago, I was always checking my phone, hoping you'd call or text. Wasn't your ego less bruised by then?"

"Hell no! I figured you'd moved on with ten other college guys and that you had a whole new life, so why would you want to hear from me?"

"Because I loved you. I wanted you. *Want* you."

He doesn't say anything for a while, making me nervous. He finally replies, "It seems like we've wasted a lot of time. Let's not waste anymore." He starts kissing me.

"I promise to work on this relationship stuff," he says between kissing my neck and breasts. "I may be a stubborn asshole from time to time."

"Oh, *really*? I hadn't noticed." I laugh.

"I give you complete permission to let me know, in any way you want."

Since he's confessing, I feel I should do the same. "And I may be always looking for the other shoe to drop. I don't come from a great family and don't have any healthy role models in the relationship department, so I guess I always assume they won't work out. My last one was exactly like my friends in high school, only richer and more demanding. It never mattered before, but with you . . ." I feel shy and terrified to admit to him, and myself, that he matters more than any guy I've ever been with. But I've come this far, so I have to push myself to keep going. "With you, it matters. A lot. And I think that scares me, so I try to blow it up before you do. Self-preservation."

"That shouldn't make sense, but it does," he says, and I feel my whole body relax. "So, we both have some work to do. I'm all right with that, are you?" I nod. "There's something else you need to know. I never went to bed with that woman back at the apartment, never. I didn't latch the door by accident. I was just so beat. I was dreaming about you, so when I felt someone, I thought it was you. I wasn't even awake when she came in."

"Sadie sort of pointed that out to me. Seems like we need to start trusting and talking to each other a lot more."

"I can do that," Jase says, looking at the clock. "We'd better get to the hospital. Brook will be up by now and probably throwing a fit. How soon can you be ready?"

"We're not going, at least I'm not. The doctor said that we can't see him for a week. He's probably in jail by now. You can call if you have to, but I think our time will be better spent looking for some rehab places and learning more about their programs. For now, Brook's recovery is out of our hands."

"All those rehab places are the same. It's your money, but I'm going to pay you back, every cent." He sounds irritated.

"Jase, have you read much about addiction?"

"Why bother? He's just like my father. He's just using a different drug."

I take a moment to gather my thoughts. His father has been another "no-go" topic. I don't want to piss him off when we're finally in a good place, but there's no way we can get through this if he doesn't face his father. "Jase," I caution. "I know your dad put you in a terrible position, and it's not fair how much you were responsible for at such a young age." I stop there and look for a reaction. He's still listening, so I continue, "Your father wasn't always a hopeless drunk. Annie has shared some really wonderful memories of him. Not just with his kids, but while he was married to your mom. I think her passing is what tipped him over the edge. Annie said that your father never got a DWI. He didn't want anyone to get hurt. She told me he just walked to the nearest grocery store to buy his liquor. He held on to his home as long as he could because he hoped to get better and be a good father. You assume he loved only alcohol, but don't you understand he was trapped in his addiction? He had a disease. He was an alcoholic."

"I don't want to hear any more of this crap."

I look at him, picturing the little boy who needed a dad. I understand more than he knows. I also understand he won't be able to help his brother until he reconciles his feelings about his father.

"Someday you're going to have to try to forgive your father, Jase. If you don't, you will start to resent Brook in the same way. Do you really think Brook wants to be a drug addict? Can you say that your brother was *never* a good man, that he never loved his daughter, his aunt, and you?"

"It's different."

"No, it's not. Your brother's an addict too, but what they're using is just different."

He doesn't say anything, so I leave it at that. He hasn't mentioned the "love" conversation. I don't know what I feel about it—scared, hopeful, wary. Probably all three.

He looks around the room, then at me, and we both start laughing. "Kat, never pictured you as the Barbie pink type."

"It was all *Henri*"—(I smile as I exaggerate his name)—"my mom's interior designer. Don't you know that pink was *the* color while I was in high school? Mom thought it looked très sophisticated. It will grow on you! Anyway, I'm going downstairs to get us some food. Mom and Dad were here a week or so, so the fridge will be stocked." I can't believe it. It's been only a few weeks since I reunited with Jase, but so much has happened. Some things—his kindness, his intelligence, his beauty, way too much to call merely handsome—are still there.

"Kat," he says as I head toward the doorway.

I look back at him. "Thanks for all you're doing. I don't think I could go through this without you."

"You're welcome. Thank you for letting me in. I know this is hard.

And one request?" He gets a mischievous look on his face. "Well, that as well." I laugh. "But what I was going to say is please talk to Annie. You don't have to change your mind about your father, but just listen to some of her stories."

Chapter 21

I head to the kitchen to gather up my stuff and decide to make coffee first. A few hours of sleep and adrenaline are only going to carry me so far. I hear Jase rattling around in the room while I wait for the coffee to brew. Just as I'm leaving with my to-go cup, I hear his voice say, "Hi, Annie. Yeah, yeah, he's all right. He had a lot of drugs with him, so he has to go to jail, but he'll be in their detox facility. No, nothing I can do about that right now. I was wondering, well, if I could ask you a bit about my dad."

I smile to myself and gently close the door behind me.

I go into the study with my computer to research the best programs. My research leads me to several rehab facilities with the best statistical results. Unfortunately, none of them are anywhere near Pennsylvania.

I know that it is a good idea to remove Brook from his drug connections, but I'm worried Jase will never go for it. It seems that for Brook to have any chance of really getting clean and staying that way, the program needs a medical detox: six months of inpatient treatment, followed by six months in an outpatient sober living facility. Some of the preferred facilities even have a list of businesses who will hire those that finish the program. They do whatever it takes for patients to stay sober in the real world. I settle on my top three choices and print out descriptions of all of them. Now I just need to convince Jase that this is the right thing to do.

His head peeks through the door, just as the last few pages finish printing.

"Kat?"

"Huh?"

"I need to get back to Camdan so I need a ride. Sorry."

"Well, I did kind of kidnap you. Let me get into my jeans and we'll go." I pour another to-go cup and hand it to Jase. Then we're out the door and on the road. We don't talk much. What can I say after all we've been through? Brook and jail, introducing Jase to my silly pink room, research on the best picks of rehabs for his brother, the L word, what he and Annie talked about—none of these are casual conversations. We both need time to process everything before we dig deeper.

Mike had picked up Jase's car, so it was back at his apartment. I drop him off in front. Before he shuts the door, he leans in to kiss me and whispers, "I haven't forgotten the L word," and he's gone. I try to digest this interesting piece of news.

I get back to the motel, wave to the staff, and head to my little suite. I crawl into bed, desperately needing a nap, and succumb to slumber.

Jase calls later that afternoon to ask if I'd like to have dinner with Annie and Brooklyn.

"Two of my favorite people. Of course."

He picks me up after class and we head to Annie's. I rustle my bag, debating whether I should talk about the rehab choices now, but I decide to let it go. I don't want to start a fight before dinner. After some moments of comfortable silence, he says, "So, I called Annie today."

I pretend I don't know this and nod for him to continue. "She shared some stuff with me about my dad. She said he wasn't always an alcoholic. When my mother was alive, and even a few years after she passed from colon cancer, Annie said that Dad was an amazing husband and father. He loved us, and my mom, who I barely remember. Annie said he lost his job because of a reorganization, a fancy name for laying people off. He couldn't find another job except stocking shelves at the nearest Walmart. I thought he lost his job because he was a drunk, but I was wrong. There wasn't much to do unless you worked at the Mill or one of the stores in town. They had no openings. Dad got depressed, and that's when he started drinking. Those were the times, the bad times that I remember. But Annie reminded me how my father coached and cheered me on at T-ball and soccer. And our Saturday-night dinners at Annie's, when Brook and I had silly, messy food fights. Sometimes Dad joined us. I didn't remember any of that. I only remember him passed out on the floor and having to feed Brook and get him ready for school. How terrible he'd look and act after a bender, how much I resented him and never, ever wanted to be like him. But Kathleen is right. My dad was more than just a drunk."

He has a dreamy look, and I assume he's picturing his youth. Some of the pleasant times, not the terrible ones, and I place my hand on his.

He takes a deep breath and continues, "After he died, I just put all of my energy into work and caring for my team. Brook seemed old enough to start doing things for himself, and I guess I was too wrapped up in work to see what was going on, big picture."

"Hey, don't do that to yourself. You are a great brother and a wonderful uncle and nephew. Brook's addiction is bigger than you. It's bigger than all of you, but we can get him the help he needs." We pull up to Annie's. "I'll leave it at that."

He leans over to kiss me and says, "You know, you're pretty smart about some things."

"Oh, I assure you, I am smart about most things. Now, let's go. I see a little girl about to lose it if we don't go in there *right now*."

After a delicious dinner of roasted chicken and fresh greens from Annie's garden, no less than eight rounds of freeze tag in the yard, and four rounds of Sorry, Jase and I say our goodbyes. Brooklyn can barely stand, she's so tired, but she tries to convince us to stay anyway.

Jase gives her an extra big twirl and hug, and I remind her that I'll be there tomorrow to play more freeze tag, and we can even make cookies. That does the trick, and she finally releases her grip on us. I wonder if she knows something is wrong. Then, I think, of course she does. She may not know the specifics, but kids always know when something is amiss. I always knew when Mom was out of it.

We head back to the motel, and Jase follows me up to my room. He undresses and crawls into bed. "Please make yourself comfortable, "I say, "but first I want to show you some of the research I did today." He sighs. I know I'm being a buzzkill, but this is important. "You know Brook needs more care than just detoxing, right?" He nods. "And from what I understand, he's had two thirty-day inpatient programs, three outpatient programs, numerous detoxes, and he failed drug court, twice."

"Why are you rehashing all of this?" He's getting irritated.

"I just want to make sure I have his history correct. From the research I've done, the best chance he has is with a yearlong program that will combine—"

"Yearlong! No way. That will cost a fortune, not to mention Brooklyn will be fatherless."

She may be fatherless either way. "I told you, don't worry about the cost. I've got it covered."

"I can't let you do that, no way. I can handle this—"

His self-reliance is pissing me off, so I interrupt. "How? Quitting school? Maxing out credit cards? Working even more hours at The Bar? There are only so many hours in a day, Jase, and you're already utilizing every single one. You're in a difficult business program, building equity in The Bar, taking care of Annie and Brooklyn, trying to find out what to do around your brother's situation, and that doesn't even count me or whoever else you might be seeing."

"I've figured it out before. I can figure it out again."

"You never did figure it out. If you knew what to do, why is Brook going to jail? Jase, you can't afford the best program." As soon as I say it, I want to take it back. The look on his face is as if I slapped him and then ran over his favorite pet. *Damn it, why did I go there?* His pride might never let me help him now.

"This is why I never get involved with women, especially women who think they can hold me with their daddy's money."

The conversation is deteriorating, and as much as I want to plead my case, I need to get him to listen. I know his ego is at stake, so I say, "Like I told you last night, I didn't plan on giving you anything. I was thinking of lending you the money. You can start to pay me back after you graduate. We can even have a legal contract drawn up if that's what you want. I'll charge interest."

He still looks angry, but he uncrosses his arms, giving me an opening. I sit on the bed and make my voice softer. "This isn't about helping you, Jase; it's about Brooklyn. I love that little girl and would never forgive myself if I didn't do everything I could so her father can be in her life. And for Annie. She's lost so much already; I don't want her to lose her nephew." He says nothing. He looks confused and defeated. He's staring out the window.

"You're right. Annie can't handle another call from the cops. But I insist it's a loan at fair market interest rates. I can probably start paying you back—"

"I know you're good for it," I say. "I also know where to find you." I laugh. "Now, can I show you my research?"

"Babe, can we look at it tomorrow? I appreciate it, I really do, but I don't think I'm ready." I'm not about to argue. Seeing him naked under the covers makes me shed my clothes in no time. Later that night, while he's holding me, I hear him whisper, "Kat, there aren't any other women." I close my eyes with a smile.

I wake in the morning to the smell of fresh coffee. "How about some coffee from the man still groveling before you?" Jase teases. I'm disappointed to see he is dressed in his usual jeans and a casual white shirt, no undershirt, but I get over it when he hands me a cup of coffee. I open the lid and see he remembered half milk, half coffee, just the way I like it. He throws me my nightshirt and crawls back into bed with me. He has my stack of papers in his hand. He shows them to me. It's information from my search the night before. He must have found them on my printer. "Here are my three top choices." I start explaining the difference between the treatment options. We both agree that a facility in Northern Arizona seems to be the best fit for Brook. It's halfway between Sedona, which can be a magical city of art and nature, and Northern Arizona State, a college renowned in the state.

I see the worry on Jase's face. "But all the way in Arizona, for a whole year? I don't know if he can handle that. I don't know if I can handle that. What do I tell Brooklyn?"

"Let's not worry too much about that now. I'll call them and see what their availability is, and we'll take it a step at a time. I'm going to print another copy and top off my coffee. Want anything?"

"I'm good. I'm going to grab a shower here before class. Want to join me?"

"I hate to say it, but I have to take a rain check. If you leave before I get back, the door locks automatically. It's my morning to drop Brooklyn off at camp. But tonight?" I ask.

He just smiles back at me. I almost change my mind about leaving. I remember our "shower" at the church camp.

I smile all the way down the elevator, through the lobby, and toward the business center, on my way to find out more information about rehab centers. It's probably why I didn't notice the blond man until he is right in front of me, grabbing my arm.

"Richard, what are you doing here?"

"Well, it wasn't easy, but I was able to talk Mara into telling me where you were. There are only so many places to stay in this shit town. I can't believe this is where you're from." Richard looks around the lobby in disgust. "It's a long drive, so we can stay here tonight, but we're out of here first thing in the morning. I've chosen a couple of apartments for us to look at later in the week, and I assume you want a Tiffany design for your engagement ring. We can go early next week to pick one out."

"Excuse me?" I am incredulous. "Richard, I told you I don't want to see you anymore. We're over. I'm not moving in with you, and I'm *not* getting engaged to you."

"Kathleen, you've been here long enough. It's time to get back to real life."

"This *is* my real life. And not that it matters, because you don't have any say in it."

"Get your stuff together, and we can straighten things out on the drive. I saw your house is for sale, so I assume all your belongings are here. I'll help you load up the car and drop the rental. We can leave first thing."

"*We* are not doing anything, because *we* are no longer a couple!" I'm nearly shouting at this point, but he infuriates me. It's just like my father all over again: not listening to me, thinking he knows best.

Richard looks surprised. "Who are you fucking? That's the only reason I can think of why you're acting like this. Whatever redneck you screwed will get over it. Now let's get going." He grabs my arm again, only tighter.

"Let go of me!" I feel a slap on my cheek, and just as suddenly, his hand is released from my arm. Jase, with damp hair and a menacing look, pins Richard against the wall. "She said let go of her. And as for the redneck she's fucking, you're looking at him."

"Get your hands off me. This is an Armani shirt, you hick. I'm pressing charges," Richard yells, but I can see he's scared. Jase can look intimidating if he wants to.

"If anyone is pressing charges, it's me," I say. I look to the receptionist in the lobby, and she nods and points to the phone she's holding, silently telling me she has probably already called the police.

Richard's face becomes red and sweaty. He looks at me and pronounces, "I don't know what I saw in you. You're just a small-town girl who I generously spent my time with. Just so you know, you little bitch, I have never been faithful. I fucked half of your sorority sisters, and you didn't even guess it was happening. Have fun with your cheap little life." He storms out of the motel.

"Ms. Hill. Is there anything we can do for you? We've already called the police, but we can call it off if you want. I'm so sorry that happened," the receptionist says.

I'm still in shock, so Jase answers for me. "Thank you, Sarah. I think I got it from here. Tell the cops it's all right; they don't need to waste their time. I'll stay and make sure he's out of town." That would be great." He puts his arms around me and starts to escort me to the elevator. "Actually, Sarah, there is one more thing you can do. Can you send some ice up to our room? I think she may have some swelling on her cheek."

"Of course, anything for Ms. Hill. We've enjoyed having her here."

Once in the room, he tells me to lie down for a bit. I protest that I need to get Brooklyn, but he says, "You are in no state to drive. I'll text Annie. I'm sure she'll be fine taking Brooklyn. Let's ice this first so it doesn't swell." The ice arrives, and Jase wraps it in a clean washcloth and gently puts it on my cheek. He lies down next to me and pulls me toward him, laying my head on his chest. "Do you want to tell me about it?"

I hesitate. "Well, you probably guessed that was my ex-boyfriend, Richard. I broke up with him right before I came here. He . . . was trying to get me to go back to Chicago with him. He never listened to my voicemails or our conversation when I said we were over. I knew he was a control freak, but I never thought he would hurt me." Tears well up in my eyes, but I refuse to cry about Richard, so I wipe them away.

"Babe, there's something I've been wanting to talk to you about, and now seems like a good time." *Oh God*, I think. *He's going to dump me. I'm too much trouble. First my dad; then my crazy ex-boyfriend.* "Maybe it's time for you to move out of this motel."

Oh no, he wants me to leave!

He sees my face. "I mean, it's nice and all, but do you really want to be living in a motel?"

"I don't have anywhere else to go. My parents are selling our house and—"

"I know, babe. What I'm saying is I want you with me. I know I don't have the right to ask you in the middle of this crazy mess. I understand if you say no. It's a shitstorm right now. But I'd love it if you would come live with me. I can't guarantee room service." He laughs. "Or that my bed will be as comfortable as this one. Sometimes we also have to use an uncomfortable couch when a four-year-old stays over, and she'll wake you up earlier than you'd like most mornings. I understand if you want to stay here. My place is small and not that great and—"

I silence him by kissing him. When we come up for air, I say, "I'd love to. There's no one I'd rather wake up to. You know how much I love your niece."

I get his special smile. "Great! Why don't you check out today, and we can move your stuff tonight?" He glances at his phone. "Shit!"

"Go, go!" I say. "I'm fine. I don't want you to be late for class."

"No way, Richard could still be outside. It's okay. I'll just email the professor."

"Not a chance. I'll call the front desk and have them escort me to my car. I will not be the reason for you to have to miss a class. I'll be fine."

It takes some convincing, but he finally leaves, agreeing to meet me at Annie's when I'm done babysitting and he's done with class. Then we'll move my stuff to his apartment, "our home," I guess I should call it now. I lay back on the pillows and sigh a contented sigh. I finally have a boyfriend I love and respect and feel safe with. And I think I have a way to get Jase to let Brook into treatment.

Chapter 22

The next morning, I arrive early at the Police Department and walk into Detective Donovan's office. I heard he was the head of the Drug Task Force in southwestern Pennsylvania. He stops what he is working on and rises to greet me.

"Miss Hill, hello. What can I do for you?"

Of course he knows me. Why even try to pretend I'm not a Hill.

"Just call me Kathleen. It's really about how I can help you. I want to work with you."

He looks surprised, then amused, which I assumed he would, so I came prepared. "Here's my résumé and letters of reference. As you see, I worked in Chicago at a shelter for youth, many of whom faced addiction issues. I have a degree in psychology and business, so I am quite versed in statistics. I want to work with your Drug Task Force. I . . ." Some of my bluster is waning, and my emotions are taking over. "I . . I need to do something that matters."

The detective looks over my materials. "Can you briefly outline what your proposal is?"

"As I said before, I have a degree in business, with a focus on data analysis. In other words, I look at patterns and connections in information. For instance, like what drugs are coming into the area, so we can alert healthcare facilities and decide what police information might be needed. I'd like to design a system to track drug activity in this part of the state. That would mean your department would give me information related to drug arrests, where they occurred, drugs seized, and overdose statistics. We would probably need to get additional information from hospitals, detox beds, the fire departments, schools, and, if relevant, your undercover officers and confidential informants. Using all the information, I will search for patterns. These correlations could help identify clusters of the most dangerous drugs, where they came from, and who sold the drugs. Right now, I know we will start with the low-hanging fruit, but with time, we will be able to move up the food chain."

He's looking at my paperwork again, which makes me nervous. He finally says, "I'm impressed, Kathleen. Right now, though, we're vastly understaffed and underfunded, so there is no way I can afford a project like this."

"I don't expect any payment. I'll work for free. We can call it a technically true internship. A letter of recommendation, if my work proves useful, will be enough."

He looks at me very seriously. "We could certainly use all of the help we can get, especially this kind. I need to talk to the other members of the task force because you will be working under them. Lots of the cops are on SWAT. When we do a raid, we need people trained to work in very dicey situations. The rest are detectives. We have some other administrative people to help with paperwork. You'll need clearance to get access to this information." He hands me an employee application. "Fill this out and sign it. Next, go to booking and have your fingerprints taken, and they'll do a background check for previous felony or drug convictions. I'll start a file on you and keep what you gave me. It's not that I question your integrity, but you're going to work on classified information. If everything checks out, I can get back to you by the end of the week. Then we'll have you come in, meet everyone, and finalize a regular schedule."

I stand up and extend my hand. "Thank you for your time. I can see that you're busy."

He shakes it and answers, "Unfortunately, I am. I think your help can make a difference, Kathleen. The more we know about the kind of drugs being used, and where they come from, the better."

For now, I keep my visit with the detective to myself. If it doesn't go anywhere, fine. If it does, I can tell Jase about it. Not that I'm trying to lie to him, but there's a good chance it won't even happen. The task force might just see me as "more work" for them or feel uncomfortable that I'm a Hill and a lot of the drug problems in this part of Pennsylvania are associated with the closure of the steel mill—our family's steel mill.

I return to the motel to pack my stuff. Jace walks in an hour later and gathers my two suitcases. He looks heartbroken, so I walk up to him with a hug. I don't say anything. I know he'll tell me when he's ready.

"I talked to the doctor. He's been giving Brook extra attention. He was our doctor for a few years when we were growing up."

I stand there with my arms still around him.

"The doctor said it's been tough. Brook's been an addict for a long time. Going through detox and trying to keep the wound clean makes him feel very, very sick. It's been a long time since Brook even tried to stay sober. If he gets through the week okay, he'll get transferred to a low-security jail. Then I can visit him. I'd like it if you went with me, just to be there." He takes a deep breath. "He's been asking about Brooklyn."

"Of course I'll go! That's a good sign. If Brook wants me there, I can tell him all about his daughter and her antics. For all of Brook's challenges, I do believe he wants to do what's best for Brooklyn. He was willing to give up custody because he couldn't take care of her." Jase swallows. I see that his eyes are full of tears. He holds me tighter. I know that we have moved to a deeper connection than ever before. I'm so moved that he trusts me with his feelings and wants me with him.

"Let's get out of here. I have an apartment to organize!" He smiles down at me, gives me a gentle kiss, and picks up my suitcases.

When we reach the entrance level, I walk up to the reception area, reach across the desk, and give every person a hug and a fifty-dollar bill. They are all very appreciative. Most people probably forget that they even exist. "Thank you all for everything, especially your kindness and support around the thing with my ex." Then I turn around to start my next adventure, as official girlfriend and roommate to Jason Thompson.

I follow his car to his—actually our—apartment. I know things are crazy, but I'm giddy about the move. My life has taken a 180-degree change in less than two weeks. I've been leaving detailed lies to my parents every two days. Luckily, Richard didn't say anything to them or my sorority sisters. No doubt he doesn't want anyone to know the details of our breakup. I shake myself out of the weeds and park my car next to Jase's. We walk in the back door and up the stairs. In front of it, he puts my things down and reaches into his pocket. Then he hands me a key. "Babe, go ahead and open the door to your new home." I open the door. Now it's mine too. I'm totally exhausted but also happier than I've ever been in my life. I put on a nightshirt, and Jase strips to his boxers. We hit the sack and instantly fall asleep.

When I open my eyes, I feel Jase wrapped around me. I'm so glad he's a spooner. I turn around and start kissing my way down his body. I take him in my mouth and suck on him, moving my arms around his back. He sits up and moves my legs around him; then he's inside me. We can't stop kissing, and he keeps moving in and out of me. My arms are around his neck as he finds his release; a minute later I join him. I don't want to move yet, and it appears he shares my sentiment. We sit, locked into each other as our breathing slows down. I love feeling his heart after making love. I feel safe and satisfied. I let go of his neck and look into those amazing, deep brown eyes. He just smiles back. "I wish we could stay this way all day," Jase says. It was the truth, but an impossibility. I have too much to do, and so does Jase. I move and break the connection. I look around the room and laugh.

"What, Miss Hill, you don't like my decorating?" Light purple paint and multicolored stick-on unicorns surround me. I grab a giant T-shirt and panties from the floor, and when I get off the bed, I inadvertently step on something soft and squeaky. I look down. It's another unicorn. "Never knew you had a unicorn fetish," I say. "If you like them so much, I can buy you more." He looks at me the way he did when I first met him: part smile, part smirk.

He gets up, pulls up his jeans, and walks into the main living area. "Coffee, Kat?" I answer with a resounding yes. "French press on its way!" *Perfect. Everything is perfect.*

I start picking up the mess we dropped by the door when we got in last night. "Kat, I have a test in an hour; then Mike needs some help at The Bar. I'm sorry. Just leave all your stuff, and I can help when I get home."

"No, I'm fine. Plus, this way it will be easier when I rearrange everything and throw half of your stuff out," I tease. He looks shocked at first but then laughs. We kiss goodbye, and I head to my overstuffed suitcases to start the unpacking process. I open the closet in the bedroom. There are a few children's pastel dresses, two suits, some ties, a lot of The Bar T-shirts, and a sports coat. I recognize one of the suits from Sadie's wedding. I wish Jase was here so I could peel it off him. But, back to business. There is plenty of room for my clothes. Behind me is a white IKEA dresser. Jase thoughtfully left me four drawers. Then my phone rings. It's Detective Donovan, so I answer.

"Well, Miss Hill, you made a very compelling argument for yourself, and I ran it by my supervisor, who agreed to it on a trial basis. When can you start?"

"Monday. I can be there as early as you want, and I can stay as late as you need me to."

"How about eight to five?"

"No problem."

"You'll be working on a department PC that's linked to sensitive state records and data."

The next couple of weeks pass in a blur. I'm totally booked, but I relish it. I still babysit Brooklyn and help Annie two afternoons a week. The other days I spend at the police station working on my analysis. Jase is amazingly supportive of my work. The drug problem is personal to him. He has friends on the force. Some have known him from Hilltown, others because of The Bar. Jase is equally busy, so sometimes we don't see each other until late at night. Then we make sure to connect under the covers.

The special drug enforcement team is an impressive and formidable group of officers. At first, I was intimidated to learn that most have undercover experience. I admire them, putting themselves at risk to save people they don't know.

My first week was spent setting up the site. From there, we got other law and health departments in the state to share information with me. Detective Donovan was a huge help. He is very well known and respected in the state and was easily able to influence any reluctant people that my data could make a difference.

After the first week of implementing my software, I began learning more about black-market drugs on the streets. Then, I start following the dead bodies. It was scary to learn that our state has one of the highest rates of illegal drug use and overdoses in the nation. Kensington, a small area of Philadelphia, is known as the largest open-air drug market in the United States. Brook was saved from his overdose of fentanyl. It scares me because its potency is fifty times stronger than heroin. Addicts get hooked on the stronger high. Death and ODs are the norm. There is still a low percentage of trank usage, but it is a frightening, emerging trend.

I call over Detective Donovan. "It looks like there is a recent batch of bad meth in the area. There are a lot of hospital OD check-ins by users in Wilmington, Delaware, and surrounding areas. We're seeing frequent and increased drug use. It looks like Brook's fentanyl came into Hilltown from Wilmington. It was probably headed to Philly."

The detective leaned over me to look at my statistics and to enlighten me about the meth world. I like hearing that I'm making a difference. "Kathleen, fentanyl may be in less supply now because more people are learning about it. Because the drug is so lethal, dealers see that a lot of their customers are dying—not good for business. We have, however, more tools for opioids. We can stop an overdose with Narcan, but we have to get there early. Still, the cartels are adept at hiding their product. They've been getting smarter. They order the separate ingredients from China and send them to 'cut,' another word for mixing them with fillers once it's in the States. We've gotten better at finding the shipments, but we're still playing catch-up. We need a lot more manpower to find all the drugs. You can't know what you're getting if you're buying any drug on the street. I've seen it all: pot laced with PCP, fentanyl pressed into pharmacy-grade-looking pills, meth mixed with coke."

I nod. He continues, "Kathleen, let me tell you about methamphetamine. Addicts are called 'tweekers.' That's because they are constantly twitching, and many users think that there are bugs or other things in their bodies. They start digging and picking at their faces and body to get rid of hallucinations. Tweekers can stay up for days. Their teeth rot, they lose lots of weight, and they have tons of infections. Users can become easily agitated and provoked into violence. I'll let first responders and hospitals know about this development. This could save a lot of lives." I have to pat myself on the back. *Yeah!* I did something good.

The next day is spent babysitting Brooklyn. I arrive at Annie's early to start baking cookies. Once I'm done, I'll pick up Brooklyn. She hasn't been her usual peppy self and has asked to see her father a few times. We keep stalling her, but she barely ate her dinner last night and refused a treat at bedtime. That was a first. I hope my aunt Kathleen's special chocolate chip cookies bring a smile to her face.

I'm rummaging through the cupboards for baking soda when I hear footsteps outside. I assume it's Annie, early from her bridge group. "In here!" I call. "Follow the soon-to-be smell of melting chocolate."

I'm reaching behind the flour when I feel something smash my head, and then—

Everything is foggy. *I feel dizzy, my head hurts, and I'm sick to my stomach.* Even more so when I see the dirty mattress I'm on. The room is dark, and I don't recognize anything. I vaguely hear voices but don't understand what they're saying. *Where am I? How long have I been asleep? Am I having a nightmare?* The only thing I remember is baking cookies for . . . oh no! Brooklyn! She'll be stranded at school, wondering why I didn't pick her up. I try to sit up, but my arms are chained to something, and I fall back down.

The voices come closer, and I struggle to focus my eyes. A dingy, yellow light is above me, and I see the shadows of two men coming toward me. One with rotten teeth, a shaved head, and a big scratch on his face, says, "You're a scrappy one, aren't you?" And then spits in my face. "That's for the cut and bruised shins. You better behave yourself; you will not like what we do to you if you're bad." He laughs a sick, phlegmy snicker.

"Let me go!" I yell. "Do you know who I am? You are so screwed when my family finds me, and they will find me." I tug against the chains and kick my feet while they laugh at me.

Scraped Cheek says to Covered in Tattoos, "We may have to knock this bitch out."

"Especially if she keeps screaming," the other one says. They sneer at me and then leave the room. I can hear their muffled voices and footsteps above me. One says, "Give me some of that, but not too much. We need to make sure we're ready when Boss Man comes. He says we need to keep her alive until he sees her."

Another voice says, "Hey, go easy on that. I don't want to have to Narcan her ass. When's he coming?"

"He's supposed to come by tonight or tomorrow night."

The footsteps move to another part of the house, and I can't hear them anymore. I scream, "Help! Let me out of here, you fucks!" But my throat is so dry it hurts. The cement walls and floor tell me I'm in a basement, so probably no one can hear me outside anyway. From the looks of the graffiti tags, dingy mattress, and needles around me, I'm guessing I'm in one of the drug houses. Those guys probably work for one of the higher dealers; they seem pretty small-time, definitely not in charge. But who do they work for? And what do they want with me? Fear creeps in, but I hold it at bay, racking my brain for my research. How can I get away from them?

I must have fallen asleep because I'm startled awake by the sound of footsteps again. I am so thirsty, and my lips are cracked. My head still hurts, and now I need to pee. "Hey!" I yell. "I need to go to the bathroom. Hey!"

Finally, the door opens and I hear footsteps descending the stairs. "You're becoming a pain in my ass," I hear from who I now recognize as Scratched Cheek.

"Can I have some water?" I ask, trying to hide my fear. I can't let them know I'm afraid. "And I need to go to the bathroom."

"Here's a pussy towel," he says as he approaches. He's holding a dingy towel, and his hands are all scraped up, his nails dirty and bitten. He lifts me from my waist, and I stiffen. I relax when he places the gross towel under me and lets go of my hips.

"Pee on that," he says and walks away. When he opens the door at the top of the staircase, a beam of light shines down. I hear their voices. "Remember, we need to use the good shit. Soon, we can do whatever we want to her. I vote a trip to Kensington."

Kensington? Wasn't I working on that? Yes, after tracking the meth from Delaware, I was finding a lot of ODs like ours in the Kensington database. I think that's where the latest shipment to Hilltown came from. I remember meeting with Detective Donovan. I twist my body and try to free my arms. The chain rattles against the pipe it's attached to and makes a *clang* sound. A shadow emerges from the corner. I guess I wasn't alone after all.

"I need to pee," I say with as much conviction as possible.

"What you need is to shut up," the man says. He comes closer, and I notice a needle in his hand.

"No, no, no!" I shout, twisting my body and flailing my legs.

"Don't make this hard on yourself, bitch," he says as he moves toward me, where my legs still can't reach him. Scraped Cheek yells to Covered in Tattoos, who is just outside the room, "I need help with this whore." He grabs my wrist to hold it still. I'm no match for them, especially not chained to a pipe. I feel pressure on my right arm, then pain, like an intense spider bite. *What if I OD? What if they kill me? I'm so scared. I'm so scared. I'm so scared.* It repeats on a loop until it's replaced by a warmth that seeps through my body. After that, nothing.

I don't know how long I've been here, but I wake up soaked. My throat hurts, and I can hardly breathe. What is going on? I have no idea if it is day or night or how long I have been here. The stench of vomit and something else sour and vile overwhelms me. I look down at my shirt and see that I am covered in puke and sweat. I'm scared to look more closely, but I do, and I'm relieved that my pants are still buttoned and don't seem to have been removed. Both my arms hurt from being chained, but when I look at them and see the bruise forming on my right arm, I remember. The pin prick, then darkness. Screaming is futile. My throat hurts too much, and besides, no one will hear me down here. *What am I going to do?* Surely, Jase and the detectives are looking for me, but will they be able to find me? I don't even know if I'm in Pennsylvania anymore.

The door opens, letting in a beam of light again, and I chant to myself, "Please go away. Please go away." I remain perfectly still and hope they stay upstairs. My heart races when I hear footsteps descending.

One of the men from before, Scraped Cheek, also has rotten teeth and a shaved head. He approaches. His breath is sour, his lips cracked, and his eyes bloodshot. "Back to sleep," he says as he pulls a syringe and baggie out of his pocket.

"No, please, no more drugs! I'll be quiet, I promise." But I can barely talk. "Can I have a little water please?" I'm trying to stall him so I can come up with a plan and sweet talk him with kindness. "Please, I'm so thirsty, and my throat really hurts."

He pauses and looks at me. "You sure are a princess, aren't you? What do you think this is, room service? You don't seem to understand that you are not in charge here. We are." He points to the other disgusting man. "And we can do whatever the fuck we want. You may be hot shit out there"—he points to the windowless wall—"but you're nobody in here."

"I get that. I'm sure you are the man in charge here, so no one will mind or even needs to know if you give me a glass of water, right?"

The flattery seems to work, and I can see he's considering it. Or at least not filling his syringe. He smiles a slow smile. "Nah, I don't feel like going back upstairs. What about you?" he asks the other man, who shakes his head. "I'll hold her down again." The first man has the baggie of powder and takes a spoon and lighter out of his other pocket. *Think, think, think,* I say to myself, but my brain isn't working right. It's still fuzzy and aches. The powder starts to turn to liquid under the flame and bubbles just when I hear a door bang open, tons of feet stomping above me, and lots of shouting. Covered in Tattoos looks around the room with panic. I can see him looking for a place to hide or exit, but there aren't any. He's stuck. The shouting from above increases, and I hear a bullhorn outside say, "The premises are surrounded. Come out slowly with your hands up."

More scuffling and what sounds like things being thrown and bodies wrestling comes from above. "Where is she? Where is she?" I hear, and my heart races. *It's Jase, thank God!*

Another voice says, "I bet she's down here," as more light shines down the stairs. Scrapped Cheek hides behind the stairwell, and I scream, "He has a needle, and he's behind the stairs."

Several men in full SWAT team attire run down the stairs. They have Covered in Tattoos on the ground and at gunpoint in no time. One of them approaches me and asks if I'm all right. "Yes," I croak, tears pouring out of my eyes. "John, go get the cutters from the van. She's chained up."

A man runs up the stairs as others shine flashlights in every corner and crevice of the basement. John, one of the SWAT team, looks me over and studies my arm. I feel so ashamed. I'm covered in pee and vomit, but even worse is the needle mark and bruise on my arm. His face remains completely neutral, which I appreciate. No judgment or pity, which would be just as bad.

John, a member of the task force, comes back with a huge contraption in his hand and some blankets. He's followed by Jase, who runs to me and grabs me in a huge embrace. He grabs my face and studies it. "Did they . . . are you . . . God, Kat, I'm so sorry." He kisses me. I feel dampness, his tears. John frees my arms from the chains, and I wrap them around Jase. I can barely feel them; they are so numb. Jase looks up at me and helps John wrap me in blankets. Two men approach with a stretcher, and all hands are placed on me, gently lifting me onto the stretcher and then up the stairs.

Some members of the Drug Squad have Scraped Cheek at gunpoint on the ground, and SWAT men are swarming everywhere. Any and all furniture is tipped over; the place looks like a tornado hit it. Beams from flashlights are making arcs outside, and I see the flashing lights of police cars. More men are handcuffed and being escorted into the waiting cop cars. Jase holds my hand to the ambulance while an EMT looks me over. The EMT scans my eyes, cleans up my injection site, takes my blood pressure, and monitors my heart rate.

"Ma'am, I don't mean to be intrusive, but do you think . . . do we need . . . would you . . ." From the flush on this young EMTs face, I intuit he's wondering if I need a more thorough examination than what he can do by lifting my shirt.

"I don't think that's necessary," I say.

"I'm right here, babe," Jase says over and over again. "I'm right here." They close the ambulance doors, and he caresses my hand and chants this all the way to Park City Hospital.

Chapter 23

Inside the ambulance, the EMT places an oxygen mask over me and secures a heart monitor. He inserts an IV attached to a saline line. As he hangs the bag, he says, "I'm adding some Ativan to help with possible shock and to keep you relaxed. You've been through a lot in the last couple of days." He pulls another blanket out of a steel cupboard and places it around my shoulders.

I remove the oxygen mask and nearly scream, "Couple of days? Is Brooklyn all right? I was making her cookies and then—"

"She's fine," Jase says gently. "Annie came home probably a few minutes after they—" His voice catches, and he takes a moment. "After they abducted you, so she was able to pick Brooklyn up. We're more focused on you right now."

"How did you find me?"

"Well," he says, rubbing his chin. "When Annie came home and saw you weren't there, but your car was, she just figured you were out for a run. But then she saw flour and baking soda spilled all over the floor and knew something was wrong. She called me, and I called the police immediately. They said it was too soon to file a missing person report. That is, until I told them who was missing." He grins at me. "You have quite the fan club down at the precinct. I thought I was on good terms with the cops in this town, but you . . . they love you."

"They are amazing men, but you, you are my knight in shining armor."

"Well, I had some help. A lot of help. When Detective Donovan heard you were missing, he brought in the whole drug enforcement team and SWAT team. He said SWAT could enter without a warrant. Thanks to your research, you guys were closing in on some big dealers. The tricky part was finding where they were hiding you. And for that, Brook was incredibly helpful."

"Brook?"

"Yes, he knows all of the flop houses in town and where to get what drugs and who is selling them. Over the years, I've looked for him in a few of these drug dens, so I knew some as well. We went house to house looking for activity, you know, lots of people coming in and out. Most of them are abandoned, dilapidated drug-shooting alleys, not really where drugs are sold or where the dealers hang out, so we . . ." I drift off because next thing I know, we are at the hospital and someone is pulling me and my stretcher out of the ambulance. We wheel down a hallway and into a room where they fill the emergency physician in on all my vitals. He takes notes, sets me up with new monitors, and adds another saline bag to my line. "We need a rape kit done ASAP," he says to a nurse.

Jase's face pales. I reach my hand out to him. Two women enter the room and identify themselves as a nurse and a social worker. They do a quick exam to check my vitals and then start to explain the procedure. I start to drift off again. The Ativan is making it difficult to stay focused. But maybe that's not such a bad thing. They explain that they need to conduct a pelvic examination and body scan for DNA to determine whether I was sexually assaulted.

"It might be uncomfortable, but we'll try to be gentle and get done as fast as we can," the nurse says. I doze in and out, waking sometimes to a cramping feeling in my abdomen or when they need to move me to check for scratches on my body.

"I can't see any tearing or damage to the area," the nurse says.

"I'll take a swab to make sure there isn't anything we missed." She finally removes her speculum and says, "I'm sorry we had to do that, and sorry there was a reason to do it." She pats my arm and makes sure the other nurse has all she needs to take to the lab. "Someone is waiting outside for you. Shall I let him in? I want to explain to you what's next and can do that in private, or if you want someone else to keep track of this, I can call—"

"Let Jase in. He'll want to know and will remember everything if I don't."

She leaves and momentarily returns with Jase. He's still pale and in shock, but he gives me his full smile and pulls a chair next to me. I nod that I'm all right, and we give the nurse our attention.

"We have blood samples to test for HIV, pregnancy, hepatitis, STDs, or other infections you might have gotten. The blood tests will give the team much more information. I also swabbed several areas, and this may reveal DNA and any signs of semen."

I squeeze Jase's hand, but his eyes are glued to the nurse. "I talked to the police, and only two syringes were found at the scene. It doesn't look like they were particularly used, dirty needles, and it looks as if she only has one puncture mark. Hopefully, there won't be any withdrawal symptoms." She tells us the lab results should be in by the morning and double-checks that she has all my correct contact information.

"Is there anyone else we should notify?" she asks. "Parents or a family doctor?"

"No, I'll handle that," I say.

The ER doctor enters and repeats some of what the nurse already told us. He speaks to Jase, as if I am not there. "I'll keep her on Ativan for the next couple of days if she needs it. If she wakes up and has any cravings for narcotics, we'll give her Suboxone, which helps with those. I doubt it will be a problem. Luckily, she was only missing for thirty-six hours, so it's unlikely that there was enough time for the drugs to become addictive. It's not always true, so keep an eye on her."

My brain spins with this information. Possible addiction, rape kit, semen, it's all too much. When I feel my lids become heavy again, I welcome the darkness and drift off.

I wake up with Jase's hand on mine.

"Hey," I say, still groggy.

He just stares at me. "Jesus, Kat, I was scared I'd lost you."

"You can't get rid of me that easily." I'm trying for levity, but it fails. "Hey," I say until he looks me in the eye again. "I'll always come back to you."

A woman enters the room and introduces herself as Lisa McClain. "I'm a social worker who was there for your examination. Now I'm here to give you information after you leave the hospital. You've been through a lot, both emotionally and physically. Many patients don't want to think about it. That's normal. I'll leave some information you might find helpful when dealing with the emotions that may come up. Post-traumatic stress disorder is very common after what you've gone through. Many report feelings of panic, claustrophobia, nightmares, and even feel like they're back in the dangerous situation again. Sometimes there is a trigger, something that reminds you of the incident, and sometimes these feelings come up for no reason. It can happen any time and can last a few days, months, or even longer. I just want you to know that it's not something that should be ignored. It doesn't mean that you're weak." She looks at me. "I've included a list of practitioners that specialize in PTSD, as well as support groups. Sometimes it's good to feel that you're not alone. Please remember that I'm just a phone call away if you need to talk. We also have a support group sponsored by the hospital, and you're very welcome to join it anytime. Now I'll leave you to rest."

"Thanks for the information," Jase and I say in unison.

Once she leaves, Jase looks at me with concern. "How are you feeling?"

"I just want to go home and put this all behind me. When can I leave?"

"Babe, I know you do, but you almost died. That is serious. If I was scared shitless, I can't imagine what you're going through."

"I was terrified, but I wanted to know who they were working for so I could tell Detective Donovan. Jase?"

"Yeah, Babe?"

"Can you call Sadie?"

Jase looks at me seriously, then smiles. "You are too much. Of course, I'll call her. And in case you didn't know, Kat, I love you."

"You love me?"

"You know I—"

"I know." All I can do is smile.

Chapter 24

I am finally released from the hospital once everyone is reassured that I no longer have narcotics in my system and was not sexually assaulted. I'm welcomed home with a dinner at Annie's, where Brooklyn makes up for lost time by informing me about Snowflake's antics and how she's ready for freeze tag.

"Kat needs to rest. She's tired," Jase says.

I am tired, but at the same time, I've asked him not to baby me. When I'm at home or with people, I want to be seen as the Kat I've always been, not the poor Kathleen who was kidnapped.

But I was kidnapped, I think. I quickly move on. *No need to revisit that. I was in danger for such a short time.* I take my usual deep breath and sit down to supper. But I feel my heart racing for no reason.

Annie outdoes herself with a roasted chicken, salad, French bread, and sautéed asparagus. Chocolate cake is dessert, which Brooklyn can hardly wait to get her hands on.

Annie took Brooklyn to see Brook a few days ago, with a lot of preparation for the visit: the screen between them, the orange jumpsuit, and her father's exhausted face. It seems to have gone well. Brooklyn doesn't seem traumatized. I guess seeing her dad behind a plexiglass barrier is better than not seeing him at all. Children can be resilient, especially one who is so loved.

I've talked to Sadie a few times. She wants to nurse me. "Maybe a little later. Jase has been taking good care of me."

"Later will be fine. I'm glad you have your gorgeous nurse."

"Sadie, I wouldn't have him if you hadn't told me to go for it." We laugh and say goodbye.

I follow the smell of coffee the next morning and notice a small suitcase on the floor and Jase sitting at the table with a huge smile on his face.

"What is going on? Is Brooklyn here? I thought she was coming back to us today."

"Nope, I'm whisking you off for a weekend in Pittsburgh. I know it's not that glamorous, but personally, I don't really plan to leave the hotel at all, so it doesn't really matter where we are. I've already made reservations for a suite at the Grand Hyatt and checked out some great restaurants, but room service would suit me. I've already called Detective Donovan and Annie, and they both agree you need a vacation. What do you say?"

It takes me a minute to switch from thinking I'd be running around with Brooklyn for the next two days to being on vacation with Jase. "I'd love that. When do you want to leave?"

"As soon as you're ready. We're already packed," he says, pointing to the suitcase.

A few hours later we walk into an amazing lobby to check in. Pittsburgh has come a long way since I was a little kid, and it was known as a steel town. They've upgraded their hotels and downtown area to attract tourists and new inhabitants, and I'm pleasantly surprised by the opulence of the hotel. When I snuck into Pittsburgh with my high school friends, we always got the cheapest rooms in the better hotels. We wanted a nice place, but we needed to hide it from our parents, so we all paid cash.

The lobby has a *huge* gas fireplace. On one side, there are comfortable chairs and coffee tables where patrons are enjoying cocktails. We walk by and see the other side. It looks like an elegant restaurant.

When we get in the elevator, Jase presses the fifteenth-floor button. After I leave the elevator, Jase takes the keycard, revealing a beautiful, modern space with a view of downtown. After taking in the view in the living room, I walk to the bedroom and follow a path of rose petals to the bed. Petals lead to a box of Fran's chocolates from Seattle, my favorite. By the side of the bed is a chilled bottle of Crystal Champagne, a small plate of fresh strawberries, and a beautifully wrapped box.

"I can't believe you got all of this together." Tears fill my eyes and I start crying.

I wonder if this is what the social worker warned me about, heightened emotions. But no, this has nothing to do with being kidnapped, I decide, and everything to do with the generous, sexy, smart man standing in front of me. He knows me so well.

I wrap Jase in my arms and start kissing him. I want to break in the bed immediately, but he has other ideas. He pours two glasses of Champagne and says, "Hey, babe, why don't you open our present?"

"Our present?"

"Just trust me."

I slowly start to unwrap the beautiful box on the bed.

"Kat, just rip it open." That wasn't done in our family. Just like everything else, I was expected to demurely take off all the tape and gently unwrap the gift. The gift inside was always expensive, but never special. I just got used to slowing down the unwrapping process so I could plan my fake appreciation. But today, I rip the paper off and open the box to see the most beautiful undergarments. One is black: shorts with lace and a little pair of matching panties. The other is a long, beautiful, white silk see-through nightgown.

"See what I mean? Wait, I think there's something else." Jase reaches down, opens his suitcase, and hands a bag to me. Inside are a comfy pair of pajamas, a box of microwave popcorn, and my favorite pillow from home.

"I can't believe you remembered!"

"I remember everything about you. Kat, if all you feel like doing is resting or watching old movies, I'm cool with that. I know you might not want to do . . ."

I reach for him. "Jase, I want you. I want you to take all the fear away."

We look at each other and start to quickly undress. The sexy undergarments will be for later. Jase grabs the blankets off the bed, the petals falling on the floor. He picks me up and gently puts me on the bed. He removes the rest of my clothes and starts to kiss every part of my body, moving down to my clitoris, where he continues kissing and licking me. Like always, I quickly find my release. He enters me. It only takes minutes for him to come. I don't mind. I know we are both desperate for each other. There will be plenty of time for slow lovemaking later. I pick up my Champagne and open the chocolates, choosing my favorites.

"Let's stay right here all weekend," I say to him and lean back on his chest. I think, *I'm safe here, with Jase to protect me.*

"That is a great idea, Ms. Hill."

The "do not disturb" sign stays on the door. We spend most of the time in bed, eating, laughing, making love, talking, and making more love. It makes me realize how busy we've both been. Jase is always in motion at home. Going to class, the bar, school, Brooklyn. Adding to his load are Brook and me. The weekend is the first time this summer I have seen Jase rest, with no responsibilities.

Jase shares his plans to better organize the first establishment, The Bar, while he and Mike open a second place. Frank O'Leary, The Bar's owner, has been letting them lease to own The Bar and will be a financial backer to their second establishment, asking only for a percentage of the profits. They already have the name picked out, The Rebar, to honor the state's steel mills. It will be more of a casual restaurant and coffee/wine bar. Other than Starbucks and a coffee stand on campus, there aren't many choices in Camdan. They've already picked out the location: a failed dress shop a few blocks away from the campus. The Bar has doubled its revenue and brand name since Mike and Jase started managing it. I'm confident that The Rebar will be successful as well.

I'm honored that Jase is sharing his dreams with me. I'm so proud of his success. I feel a little jealous too. I wish I was more certain about my future. I've gotten job offers from some firms in Chicago, but nothing I'm excited about. Not only are the firms boring, but they are in Chicago. I also feel unsettled. A low stream of anxiety is inside me. It's getting harder to hide.

I share with Jase how satisfying my work with the Drug Task Force has been because I feel as if I am making a difference. "I feel guilty for abandoning Hilltown and not understanding what my father had done to it, and working with the police helps me forgive myself for leaving."

"Kat, no one blames you for the Mill closing. We know you are not your father. Hell, I left too. So did a lot of people."

"It's more than that, I guess. It's that the work I do with the police can literally save lives. Working in finance or as a manager for one of the firms does not save lives. It just makes rich people richer."

"Maybe there's a position for you with the task force."

"I'm not trained properly. Plus, their budget is already stretched so thin, I don't want to use any of their limited resources." The truth is that I don't want to have to go into the precinct. I don't want to stare at that computer screen, tracking overdoses and deaths. I could have been one of those statistics.

Jase can see my mood is shifting away from our sexy, relaxed weekend. "We only have a couple more hours here. Do you want to talk job ideas?"

"God no, we can talk about it later!"

"Great, because I already called room service for some whipped cream."

Once we're home, I'm glad that Jase resumes his classes and goes back to work at The Bar. I was afraid he'd want to stay home and watch over me, but to be honest, I'm beginning to think that's what I need. Tethered to him, I wouldn't feel afraid of the walls closing in.

As soon as he leaves for class, I head to the precinct to see what Detective Donovan has found out since I've been gone. I set up the meeting. I stand outside the door of the building, officers greet me, but I'm not able to go in. I'm frozen. I get out my phone and call the detective. I tell him that I overbooked myself, a lie. I drive back to the apartment. I feel safer there. But it's past time to tell Jase what's going on.

I call his cell and he picks up on the first ring. "Hey, babe, what do you need, or is this just a love call?"

"Can you come home? Now."

"Be there in ten." He hangs up. I sit down on the couch, trying not to think.

Jase walks in and looks at me. "Kat, I know that you've been struggling."

He's noticed. So much for hiding. Tears fall from my eyes. I'm so embarrassed.

He continues, "Yes, you were found quickly, but going on like it never happened would be impossible for anyone. You're strong and brave, but seeking help doesn't mean you're weak. I'm calling Lisa McCain. Part of loving you is taking care of you. It's not a burden. We're here for each other, in every way."

"But I'll be over all of these feelings soon."

Jase answers, "I was going to talk to you about what's been going on. I see it on your face, and sometimes you cry out at night."

Jase retrieves the social worker's card. A few minutes later, he hangs up. "You have an appointment tomorrow at ten with Lisa at the hospital. She wanted to work with you herself since she knows your case. I'll take you."

"You don't have to—"

"Yes, I do, and you are not a burden."

The next day, my real healing begins.

Chapter 25

Lisa's office is in a building just adjacent to the hospital. I walk in. It's painted a soft green and has a comfortable couch and armchair. Lisa's light teak desk is not imposing; it just blends in. She welcomes me. I sit down and immediately burst into tears. I can't seem to stop.

"Kathleen, what's happening is normal. I know it's hard to believe, but it's true. From what Jase said, you're having a lot of anxiety. We'll start with what is going on now. Later, I'll teach you some techniques that will help you in the 'real' world." The hour flies by. I leave with a short to-do list, designed to give me some time and space. "Take away the 'shoulds,'" Lisa says. I've never done that in my life. I'm used to go, go, go! And *always be perfect.*

Jase picks me up, hugs me, and helps me into the car. I book another appointment with Lisa. I also sign up for a support group in Camdam with people who have similar issues. I'm relieved to know that there are others like me.

The first call I make is to Detective Donovan to tell him I'm taking time off.

"Kathleen, come back whenever you want to. After what happened, I wasn't sure you'd even want to continue. I'm glad you are still interested. I'm just sorry we don't have the budget to pay you. You've been so instrumental."

I dismiss his compliment and ask him to fill me in on what happened since I was rescued.

He answers, "The first dealer was shot trying to escape, but the other one is willing to flip. If he has any chance of surviving, it will be in the witness protection program. Of course, that will depend on what he gives us. We now know what gang is selling in this region. They're called the Surenos Thirteen. They are based in Mexico and work with a larger enterprise, the Gulf Cartel. They're known for being one of the most violent gangs in the drug market. They kill without mercy, even women and children. They've made Mexico into what Colombia was in the eighties, only worse. The dealer who was killed was part of this gang, a lower-level member. He was tattooed with their symbols. The other dealer confirmed it as well. It will take a lot to bring all of them down, but at least we know what we're dealing with. You won't have to worry. Police have a large footprint in Hilltown now."

"But why did they want me?"

"Word had gotten out about the research you've been doing, and they were able to tie you to Brook. Brook has some dealers that he owes a lot of money to. Put the two together, and they were probably trying to send a message. They didn't think long-term. They didn't know you were such an important person. I originally thought it was for money, but they would have reached out with a ransom demand, so I think it was a warning for us to back off."

"But you're not sure?" I ask.

"As you know, there are lots of unknowns in the drug world. Trust me, though, we will not let them get to you ever again."

When I get back to our little apartment, I find Jase knee deep in what looks like bed parts and a new mattress standing up in the corner of the bedroom. It doesn't seem to be going well, and I can't help but laugh. He gives me a dirty look, but then he laughs as well.

"Remind me never to buy anything at IKEA again. I wanted to surprise you with a new bed, but it's taking longer than I thought."

"What was wrong with our old bed?" He gives me the same look, and I laugh again. "Okay, it wasn't really a bed. The mattress is pretty lumpy and canoe-shaped, so we always rolled toward the middle, not that I really minded that part."

I see he has it handled, sort of, so I head to the kitchen to make tea. As the kettle whistles, I have an overwhelming desire to call my mother. I don't know why. Maybe because she is someone who truly loves me unconditionally, like Jase. Jase insists on making the call, gently reminding me that my mom is fragile. "Kat, you don't need her possible hysteria right now, and I assume you don't want your dad to know anything." As always, he's right. Jase goes into the empty bedroom to make the call. I put my ear to the door to hear the conversation. "Hello, is this Caroline Hill?" Jase waits for her answer. "I'm Jase Thompson. Kathleen is in Camdan with me, not in Chicago. She came here after seeing you at your Hilltown house. She went into town. Kathleen was never one to close her eyes when she feels like something's off." There are frequent silences while Jase listens to her. "Before I tell you more, I need your word that you won't tell any of this to your husband, that means *anything*. If you can't do that, I'll hang up now. It's what Kathleen wants. Do you understand? She wanted to notify you because she knows you really love her, like I do."

More silence. And then he gently and carefully explains what happened. I look into the room. He gives me a thumbs-up, so I mouth, *I want to talk to her*. A moment later, he hands me the phone. "Hi, Mom."

"Oh, dear, I can't believe all of this! It's so terrifying. That town has really gotten so dangerous and—"

I start to regret talking to her, but I take a deep breath. "Mom, I'm fine. I just, I just . . ." And I start crying.

"I'm hopping on the next plane. I'll be there tomorrow."

I protest, tell her she doesn't need to come, but she insists. And in that moment, I need a mom. "All right, but don't bring Dad. I can't deal with him. You can stay at a hotel or, better yet, with Jase's aunt Annie. You'll love her."

A long silence. Maybe it's too much for her. But I really want to see her. I'm just hoping she can keep it together this time. I want my mother, not the frightened, sad woman who spends most of her life shut in a set of rooms. She wasn't always that way. When I was little, she was so much stronger.

"Okay, dear, I'll say I'm going to a spa retreat."

"Okay. Good. So, tomorrow? I'll talk to Annie to arrange your stay."

She doesn't say anything, and I know I'm overwhelming her, so I remind her she can call our travel agent and just text me the flight details. We'll take care of everything else. "And Mom, thank you for coming. It will be good to see you."

Jase smiles at me when I hang up but then asks why I don't look happy. "I'm afraid she won't come. She'll call back to say she's sick."

"You know your mom best, but I heard a determined, committed woman. I think she'll surprise you. Now, come on and help me put this bed together."

That weekend, we head out to the mall to find more furniture, avoiding IKEA this time. We find a beautiful, distressed armoire in a consignment shop and a rug on sale at Macy's. We splurge on new sheets and a duvet cover, which we christen with our new bed as soon as we can. And then I suggest we go to the paint store. "There's a cornflower-blue color I've had my eye on for a while." Eight years of living in my pink bedroom was more than enough, and Richard would never dream of any color but taupe or white for his walls. He wanted it to feel like a museum. I finally get to create a space that feels right for me, with the guy who is right for me.

Chapter 26

I walk into the precinct on Monday morning just for a visit, and all the officers cheer on my arrival. I find that my fears are confirmed. We are dealing with far bigger shipments and dealers coming from the cities, and meth is also on the rise. Following the bodies is even more complicated than it was before. I leave at noon and stop at a sandwich shop the cops swear by. When I get my sandwich, my phone rings. It's my father. I decide to take it. I have to get him out of my life sometime. The sooner, the better, I decide. I can't avoid him forever.

"Hi, Dad," I tentatively answer.

"I called Richard about plans between you both, and he told me you left school and are living in Camdan with Jase Thompson. Kathleen, what is this nonsense I hear that you are working with a drug team? I did not pay for you to go to one of the best schools to slum it with some drug lords. And why are you even in that town still? You need to get back to Chicago and Richard."

"Father, Richard and I broke up, and I decided to graduate early and skip the formal ceremony. I have a double major, by the way, in psychology and business, and I don't have any reason to go back to Chicago except to get my stuff. I'm building a life here now. I want to help Hilltown from the mess you—" I pause, not wanting to incite him too much—"from the problems that arose when the Mill closed. I live with Jase now and we're—"

He cuts me off with a scoff. "Kathleen, Jase Thompson will not be able to provide for you in the way you are accustomed. And that town is dying. Let it die and move on with your life. You have such a promising future and so many opportunities available to you. I know. I'll just call Jed over at—"

"No, Dad!" He and I are both surprised by my tone. I've never shouted at my father. I take a deep breath. "I don't want to work for Jed Barrons. I'm not exactly sure what I'm going to do, but I'll figure it out. And it will be here in Camdan, not in Chicago, and not in Philadelphia."

He takes a beat, which is never a good sign with my father. "Kathleen, I will not support you in this juvenile idea of 'saving' a town or some puppy-love crush you have on a mill worker. Pack your things and come to Philadelphia and I'll line up some interviews for you."

"No, Dad, I'm staying here."

"Not on my dime, you're not. If you refuse to come back, I'm cutting you off."

"Then cut me off," I say and hang up. I'm shaking as I do, so I sit down on a bench outside the sandwich shop to regroup. No one hangs up on Jonathan Hill, no one. I know he meant it about the money. I do a quick calculation and realize I have enough to live for another year in my college account. It's under my name, so Dad can't just take it out. Instead of feeling scared, I feel liberated. Dad is no longer "the king." He's just one of many millionaires in a city full of them. He can't hurt me, and most importantly, he can't hurt Jase.

Next, another call comes in. It's my mom. *Geez. Is it family day?*

"Hey, Mom, why didn't you text me your flight info? Are you not coming?"

"I'm already here, dear. Well, in Pittsburgh. It seems that the Courtyard has a shuttle to Camdan. Students and their families fly into the airport to get to Southwestern. I should be there in two hours. I'll let you know when I'm settled. Goodbye, sweetheart."

There is something new about my mother. In the past she wouldn't have made arrangements by herself to come to a city she didn't know well. The only place she ever went alone was Canyon Ranch Spa. She didn't sound guarded or drugged. Something has changed. Maybe she's growing up, like I am. *Don't get your hopes up, Kathleen,* I remind myself, but I can't help but feel good.

I place a quick call to Jase, and he volunteers to come with me to the hotel. "No, Jase, I think I need to see her and catch her up on my life. Then I'll bring her to The Bar, which will be quiet since classes are over and it's still early."

I can't totally relax. I head back to the apartment and pick up the paintbrush. I'm done with the bedroom. Now a creamy yellow for the main room. Nothing like mindless work to keep my mind off everything uncertain in my future.

Exactly two hours later, my cell rings. It's Mom. She's at the hotel. I say, "Be there in fifteen minutes. I'll meet you in the lobby." I get there in ten, and the front desk calls her room.

"Mom!" I say as soon as I see her. I grab her in a huge embrace. She grips me with a bear hug, knocking the wind out of me. We both look at each other and, in unison, say, "You look great!" I know why I do. Living with the love of your life will do that.

My mother's changes are more subtle. She's still too thin, but it looks like she's gained about ten pounds; her green eyes are clear, so she's not drugged up; and she has a beautiful, full smile on her face. She's also wearing jeans and a white shirt with simple gold hoops. Her once long platinum-blond hair, she had cut in a low bob. The color is now more of a light brown. She's had darker shades mixed into her color, and it looks better, more real.

Once we catch up, I tell her about my talk with my father.

She studies my face. She reaches for my hand and says, "Honey, your father uses his money to hold over people. You know that."

"More like control them." I snort.

"Now, tell me about Jase."

"Mom, I really love Jase. I can't wait for you to meet him. He's nothing like Richard or the other guys I've dated. He's devoted to his family, his town, and me. He makes me want to be the same. A better person."

"Nothing about you could be better," she says.

"Thanks, Mom, but you know what I mean. Dad has always been about . . . himself and money. The Thompsons are so different. They care about each other and take care of each other and—" I stop when I see the hurt look on her face.

"I'm sorry, Mom. I don't mean to say you didn't care for me. You did your best, but you know our family never looked out for each other. Being with Jase and his family makes me long for that."

"We don't need to sugarcoat it, Kathleen. I haven't been a very good role model. But I am working on myself. I'm feeling stronger, but I have a long way to go."

"You know I'm working with the police, tracking drugs. I feel so fulfilled each day, as if I'm making a difference. Helping this town, the one we destroyed, get back on its feet."

She stares at me again. "But I can see it's more than that. It's the look you got as a child when you were taking on a new cause for refugees or setting up your lemonade stand to help rescue dogs. You get a glint in your eye, and you have it now."

"I only wish Dad could understand that."

"He never will. Meanwhile, I have some news for you."

My heart skips a beat. That is usually followed by something bad.

"Remember your aunt Katherine?"

"Of course. I make her cookies all the time."

"Well, she left you an inheritance that becomes yours when you turn twenty-two. Knowing my sister, she planned that for when you graduated from college, perhaps predicting you would want to do something your father didn't approve of. It's been in a trust since she died. I don't know the exact amount, somewhere around four hundred thousand. It's certainly enough to live on for several years.

You don't have to worry about your dad cutting you off for a while."

"What? Why didn't you ever tell me?"

"She didn't want you to know until you were twenty-one. She wanted you to plan your own future and follow your own dreams. Money can help with that, but it can also be a curse, as you know."

My head is spinning, and I have a bunch of questions, but my phone rings. I look down and see it's Jase. We're late. We were supposed to meet him at The Bar twenty minutes ago.

"I'm so sorry. We're on our way!" I say as a greeting.

He just laughs and says, "Take your time. I know you two have a lot to catch up on."

My mother looks fascinated when we get there. As usual, Jase has mostly women on his side of the bar. Mike is also holding court with several women, all at least ten years younger than him. He excuses himself and walks up to us. "Kat, you didn't tell me you had a sister." I roll my eyes as he takes my mom's hand in his and introduces himself as the owner. Not a co-owner, I notice, but I stop myself from correcting him when I see the blush on my mother's face. She had the same look as when we traveled together. If Mike can make her feel like that again, I'll forgive his arrogance. I will, however, keep my eyes open to make sure he doesn't go too far.

I walk to Jase and give him a big, sloppy kiss. He picks me up and deepens the kiss. Take that, coeds! I offer to barback with him, but he says, "Don't be ridiculous. Your mom is here. I was just helping Mike out until you guys got here. But let's grab a table."

"How's the visit going so far?" He leads me to a four-top and takes a chair out for me.

Once we're seated, I grab his hands in mine. "I didn't realize how much I missed her. I mean, for years, I've been missing her. We barely kept in touch while I was in college, and even before that, well, she was emotionally absent. But look at her now."

We both watch as she talks to Mike. I know she doesn't have experience with men, but she's smiling, even laughing at something he said. I've never seen her laugh like that with my father, ever.

"Ahh, another woman falling for Mike's charms. I'll tell him to cool it. I'm sorry if this is making you uncomfortable. "

"Hopefully Mike will lose interest soon, like he always does." I laugh.

My mom is making her way toward our table, with Mike minding the bar. We order burgers and fries, and I almost faint as I watch my mother shovel fry after fry into her mouth. So much for her latest diet and health kick. At home, we never had fried food or even rich food; it was one grilled chicken breast or poached salmon after another. And even then, she'd hardly eat, but now she's devouring her burger. A veggie burger, but still. And when Jase offers to get her a glass of wine, she says, "No, thank you, but I'd love a Perrier." I'm shocked. No wine?

She asks Jase a bunch of questions about the business plans for the second bar and has a lot of good ideas on how to distinguish the two places.

"I'm thinking, for The Rebar, a foodies spin on comfort food," Jase says. "Like homemade mac and cheese with hatch chilies, Annie's roasted chicken with an apricot compote, and, of course, Brooklyn's favorite, Aunt Kathleen's chocolate chip cookies served warm with vanilla bean ice cream."

"Stop, you're making me hungry again." She laughs. "Annie sounds like a wonderful woman. I've heard nothing but amazing things about her."

I look to see if there is any resentment or jealousy, but she seems genuine. I look at Jase and raise my eyebrows. He understands what I mean. He nods. I love our telepathic way of communicating. I always thought that was a myth, seeing as my parents never had it, but I've seen it before with Sadie and Lou.

"Mom, do you want to come to dinner at Annie's tomorrow? You could meet Brooklyn and—"

"I'd like that very much," she says before I can finish my sentence. "And although this has been so lovely, I better call it a night. I'll take an Uber back to the hotel. Stay here, darling, and gentlemen, I'll see you tomorrow."

Mike walks over to the table and offers to drive my mom to the motel.

"That's not necessary," she says. "I'll just—"

"Uber is unreliable around here. I insist."

She excuses herself to go to the restroom, and Jase reminds him that he is supposed to be watching the bar. "Oh man. I forgot. Jase, will you cover for me? It will only take me twenty minutes to run her back."

"If she's all right with it. But cool it with the flirting. She's married to a real bastard."

My mom agrees to the ride, and Jase heads behind the bar, so I head home. I'm kind of glad Jase is working. I have a lot to think about, and I want to sort some things out before I share with him. My mom's news about my inheritance is huge, but I don't want it to drive a wedge between Jase and me. My family's money has always been a sore spot between us, and I need him to see that this is different. It's not sin money from my dad, but it could be a way to make a lot of dreams come true.

Chapter 27

When I call Annie the following morning to ask if my mom can join us for dinner, she says, "Of course! I'd love to meet her. I'll make my special chili. No, wait, that's not nearly fancy enough. How about we grill steaks, or is she a vegetarian? Oh my, maybe—"

"Annie, Annie, she'll eat anything you make, really. It's not Princess Di; it's just my mom. We've been raving about your roasted chicken. Let's just do that and a salad. I'll come over around three and help you."

"Chicken, really? That's so boring. What about—"

"Annie, she'll love it. And she'll love you. See you at three."

After hanging up, I call my mom to make the plans for the day. I assume coffee and brunch, then shopping, but she surprises me. "I want to see where you work. I want to meet the detectives."

My mouth drops open. "Really?" I ask.

"Yes. I'm so proud of you, Kathleen, and I want to see you in action."

"Are you sure you're not just living out your *NCIS* fantasies?"

My mom is like a grade schooler on a field trip at the precinct, wanting to see everything. Detective Donovan seems irritated at first, but before I know it, they're sitting side by side at his desk as he shows her our database and how it works. She catches on to the algorithm quickly and is dismayed by how many sources come from

Philadelphia. "Yeah, Kathleen has done amazing things, and it almost cost her her own life," Detective Donovan replies.

Mom suddenly looks a bit pale. We haven't talked about the kidnapping since she's been here, and I guess this is the time.

"Mom, it was only for a little over a day. I'm fine. I am seeing a therapist and am part of a support group, so I can move on."

She shakes her head. "Are you sure you're all right and safe? Maybe you should take a break from your police work."

"I am," I reassure her. "I'll probably be on leave for another week or so. Mom, the police officers are very protective. They'll be on triple duty looking out for me." Detective Donovan reaffirms this statement. "There is now a small precinct in Hilltown with officers specifically trained in drug-related crime, so it is far less dangerous than it was."

My mom's eyes are filled with tears. Not of sadness; it's pride. I can't recall her ever looking at me this way, even as salutatorian of my high school or at my cotillion ball. "It doesn't surprise me at all," she says. "I always knew you would do great things. But as your mom, I'm scared for you."

"Mom, we can talk more about it if we need to later. Just know that I'm doing well."

After the precinct trip, my mom insists on joining me at Annie's to help. Brooklyn opens the door holding Snowflake. "Hi, Kathy," she says, grabbing me in a hug and squishing a not-too-thrilled Snowflake.

"Hi, Kathy's mom. I'm Brooklyn."

"I'm Caroline. Nice to meet you," she says, extending her hand.

Snowflake shakes loose, running under the coffee table. "Want to see my room?"

My mom laughs, surprised by Brooklyn's openness. But I'm not surprised at all. That girl loves an audience and especially a new audience to show all her things to. I imagine they will be busy for at least an hour and whisper to my mom, "You can say you need to help us in the kitchen at any time."

"I'll be fine," she says, squeezing my arm. "It's been years since I was invited to play dolls."

If ever, I think. Somehow, I can't imagine my mom sitting on my floor with me playing Barbies. Come to think of it, I don't think I even played with dolls. My dad always bought me "educational" toys and claimed Barbie and American Girl dolls were for "plebeians." I had to look the word up in a dictionary.

Jase arrives just as we're getting the chicken out, and my mom and Brooklyn return from the backyard, where Brooklyn was showing my mom their garden.

"Annie, it smells wonderful," my mom says. "And your garden is miraculous. How do you get your hydrangeas so healthy? And your tomatoes! Brooklyn and I must have eaten a dozen right off the vine. I've never tasted something so good, even at farmers' markets."

"The key is the fertilizer. Sometimes I use eggshells with a bit of coffee grounds. You want to get the pH balance . . ."

Jase takes my hand and leads me out to the living room, letting the women continue to talk soil and manure. He gives me a big kiss and asks me about my day.

"It was fun. My mom insisted on going to the precinct and learning all about what I do."

"I bet Detective Donovan loved that," Jase says, rolling his eyes. Detective Donovan's usual gruff demeanor is hard to miss.

"She had him giving us a private tour within half an hour."

"No way! We should send her to the Middle East. Now I know where you get your charm." He kisses me again.

Eventually, I pull away and say, "She has great ideas. I'm surprised. I mean, I know once upon a time she used to help my dad with the Mill, but ever since I started school, she wasn't allowed to work outside the house. That was the end of my mom's self-esteem. I was running this idea I had of a workforce training organization by her and Detective—" I stop myself, realizing I haven't shared my idea with Jase yet. I wanted to crunch some numbers and do more research before I floated it by him, but it looks like I inadvertently just did.

"Workforce training? But I thought you liked working with the Drug Force?"

"I do, but you know my time is limited there. And with the database up and running and everyone trained on it, they don't need me as much. But what Hilltown needs is jobs. My father told mill workers they could work at the meat-packing plant, but we know that's not the same skill set. Plus, the new owner was already doing layoffs; he wasn't going to hire a bunch of locals. And with more mills closing all around the state, people need new skills. They need to be trained in technology or a trade or—"

Jase puts up his hands in surrender and says, "Believe me, I know, Kat. I was one of them, remember? But new training takes money, and as you know, that's lacking right now for a lot of Hilltown families."

"I know. But I also know there are federal grants available for workforce training, and schools like Southwestern have offices that I could partner with, and with a little seed money—"

"From your dad?" He scoffs. "That's ironic. He makes everyone lose their jobs and then you use his money to retrain them?"

"No, not his money. I've been meaning to tell you, but it's been so busy. I'll explain it all later, but my mom's sister left me an inheritance. I can use that money, free of sin and my dad's input, to start the organization. If my calculations are right, I could apply for grants this fall and be up and running next spring. I mean, it would be a lot of work, but I'd hire people to help and . . . why aren't you saying anything? Why are you just staring at me?"

"Because I'm amazed by you. I'm always amazed by you. You don't let anything stop you, do you?"

"Well," I say, feigning modesty. "So you like the idea? I only just started looking into it, but—"

"I love it. Almost as much as I love you."

He wraps his arms around me and leans in for a passionate kiss. He's just starting to put his hands under my shirt when Brooklyn says, "Yuck, stop that and come to dinner. Aunt Annie says the chicken is getting cold."

We laugh and follow her to the kitchen table, where my mom and Annie are still discussing tomatoes. The table is set with bright, cheery plates of all colors and glasses of iced tea. No wine, I notice, and I wonder if my mom refused a glass. I know Annie would have offered. Fresh flowers—white roses and sunflowers—are overflowing from a vase, and my four favorite people are all sitting around me. We toast to Annie and her feast, and my mom adds, "And to the warmth of this new family. I cannot thank you all enough for being here for Kathleen. Your love radiates, and I see it in her as well. I'm so happy she has you all. And cheers to you all and all of the good things I know are coming for you and from you."

"For you too, Caroline," Annie says. We all clink glasses and dive into the meal.

After dinner and cleaning up, Jase and I sit for a moment in the living room while Mom, Aunt Annie, and Brooklyn go look at the garden again.

"There's something else I decided," I say to Jase.

"What is it, babe?"

"After I set up this new program, I want to go back to school. I want to get a master's in social work. I'm getting so much out of my therapy. I want to give back some of what I've been given."

"Kat, I support you in *anything* you want to do." I sit on his lap and kiss him deeply.

"I was hoping you'd say that." Then I look into his eyes, and I recognize that half smile, half smirk. We're both thinking the same thing.

"I think I'll ask Annie if she can take my mom back to the hotel."

"Kat, you're just *full* of great ideas tonight."

"I'm *just* getting started," I answer with a laugh.

www.ingramcontent.com/pod-product-compliance
Lightning Source LLC
LaVergne TN
LVHW041920070526
838199LV00051BA/2676